ABOUT THE AUTHOR

M. A. Anderson has always had a love of things that go 'bump in the night,' and that's why she writes dark and scary.

She is an Australian author who writes Urban fantasy, Supernatural crime thrillers, Young Adult thrillers and Contemporary and Paranormal Romance. Books One, Two and Three in the Dark Legacy are available on amazon.com, Smashwords and other online retailers.

You can find out more about M. A. and her books on her website: http://www.m-anderson.com.au or join her on popular social media sites.

DARK LEGACY SERIES
Reece: Prequel
Dark Legacy
Once Bitten
Soul Chaser

PARANORMAL ROMANCE
SERIES
Wolf Blood
Wolf Curse
Wolf Lover (coming 2019)

OTHER BOOKS
Written as Maggie Anderson
Driving Me Crazy
Love's Twist of Fate
A Night of Passion
A Night of Passion: Clean Romance Edition
Christmas, Mistletoe and You

ONCE BITTEN

ഇ൫ൠ

M. A. ANDERSON

Bella Luna Books
Australia

This edition published 2018
Bella Luna Books, Australia

Cover photos from canstockphoto.com
Front and back cover design by Maggie Anderson

National Library of Australia
Cataloguing-in-Publication entry

M. A. Anderson (author)

Once Bitten

ISBN: 9780992513917 (paperback)

Series: Anderson, M. A. Dark Legacy Bk 2

Urban fantasy/Fantasy fiction

A823.4

To my family, friends and readers.
Thank you!

"Everything you can imagine is real."
~ Pablo Picasso

CHAPTER ONE

The hulk cornered in the dark dead-end snarled and bared its razor-sharp canines at Reece as he inched his way closer. Flanked by Andre and Ed wielding laser stunners, he led the team, ready to shoot if the beast decided to attack. Decided? Did the thing have the capacity to think? Was the human trapped somewhere inside the fur and muscle conscious of the situation, or was it purely a primal instinct for survival?

Fight or flight. Wasn't that every creature on the planet's mechanism for safety?

The three men moved in. Half way down the alley.

They had been tracking this monster for weeks, but up until tonight it had eluded them. Now it was exactly where it should be ... trapped like the dog that it was.

"Andre, fan out to the left. Ed, you take the right," Reece directed, keeping his gaze steadfast on the shadows and the impending threat lurking within them. "If that thing tries *anything* you know what to do."

"Got it." Ed moved into position beside him, arm raised, stunner locked and loaded. Andre mirrored his movements on the other side of Reece. They were ready for anything.

Something slithered in Reece's gut and a static charge crawled over the length of his tense frame. Was it the exhilaration of the capture or something else?

They continued to edge closer.

The one streetlight in the alley offering a milky spotlight between dark and darker, flickered above them, gave an electrical buzz and evaporated into the murky night.

Green mobile garbage bins crashed to the ground, one by one, their lids flipping open, the sound of cans, bottles and other contents spilling onto the asphalt and echoing off the high-rise buildings. The agitated werewolf wanted out.

"Backs to the wall *now!*" Reece yelled, his heart hammering in his chest.

Andre grabbed Ed and whisked him across the alley—backs pressed against the red bricks, weapons ready.

None of them could afford to be bitten.

Reece fumbled for the switch on the infrared headset, he hated it when he couldn't see. The alley lit up like a red neon light through the viewer. The beast was gone. He whipped his head around, scanning the entire area. *Where'd it go?* He glanced over his shoulder at Andre and Ed. Andre scanned the rooftops with his nocturnal vision and shook his head. He pointed above Reece's head.

Reece swung his anxious gaze back to the grated landing. The wolf was on the railing ready to make its escape up the fire ladder. He couldn't let that happen. He aimed Sarah's high-powered, double-chamber crossbow at his target, finger on the trigger. It was an ugly mother: big, hairy, slobbering, eyes glowing fire engine red. He squinted into the sight and aimed between its eyes, visualizing a bullseye painted on its massive forehead.

"Wait. What if it can tell us where the missing kids are?" Andre asked, moving beside him. "We have the tranquilizer rifle in the van. That would knock it out for a few hours. We could..."

"Not this time, pal. This thing's run amok long enough. Now that we have it, I want to make sure it *never* attacks anyone again. Shit, Andre, its last victim was a six year old kid. Remember the mess we found? That kid's parents will never know what happened to him."

"I know. But..."

"But nothing. This thing's got to go. Now!" Reece didn't hesitate, he pulled the trigger. Two pure silver shafts rocketed toward the roaring, drooling beast, hitting it in Reece's imaginary bullseye. The creature gave one last almighty roar and dissolved into a puddle of black sludge and fur that seeped through the landing grate and onto the bins below. "Collect some of that, if you want. You won't find anything more than we already know." Reece turned on his heel and stalked along the alley to the well-lit city street.

Ed holstered his weapon, flicked on his flashlight and joined Andre. He could feel the tension between them. "Don't take it to heart kid. He's just tired that's all."

"No. It's something else." Andre looked along the alley.

"Like what?"

"I think he's still pissed at me for not telling him I was a vampire. Before I had to, I mean. I think he's under the impression I betrayed his trust." He headed for the street.

"Nah, it's all in the past, Andre. I'm sure that's not it." Ed tried to console him.

"I thought that too at first, but now I'm not so sure. Our friendship hasn't been quite the same since."

"Ya think?"

"There's something on his mind. And I know it has something to do with me." Andre's gaze moved to his friend waiting under a streetlight beside to the van. "I guess it'll come to a head soon enough."

CHAPTER TWO

The minute Detective Charlotte Delaney entered the precinct Ned Bowers spotted her and rushed across the lobby. "Charlotte, just a minute," he called in his usual brusque tone.

She slowed her pace, gave an irritated sigh and offered him a thin smile as he approached. He was an annoying, patronizing little man and she didn't want to deal with him at such an early hour of the morning. She glanced at her watch. 8.15 am. Well as far as she was concerned any time of day was too early for Ned.

"Morning, Ned, what can I do for you?" she asked, continuing toward the elevator, knowing by the scowl on his face he was not a happy man.

"Have you made any progress with that missing person case yet?" he asked, trying to keep up with her pace.

"And which one would that be, Ned? We do have a few," she told him, although she knew which case he referred to.

"Melinda Grahame, of course."

Charlotte stepped up to the elevator, pushed the button and hoped the doors would spring open so she could escape Ned Bowers. As acting District Attorney, he thought he had the power to needle the people he considered his subordinates. And he did a fine job of it too. Everyone he worked with hated him. "Without evidence or witnesses we have nothing to go on. It's been almost two months since the first abduction and we're running out of time. I'm bringing Reece Daniels in to help with the case."

"He's not with the department anymore, Charlotte. We don't need his assistance," Ned told her.

"Reece is good at what he does. He was always an honest, hardworking cop so I don't see the problem. We've had great success with his help in the past, on many occasions, and we *do* need it now," Charlotte countered, giving him a sideward glance, wishing she could blink and make him disappear. The elevator doors slid open and Charlotte ducked inside. "I'll keep you posted, Ned. Gotta run," she said, pressing the button for her floor and watching the DA's stocky form disappear behind the closing polished metal doors. She leaned against the back wall and sighed.

The musical tone of her cell phone cut into her thoughts. She plucked it from her shoulder bag. "Detective Delaney speaking."

"Hi, Mom, it's meee," the young male voice crooned.

"Hi, honey, what's up?" She checked her watch. 8.21 am.

"I just wanted to know what time you'd be home today."

"I'm not sure, honey. I'll try to be home before you go to sleep."

"Do I have to stay with Mrs. Jenkins? I'm old enough to be on my own," her son told her with conviction.

"Sweetie, we've been over this before and I don't have time to discuss it right now." The elevator doors opened and she stepped into the busy workroom.

"But, M-o-m."

"I have to go. I'll call you after school," she promised. "Have a great day. I love you."

Tommy knew there was no point trying to argue, once his mother made up her mind that was that. "You too, Mom. Love you."

Charlotte sighed as she dropped the phone into her bag. She loved her son with all her heart and it seemed he was growing up without her, and that made her sad. Tommy was ten now. In just a couple more years he'd be a teenager, and she wouldn't be the center of his world anymore. She wondered where the years had gone. He was the most important person in her life.

Her job was important too. Locating missing people, a lot of them kids and teens, was a satisfying occupation. The outcome wasn't always positive, although the successful cases seemed to compensate for that—at least most of the time.

She rushed across the workroom, dropped her bag onto her desk and just as she sat down the phone rang. She sighed and picked it up. *No rest for the wicked.* "Detective Delaney speaking."

The voice on the other end of the line was anxious. "H – ello, I have some … some information about … Melinda Grahame."

"What kind of information?" Charlotte straightened in her chair and glanced around the workroom, looking for her partner Josh Jamieson. She needed a trace on the call.

"I – I know what happened to her."

Charlotte's heart turned to lead when she heard the words. It probably meant Melinda was dead. "Can you tell me more?" Charlotte scanned the workroom again. Where was Josh? She glanced across to the next desk and snapped her fingers. The detective looked up. She jabbed at the receiver, mouthing the word 'trace.'

He nodded and got on the other line.

"She was taken out to a cabin in the woods and…" the voice stopped.

"And?" Charlotte coaxed, listening for any recognizable background noises. The caller panted into the phone. He was either nervous or excited, it was difficult to tell which. "Hello? Are you still there?"

"I'm – I'm here. I can't talk now. I'll call you back."

The line went dead.

"Damn!" Charlotte slammed the receiver down, her eyes moving to the detective at the other desk. He shook his head. She knew there hadn't been enough time. She slumped in her chair, rubbing her aching temples. Was Melinda dead? By what the caller had said it was a distinct possibility. Would he call back? She hoped so.

CHAPTER THREE

Melinda's eyes snapped open to a veil of black. As her terrified gaze darted around the gloom of her unfamiliar surroundings, she couldn't see beyond where she lay. She struggled to get her contorted body into a sitting position and sniffed the dense, humid air. Wherever she was it smelt earthy, like a dog's wet fur after a rain storm. She tried to breathe through her mouth but she was gagged with some kind of tape. Her hands were tied behind her, the rope travelling down the back of her legs and around her ankles.

There was something else, too. Something taped to her left hand. She tugged at it and a sharp sting shot up her forearm. Melinda whimpered, wondering who had brought her here and how long she'd been missing. And worst of all, what would happen to her?

She heard a noise. Someone crunching gravel or sticks beneath their feet. Was she out in the woods? Oh, God, a secluded location. Was she going to die? The sound grew closer. Closer. CLOSER. Another noise. A metallic, high-pitched squeal against weathered metal. Someone unlocked the door. Who was out there?

Melinda's racing heartbeat thumped against her ribs, her ragged breathing quickened. If she hyperventilated she'd pass out. She tried to take in a deep breath, her nostrils flaring to inhale the much-needed air to slow her heart rate. What would happen if she were unconscious? She shook her head to dislodge the thought. She didn't want to think about the horrible possibility.

The wooden door creaked open on rusty hinges spilling sunlight into the small space. Melinda blinked at the glare, her breathing even more ragged now. The figure framed in the doorway was male. He moved toward her, leaving the door open. Melinda squeezed herself into the corner, tears of fear spilling down her face. She would have screamed if she could.

"It's all right, Melinda, I'm not going to hurt you," he assured her. The young man crouched in front of her. He made no attempt to remove the gag or to untie her. Melinda couldn't make out his features or hair color; the brightness from outside haloed his body and shrouded the front of him in shadow, but she could tell he wasn't much older than her by the sound of his voice. "I want you to listen to me very carefully," he said. "Nod if you understand."

Melinda nodded.

"Good." He stood up, towering over her. "What I have to tell you might just save your life."

CHAPTER FOUR

That had been one strange phone call, not that Reece hadn't had strange phone calls before, he had, but there was something different about that one. Something his years and experience on the force couldn't determine. Not yet. He slid the digital phone onto the desk and frowned at it.

The caller seemed edgy. He told Reece he had information about the Melinda Grahame case Charlotte Delaney was working on, and before he said anything more he hung up. He said he knew what happened to her. Was she dead? Maybe. Was the caller the abductor? Could be. If not, he knew who was.

As Reece pondered the brief conversation, he had an uneasy feeling in his gut. He knew there was more to the recent disappearances than just normal abductions, if that's what you could call them. No abduction was 'normal', and the current cases were even more disturbing.

Andre entered the office. He'd been on an errand to the local Deli to pick up lunch for Reece and Sarah. The Deacon of St. Joseph's Catholic Church had stopped by to see how the pair was doing. It had been a while since they had touched base and it was good to see her again.

Sarah sat opposite Reece, studying him. He was clearly perturbed by the phone call. She had kept up-to-date with the missing person cases and knew there were far more sinister implications than what appeared obvious.

"What was that about?" she asked.

Reece gave her a vague look. "Huh?" When what she had said registered, he said, "Some young guy with information about the Melinda Grahame case."

Andre crossed the office and sat the brown paper bag and tray of coffee on the desk. "What information?"

Reece stood up, stretched, and moved over to the window behind his desk. He gazed out at the street below. "That's just it, he didn't tell me anything." He squinted back the glare, squeezed his thumb and index finger into his closed eyes and sighed. He was tired. "The guy seemed anxious. Said something about a remote location and rang off before I could get anything else out of him."

"Maybe you should call Charlotte and let her know someone contacted you," Sarah suggested.

Reece glanced over his shoulder. "I will. I just need some time to get my head around it first. See if I can recall anything about the call that could give us a clue to his location."

"Can the department trace the call?" she asked.

"I guarantee it came from a pay phone somewhere. Wouldn't be much point." Reece returned to his seat. He grabbed the brown paper bag and peered inside. He pulled out the deli sandwiches, slid one across the desk to Sarah, unwrapped his and took a large bite.

Andre sat down next to Sarah. "The recent disappearances have to be werewolf related. There's been too much Lycan activity in the city."

"I know. The only problem I can see is how to explain it to Charlotte."

"She's an intelligent girl, she'll understand," Sarah told him.

Reece gave her one of those 'Are you kidding?' looks. "Not unless she sees it for herself. She's a cop. Cops believe what they see with their own eyes. I should know." He looked at Andre. "Remember when you told me you were a vampire? I thought it was a joke, until I saw it for myself."

"I remember." Andre gave him a furtive glance. That *was* the issue between them, he could sense it.

"So show her," Sarah said. "She needs to be aware of what's going on in this city. How is she supposed to do her job if she doesn't have a clue what's happening here?"

"It's not that simple."

"Why?" Sarah studied his face. "You like her." She leaned on the desk, a broad smile spreading across her face. "You do, don't you?"

"She's *a friend*, of course I like her." Reece's expression told her 'Don't go there,' but she ignored it.

"No. It's more than that." Sarah shook her head. "You care for her. It's written all over your face."

"I care *about* her, just like I care about Andre, and you and Ed and Adrian. That's all." Reece was adamant.

"Have it your way," she conceded, raising defensive hands, although her woman's intuition told her otherwise.

⁞⟅⟆

Charlotte was furious. She scanned the workroom looking for Josh's six foot two inch well-dressed frame. Why wasn't he here? Why hadn't she been able to get a trace on that call? The caller could have been Melinda's abductor for all she knew. It had been too good an opportunity to pass up and Josh had dropped the ball.

He stepped out of the elevator carrying a cardboard tray containing two coffees. He gazed across the workroom and when he spotted her he gave a thin smile. Charlotte didn't smile back as she watched him move toward her. She took a deep breath and counted to ten. It didn't help. She jumped to her feet. "Where the hell have you been?"

"Good morning to you, too." Josh slid the tray onto the desk.

"I needed you to get a trace on a call and you were out buying coffee?" She folded her arms and glared at him.

"I thought you'd want to kick-start your day with some caffeine. You always do."

"I just got a call from a kid who said he had information about Melinda Grahame's disappearance. If you'd been here, I would've kept him talking and maybe we'd be on our way to his location right about now."

"Calm down. What did he say?"

"That he knew what happened to Melinda and that she'd been taken to a cabin in the woods."

"That's it?" Josh gave her an incredulous frown. "There wouldn't have been enough time to get a trace."

She poked the air. "*You* should've been here."

"Did he say anything else?" Josh picked up a takeaway cup and took a cautious sip of his coffee.

"He said he'd call back."

"So we wait." He walked over to his desk and sat down.

Charlotte followed him. "Look, Josh, I need you on-the-job, not running out to buy coffee. Send a rookie next time, okay?"

Josh's intense gaze rested on her. "Whatever you say *boss*."

Charlotte wasn't sure how to take his comment. She'd been chosen over him for this particular case and knew he wasn't happy about having to work under her—his animosity was palpable. Josh had already complained to their boss about her unorthodox approach to the investigation, and she'd been called into his office for a *pep-talk*. Something she could live without. She'd worked hard to get ahead in the male-dominated establishment and she wasn't about to let some arrogant, self-centered jerk sabotage her career. If Josh Jamieson attempted to undermine her again she would have no choice but to take defensive action. And she would, without hesitation.

CHAPTER FIVE

Melinda sat alone in the dark shed, unable to believe what she'd been told. How could such a thing happen in the 21st Century? Could this be some horrible nightmare? She wished it was, but knew it wasn't. Why her? She remembered the newspaper headlines about the recent abductions, seeing the missing teens' faces on the six o'clock news. She wasn't the only one. How many were there? Three? Four? More? Melinda wasn't sure. Now her face would appear on the television, in newspapers and on milk cartons. The thought sent a shiver up her spine.

Earlier, in the glare of the open doorway, she'd noticed bloody gashes on her arms and legs and could now feel the hot, burning sensation on her skin. She hadn't felt it when she'd first regained consciousness; she had been too terrified to notice. Now she had time to sense everything about herself. Melinda also saw what had stung her hand—an intravenous drip, 'to hydrate your body and keep you alive, for now,' he'd told her. She thought he was crazy, thought he would kill her.

Still bound and gagged, Melinda replayed over and over in her head what he'd said, trying to comprehend it. "You've been attacked. Bitten by a werewolf." When her eyes grew wide with fear he repeated the words. "Yes, a werewolf, also known as a Lycanthrope. They've existed for thousands of years undetected. Lived and worked with humans. And now you'll become one of the privileged. When the next full moon appears, which isn't far off, you'll go through a metamorphosis. You'll have the inescapable urge to hunt and kill. And your prey will be human. You're not human anymore, Melinda, you're Lycan. One of our pack. And the only way you can be released from the curse is by death. I'm sure you don't want to die, do you?"

She had shaken her head vehemently. NO!

Of course she didn't want to die. She was too young. Tears spilled down her cheeks. Her tears turned to a sob and she sobbed for a long time, grieving the life she would never have, the family she could never see again, the boyfriend she loved, and the friends she would miss—but more so for the horror that lay ahead of her. She would become a *monster*.

CHAPTER SIX

Reece gazed out the window, trying to recollect if there had been anything about the call that hadn't registered at the time, anything that had slipped past him. Had there been any unusual background noises? Traffic, trains, horns, bells, voices? Nothing he could recall. He wished he could have kept him talking. The kid was scared. His ragged breathing and the choppiness of his voice told Reece that. A remote location. How many remote locations were there in California? Too many to count.

The office door opened and Charlotte Delaney walked in. Reece was surprised to see her because he'd just made the decision to call her.

"Hey, I was about to call you," he said, walking over to her.

"Something wrong?" Charlotte asked, closing the door and crossing the room with him.

"I had an unusual phone call this morning that I thought you'd want to know about."

Charlotte sat down in front of Reece's desk and looked up at him. "Ok. You want to tell me about it?"

Reece moved around his desk and sat down. "A young guy called in saying he had information about the Grahame case."

Charlotte straightened in her chair. "That's strange. Someone called the precinct this morning with the same information. What did he say?"

"He knew what had happened to Melinda. That she'd been taken to a remote location. But he hung up before I could ask him anything."

"I received the exact same phone call, only he said he'd call back."

Andre got up from his desk and joined them. "Do you suppose someone's playing a prank?" He pulled up a chair and sat beside Charlotte.

"It's possible, although he did sound afraid," Charlotte told them. "I think he could be legit."

"Can you find out where the call came from?" Andre asked.

"Wouldn't do any good. It's a certainty the call came from a pay phone nowhere near the remote location. No phones in the woods. I will look into it though." Charlotte gazed around the office and spotted the coffee pot in their small kitchen. "Hey, Andre, could I impose on your generous nature and ask you to make me a coffee?" She smiled.

Andre stood up. "Sure. No cream, no sugar, right?"

"You remembered. Thanks."

"Me too," Reece added. "You know how I take it."

Andre poured the coffee and returned to the desk. "Here you go," he said, passing one to Charlotte and setting the other mug in front of his partner.

"Thanks," Reece and Charlotte said together. Their eyes met and they smiled at each other.

Reece had come to the conclusion that he didn't want Charlotte to know what they did. He'd thought long and hard about it and he wanted to spare her for as long as he could. Sarah was right, although he wasn't about to admit it to her, he cared for Charlotte and he didn't want to do anything to jeopardize his chance of getting close to her. It occurred to him that Charlotte had come across town to see him. "Was there a reason you came by?"

"Yes, now that you mention it. I want you to work with me on this case. Are you available?"

"Absolutely." Not only would it stimulate the investigation because he already had vital information to move the case along— it would also give them time together.

∞ℂℂ

It was early evening, and Adrian was in his office working on his next novel when Reece and Andre came through the front door. He could hear them talking on their way up the stairs and walked into the hallway to meet them. The three men shared Adrian's Spanish style villa, once the home of silent movie star Rudolph Valentino, and it seemed to be an amicable arrangement so far.

Andre had moved into Reece's apartment after his had been destroyed when they'd battled his brother, Jacques. Around the same time, Beth had walked out of Andre's life saying she couldn't be with him because he had broken her trust when he'd turned her. He didn't understand that because he'd done it to save her life and knew she still loved him. After months of living on top of each other, they realized they needed a bigger apartment and Adrian offered his home. He had more than enough room.

When the pair reached the top of the staircase they noticed Adrian standing in the hallway.

"Hey, Adrian," Reece said, stepping onto the landing "How's the book coming along?"

"Good." He removed his spectacles and wiped the lenses on the front of his cardigan. Not that he needed glasses, he had perfect immortal vision. It was more for appearances sake, given his age. "How was your day?"

"Kinda weird." Reece followed the author into his office.

"That sounds ominous." Adrian sat down at his desk. "Care to elaborate?"

"You know the missing person cases Charlotte's working on?" Adrian nodded. "Well, a young guy called the office today saying he had information about Melinda Grahame."

"Will it help?"

"He wasn't on the phone long enough to give me anything," Reece said. "He was nervous. Maybe he was afraid of getting caught. Whatever the reason the call was useless." He pulled up a chair, turned it around and straddled it, resting his elbows on the backrest. Andre remained in the doorway.

"Do you think he'll call back?"

"Well, the strange thing is he also called Charlotte and gave her the same sketchy information."

"Perhaps it was a prank call," Adrian offered. "Odd people tend to come out of the woodwork when cases such as these are publicized."

"Who knows?" Reece shrugged.

"What did the caller say?"

"He said Melinda had been taken to a cabin in the woods. Doesn't exactly pinpoint where, does it?"

"No, it doesn't." Adrian gave it some thought. "What about the call to Charlotte?"

"Same thing. Although he did say he'd call back. If it is legit, I hope he does. We could use a break in this case, especially with the supernatural implications."

"Yes, you're right about that." Adrian looked across at Andre. He seemed pensive. "You're quiet, Andre. Something on your mind?" he asked, although he could sense the reason for his mood.

Andre's frowning gaze moved to his mentor. Knowing Adrian could read his thoughts he wondered why he'd brought it up. "No. I'm fine."

Reece glanced over his shoulder. "You sure about that?"

"Yes, I'm sure." Andre turned and walked down the hall.

Adrian and Reece looked at each other. "Something I should know about?" Adrian asked.

"Not that I'm aware of."

Adrian got up from his desk and headed for the hallway. "Maybe I should have a talk to him."

Reece waved him off. "No, I'll go."

Adrian sensed there was something he needed to say to Andre. "All right. You know I'm here if either of you need to talk."

"Thanks." Reece walked along the hall to Andre's room. He stood outside contemplating whether to knock, breathed a heavy sigh and continued to his own room. He knew some time in the not-too-distant future they would need to have a serious discussion.

CHAPTER SEVEN

Charlotte stepped into her apartment around nine o'clock, closed the door and gave a heavy sigh. It had been a long day. She was tired and hungry and just wanted to forget about the case for a few hours. Was that so terrible? She knew how important it was to get the missing kids back to their families, spending time with her son was important too. As she walked along the small hallway to the living room Mrs. Jenkins popped into view. Charlotte caught her breath. "Oh! Mrs. J you startled me."

"Sorry, dear, I didn't mean to."

Charlotte shook her head and gave a wry smile. "It's okay, it's me. I'm just tired."

"Your dinner's on the kitchen counter. Just pop it in the microwave." The older woman sidled past Charlotte in the narrow hallway and plucked her jacket from the coat rail near the door. She picked up her purse and readied herself to leave. "My son will be coming by to pick me up any second. Must go."

"Thank you. Have a nice evening, Mrs. J."

"You have a nice evening, too, dear. See you tomorrow."

Charlotte saw the older woman out, kicked off her shoes and padded along the hallway to the living room. Tommy was in bed.

She walked back along the hall to the second door, opened it and peeped inside. Her son was snuggled in bed sound asleep. Charlotte sighed. Another night she had missed spending time with him.

Reece's face popped into her head. It would be good working with him again. He knew how to handle the investigation, and he was thorough. Maybe having him work the case would afford her some extra time with her son. Charlotte felt as though they were slipping away from each other and that was the last thing she wanted to happen.

The musical tone of the telephone interrupted her thoughts. She closed Tommy's door, rushed along the hallway to the kitchen and plucked the receiver from its cradle. She didn't want the noise to wake her son. It was late and he had school tomorrow.

"Hello?"

"Detective Delaney? I'm sorry to call you at home … I need to see you."

The hairs on the back of Charlotte's neck bristled. It was the same young man who had called her at the precinct. How did he get her number? It wasn't listed.

"Detective? Are you there?"

"Yes, I'm here. How…" She realized she'd better play it cool or he might ring off again. "I'm glad you called back."

"Can you meet me? What I have to tell you, it's important."

Charlotte's mind worked overtime. She wanted to get whatever information he had without putting herself in danger. After considering her options, which were minimal, she asked the obvious question. "Where?"

"Out of the city where we won't be seen," the nervous voice replied. "It'll have to be in a couple days because I won't be able to get away till…" He stopped himself. He didn't want to say too much. Not yet, anyhow.

An out-of-the-way location. Why was she not surprised? She grabbed a notebook and pen. "Okay. Give me the details."

CHAPTER EIGHT

The brooding young man with dark hair and eyes gazed around the faces in front of him. He had an audience of six—three girls and three guys all aged between sixteen and nineteen. This meeting had been called to discuss the new arrival Melinda Grahame.

"If we keep her locked up until her first transformation she'll listen. She'll see there's nothing to fear, that she can to go back to her life and act like nothing's happened. And when it's the night of the full moon she can return here to the pack," Dominic offered.

None of the teens had been allowed to leave. The promise had been given for an unspecified time in the future—if they did as they were told.

Patrick paced in front of the heavy wooden bookcase laden with disintegrating books. Who was Dominic trying to convince, the others in the room or himself? Patrick glanced at the Hispanic young man and responded, "You'd better be right about that, Dom, because if she doesn't do what she's told there'll be serious consequences."

"And what happens if she won't listen?" one young woman asked, a concerned frown forming on her pretty face.

"The Alpha might have something else in mind for her," Patrick replied. The Alpha would order her termination. He wouldn't tolerate defiance.

"That's not…"

Patrick turned his serious gaze toward the male voice and jabbed the air with his finger. "Don't tell me it's not fair."

"None of us wanted to be this way, Patrick. We have to show compassion," another young woman told him.

Patrick glared at her. "Compassion?" He stalked over to her. "Who showed *compassion* when we were *bitten* and turned into the creatures we've become?" he spat the words at her. She shrank back into the warn leather sofa expecting him to slap her. He walked back to the bookcase. "We must protect the Alpha at all costs."

"Let me talk to her," the first young woman offered. Her name was Claire.

Patrick's dark gaze remained on her. "You really think you can get through to her?"

"I can try."

He gazed at each member one at a time until his dark eyes returned to Claire. "If you can't make her see reason the Alpha *will* kill her."

CHAPTER NINE

Charlotte approached the Grahame's front door, her stomach in an anxious knot. She had given Melinda's parents her word that the department would find their daughter and orchestrate her safe return. Now, almost two weeks after her disappearance, Charlotte was no closer to finding the young woman or her abductor. She knew the family was in distress. They had all but given up hope. Her parents knew the first 48 hours were crucial.

Journalists and television camera crews had been waiting for Charlotte to arrive. She ran the show, after all, and had warned them against approaching the family before she got there. The front lawn was littered with journalists Charlotte recognized as well as a few new faces eager to 'get the scoop.'

She'd spoken to Olivia and Richard Grahame on the telephone a couple of hours before, facing them now would be a different matter. Charlotte wanted to do everything she could to help the parents accomplish the task of speaking to Melinda's abductor, and to jog someone's memory about the day she disappeared. Maybe someone had seen something—anything that might steer the investigation in the right direction—no matter how insignificant it might seem, and the best way to accomplish that was through the media. The broadcast would reach every corner of the country.

As she reached the front steps of the Grahame's two-story, modestly elegant home, Josh Jamieson caught up to her, buttoning his suit jacket. Charlotte had hoped he wouldn't show. She didn't want him stirring up Melinda's parents before they faced the waiting media circus.

Charlotte climbed the three front steps onto the porch, turned to Josh and glowered at him. "I don't want you upsetting the Grahames before they go to air. This broadcast is critical. If the perpetrator is watching, it could mean the difference between getting Melinda back and not getting her back at all—alive at least."

"And you *assume* that I'm going to sabotage the broadcast in some way?" Josh looked at her, incredulous. "What kind of detective do you take me for?"

"One that's eager to make a name for himself," Charlotte replied. "And one who wants my job."

Josh smirked and raised an arrogant eyebrow. "You're very perceptive, aren't you Charlotte? I'm not about to jeopardize the safe return of Melinda Grahame, regardless of what you might think you know."

"Just make sure you don't!" She glanced at him sideways. "And, Josh, whatever I think I know, I know." Charlotte allowed the tension to disappear from her face before pressing the bell.

Josh Jamieson positioned himself behind Charlotte as she sat on the sofa opposite the Grahames. She could sense his gaze burning into the center of her back and endeavored to ignore the uncomfortable sensation. It was important for her to brief Melinda's parents, before they faced the media with a plea for their daughter's safe return, and she wasn't about to allow her partner to challenge her ability, yet again.

Charlotte wanted to prepare the couple for the barrage of invasive questions that would be thrown at them, once Melinda's father finished his appeal. She would act as a buffer should the questions become too difficult. And she was one hundred percent certain they would because the father is always the first suspect in a child's disappearance. She watched Olivia and Richard for a moment, feeling guilty for not fulfilling her promise. It wasn't as though the department had been resting on its laurels, the team worked around the clock. Melinda was one of several young people to disappear without a trace over the past couple of months, so they had to be diligent.

Josh wandered across the room, pushed the sheer, cream-colored curtain aside and glanced out the window. Not only were the television crews waiting but now a small audience of onlookers had gathered behind the barrier too. What a circus. If he had been heading the investigation it would have been handled with a very different approach. Josh turned and looked at the group sitting opposite each other. He crossed the room again and sat next to Charlotte. What could she say?

Charlotte shot Josh a sideward glance, then turned her attention back to the Grahames and tried to ignore him.

"Richard, when you go out there try to remain as calm as possible. It's important to look straight into the camera and direct your comments to the abductor. Just say what's in your heart … the safe return of your daughter … the family love and miss her…"

"Yes, detective, I know all that," Richard told her. His weary face showed all the signs of emotional strain, lack of sleep and crying.

"It's also important that Olivia be at your side. It demonstrates a united front," Charlotte told them.

Olivia Grahame leaned forward and looked into Charlotte's eyes. "Do you believe it will help? Do you think he'll be watching? Is Melinda still alive?" The mother looked tired beneath her perfectly applied makeup, dark circles under her eyes bled through the concealer like bruises just surfacing the skin.

Josh jumped in. "We can't be sure of anything in these types of crimes, but we are hopeful. If the abductor sees your broadcast it could go one of two ways, it might motivate him to do the right thing or…"

"If the person who took Melinda is the same person who abducted the other missing young people, and none of them have been found or returned, what makes you think he'll do the right thing now?" Richard asked.

"Because, at some point, these kinds of perpetrators feel remorseful and if that's the case your broadcast could be timely," Josh said.

Charlotte wanted to jump off the sofa and slap him. If she'd had her gun, she might have been tempted to use it. How dare he be so blunt. These people were suffering, for God's sake. What did he expect to accomplish? She stood up, walked over to the window and gazed outside. It was time to go.

CHAPTER TEN

The continuous ring of the telephone echoed around the office as Reece threw open the door and rushed across the room. When he reached for the receiver the ringing stopped. "Shit!" He moved around his desk and dropped into his chair. Where was Andre? Why was the office unmanned? He scanned the desktop. Perhaps his partner had left a note with some indication of where he'd gone. His thoughts returned to the call he'd missed. Was it the young guy with information about Melinda Grahame? He hoped whoever it was would call back.

He had arranged to meet Charlotte later in the day to discuss the case and any strategies they could use to push the investigation forward. He knew there were certain aspects to the disappearances he couldn't reveal to her, and that would always be a deal breaker as far as he was concerned. He didn't want her to know.

Reece wanted to put an end to the abductions, to the slaughter, to the Lycanthropic population of the city. It was a challenge that would take some time and time was a commodity they didn't have. If kids continued to disappear at the current rate the city would have an epidemic on its hands. He couldn't let that happen.

His thoughts were interrupted when three familiar voices echoed into the office.

"Hi. I didn't expect you back so soon," Andre said, as he came through the open doorway.

"Where have you been?"

Andre glanced at his companions then frowned at Reece. "With Sarah and Ed. You asked me to pick them up, remember?"

Ed walked across to Reece's desk and sat down. "What's with you, Daniels? Why are you bustin' Andre's chops?"

"I'm not." He glowered at his ex-boss.

"Sure you are. What's goin' on with you two? Why don't you just get whatever it is off your chest so we can get on with the important stuff?"

"And what do you think is *on my chest*, Chief?" Reece asked. He still called his ex-boss chief. Old habits die hard.

"You're pissed because Andre didn't let you in on his little secret back when," Ed replied.

"What are you talking about?"

"You know damn well what I'm talkin' about. The fact that he didn't tell you he was a bloodsucker." He turned to Andre. "No offence."

Andre walked over to the pair. "Ed, please leave it alone."

Reece jumped to his feet. "No. Let's get this out on the table." He frowned at Andre. "Is that what you think? That I'm pissed because you kept a huge secret from me for so long?"

Sarah stepped into the men's line of vision. "Look, gentlemen, could we do this another time? We do have more important things to…"

Reece raised a dismissive hand. "No, let's just get this done now that it's started." He turned his serious gaze to his friend. "I asked a question. Is that what you think?"

"You just said it yourself." Andre folded his arms across his chest. "I admit I was hurt that you didn't trust me enough to tell me. But that's all it was."

"It had nothing to do with trusting you, it went way beyond that." Andre paced. "What do you think would happen if people discover what I am? Do you think they'd be accepting? They'd probably form some kind of vigilante and try to kill me."

"I get that. What I don't understand is why you couldn't confide in me? Who the hell was I going to tell?"

"I didn't tell you because I didn't want *anyone* to know. I wanted a normal life, as normal as it could be. It's past history, can't we move on?"

"Yeah, Daniels," Ed spoke up. "You've been acting like a real asshole."

Reece studied Andre for several seconds before speaking again. "Have I really been a pain in the ass?"

"Yeah. Well, kind of."

Reece was embarrassed. He hadn't realized his wounded ego had affected their friendship. He thought he had it under control. He knew they needed to say something to each other, he hadn't realized it was more on his behalf than Andre's. "I'm sorry. I do understand why you didn't tell me … it's just … we're best friends, brothers. I always thought we could tell each other anything. I thought I was okay with it. Can you forgive me?"

Andre walked around the desk. He looked his friend in the eye and said, "It's a big ask."

Reece frowned at him. Had his actions damaged their friendship permanently?

A smile crept across Andre's face. "Of course I forgive you. You're my best friend. I love you, man." The pair hugged.

Sarah gave a relieved sigh. "Thank heavens." She gazed upward. "Now can we get on with why we're here? There's been another werewolf sighting. Philippe called me this morning with the location."

"Just the one?" Reece asked.

"So far." Sarah wheeled an office chair across to the desk and sat beside Ed. "We need to capture one so we can interrogate it. When the moon is waning, and the wolf returns to human form, we might be able to get the information we need."

"That's all good in theory, only trouble is where do we find one? We don't have a clue where the lair is," Ed said.

"It has to be close by," Sarah said.

"It could be anywhere within a hundred mile radius," Reece told them.

"Maybe not. With the amount of activity it has to be closer than that," Ed said.

"Let's hope the kid calls Charlotte again and gives her the exact location. Then we can storm the place and put those things out of action," Reece said. "The sooner the better."

CHAPTER ELEVEN

Melinda heard footsteps outside her prison. The sound was different this time, not as heavy on the undergrowth. Something else she noticed too, her hearing had become more acute. Her frightened gaze remained on the door as it swung outward and light streamed into the dark space. She snapped her eyes shut to shield them from the glare, then opened them enough to make out the shape of a girl in the doorway.

"Hi, I'm Claire." She stepped inside and pulled the door to.

Melinda stayed squeezed in the corner. She didn't trust any of them.

Claire took cautious steps toward her. "I'm not going to hurt you. I just want to talk," she assured her, kneeling to remove the tape from her mouth. She peeled the sticky duct tape from Melinda's skin with care.

"Ok." Melinda slid forward. In the shadows of the small space, she could see the young woman was about her age, maybe a year older, with dark brown, shoulder-length hair and slight build.

"I want to tell you some things Patrick didn't."

"Patrick?" Melinda moved closer to the young woman. She thought if she could gain her trust, maybe Claire would help her escape.

"Yeah, that's the guy's name who spoke to you," Claire told her. "There's someone else. Patrick's just the heavy who keeps us in line." She gave a thin smile. "He's the one that recruits and teaches us." Claire brushed matted strands of long, blond hair off Melinda's face. "If you embrace the Lycan way, you can go back to your life. You just have to return here every full moon."

As the realization of what Claire said hit her, Melinda smiled. "You mean ... I can go home?"

"Not yet. The next full moon is only a day away. The first time a human changes into a wolf is a scary experience. Trust me, I've been there. So have the others you're about to meet. Once you know what happens and how to handle it, you'll be able to go home." She didn't tell Melinda that none of them had been allowed to leave yet. Claire untied Melinda, stood up and held out her hand. "Want to come inside and freshen up? Meet everyone? See that it's not so bad?"

Melinda gripped Claire's hand and staggered to her feet, her legs shaking. She took an unsteady step and stumbled forward. The young woman caught her before she could fall. Melinda steadied herself and walked out of the shed into the daylight. As the warm sun caressed her skin, she noticed the gashes on her body had almost healed. How was that possible?

∞⟳

Richard Grahame hesitated as he stepped up to the cluster of microphones. Olivia moved to his side, smiled up at him, and rubbed his arm for reassurance. She nodded and Richard knew it meant 'go ahead, honey.' He cleared his throat and gazed at the sea of eager journalists and curious onlookers. When he opened his mouth to speak, static interference ran through the microphones emitting a high pitch, electronic ping. A technician rushed over. "Sorry 'bout that," he said, fumbling with the mics and sorting through the plugs and cabling. After a minute, he gave Richard the thumbs up.

Charlotte stepped onto the podium. She sensed Richard's discomfort. She covered the mics. "Are you all right? Would you prefer I talk to the media ... the abductor?"

"Thanks, I'm fine," he replied, his voice shaky. He cleared his throat and faced the microphones. "Good morning. I want to address the person or persons who took our daughter. I want you to know how much we love Melinda, and ... and that we miss her terribly. Her brother and sister miss her, her grandmother ... everyone who knows and loves her misses her. If she's all right, if she's still ... alive, we will do whatever you ask for her safe return." He glanced at Olivia, noticing tears glistening in her eyes, her trembling smile. He lost control. Turning back to the camera he blurted out, "Please give us back our daughter, can't you see what you're doing to my family? We love her … she has her whole life ahead of her. Please …"

Charlotte took Richard by the arm and led him and his wife back to the house. The media went into a frenzy with flash bulbs and questions bouncing every which way. She glanced over her shoulder and saw Josh step up to the microphones, hands raised, motioning for the crowd to settle down. Charlotte didn't like the fact that he was about to address the media.

Josh Jamieson was elated. Their boss would not be pleased that Charlotte's plan had derailed on national television. He needed to defuse the situation and put himself in a favorable light. He raised his voice and addressed the crowd. "All right, let's settle down. Your questions will be answered when you give me a chance to speak." He gazed around the sea of journalists. Some faces he recognized and there was one in particular, Sonia Edwards, he wished was not among them. She would be the one to ask the invasive questions. He would attempt to avoid her gaze and her questions for as long as he could.

The group took a couple of minutes to quieten down.

"Thank you. I appreciate your cooperation," Josh told them.

"Does the department have any new evidence into Melinda's disappearance?" One young journalist jumped in.

"At this stage we're following up some new leads, yes." Josh pointed to another young woman close to the front. "Penelope Lewis, LA Times. Do you believe Melinda Grahame is still alive?"

"We are confident that Miss Grahame is still very much alive."

"Has there been any contact from her abductor?" Sonia Edwards threaded her way through the crowd and into Josh's line of sight. "Well, Detective Jamieson, has he made contact?"

The detective attempted to hide his distaste and gave a thin smile. "No, Ms. Edwards. The abductor has made no contact at this stage. The department suspects whoever has Melinda is still deciding what his demands are."

"It's been two weeks, Detective. If the abductor wanted a ransom or any other kind of self-gratification, wouldn't he have made it known by now?" she pushed.

Josh stood his ground. "Each case is different, Ms. Edwards, nothing is cut and dry."

"Do you suspect the parents at all? Could this case be coincidental?" She continued to press. The crowd went berserk. Questions flew from everywhere.

Josh frowned at the attractive, red-haired journalist and she gave him a perceptive smirk.

CHAPTER TWELVE

The morning had been a total disaster, the afternoon not much better, and as Charlotte climbed out of her parked car and crossed the street all she wanted to do was go home, lock the door and unplug the telephone. Her cell phone had been ringing off the hook and she just wanted it all to go away. She'd promised to meet Reece to brainstorm the case and, even though she didn't feel like it, she had to keep that promise.

When Charlotte stepped onto the sidewalk she glanced up at the office window. Reece was there. She smiled at him and waved. He smiled and moved away from the window.

Charlotte entered the compact lobby and headed for the stairs. When she reached the final step Reece was in the hallway waiting for her.

"It's good to see you," he said.

"Hi," Charlotte huffed, "those stairs are killers."

Reece smiled and suggested Charlotte go inside to catch her breath.

"Do you want some coffee?" he asked, closing the door.

Charlotte plonked herself in a chair in front of his desk. "No thanks. I'd appreciate a glass of water though."

"Coming right up." He poured the water, sat the glass on the desk in front of her, and took his seat.

"Thanks," she said, and sipped the ice cold liquid.

"I would've understood if you hadn't shown," he told her. He'd seen the broadcast on television earlier.

"You saw the fiasco, huh?"

He nodded. "And your partner's little performance. Josh is an asshole, Charlotte, why do you put up with him?"

"Because I don't have a choice." Which was the truth. Her boss had made it very clear that if they couldn't work together she'd be back on the beat. She wasn't about to let that happen, not for Josh Jamieson or anyone else.

"Stand up to your boss. He'll respect you for it."

"Thanks for the advice, but I need my job. I have a son to raise, remember?" She slid the empty glass onto the desk. "I can't afford to go back to a uniform salary. Besides, I enjoy my job, I'm good at it."

"Yeah, you are. Far better than that arrogant prick you work with." Reece flashed a grin.

Charlotte couldn't help smile back. Reece had a great smile, when he cared to show it. She liked his smile. In fact, she liked him.

The office door burst open and Andre and Ed charged into the room. When they noticed Charlotte they stopped in their tracks. "Oh, hi, Charlotte." With all the excitement Andre had forgotten she was coming by.

Charlotte gazed over her shoulder. "What's the rush, boys?"

"Uh, no rush," Ed told her. "What makes you think there's a rush?"

"Oh, maybe because of the way you came charging in here just now."

Andre indicated with his eyes that Charlotte should leave. They needed to talk alone. Reece understood. He came around the desk to her. "Could we do this later, maybe over dinner?"

She gave him a curious frown. "Are you asking me out?"

"Yes. Well, not exactly, we both have to eat so why can't we do that and discuss the case?"

"I'd better take you up on that offer before you change your mind. Where and what time?" Charlotte stood up. She had a sneaking suspicion the men wanted to talk.

"How about Yang Chow's around seven? You like Chinese, don't you?" Reece glanced at his watch, although he didn't know why. Seven was a couple of hours away.

"As a matter of fact I love Chinese. Yang Chow's slippery shrimp is the best." She walked to the door, eyeing Andre and Ed. "Enjoy your *chat*." She gave Reece a smile and headed down the stairs. Charlotte found herself still smiling when she reached the lobby and realized she looked forward to their dinner date.

Reece closed the office door and turned around. "Why did you come rushing in here like the devil was on your ass?"

"We got one of 'em, Daniels," Ed told him, a gleam of triumph in his wrinkled eyes.

"What do you mean, you got one of them?" Reece frowned.

"Just what I said. What part of we got one of 'em don't you get?"

"You captured a big hairy werewolf?" Reece folded his arms across his chest and eyed both men.

"What's with you, Daniels?" Ed asked.

"Think about it for a minute."

Both men stared at him with blank expressions.

"The moon won't be full until tomorrow night. Something we didn't consider when Sarah told us about the sighting."

Andre and Ed looked at each other. "Then how the hell is that thing a wolf?" Ed asked.

"Good question. We need to see Adrian." Reece grabbed the keys to the other van and headed to the door. "Well, are you coming?"

"No can do. We have to meet Sarah at the facility. Philippe will be delivering our message to her," he said, checking his watch, "right about now."

"I'll go talk to Adrian and meet you out there when I'm done."

"Okay," Ed said. "Just don't take too long. We need everyone on board when that thing comes to."

CHAPTER THIRTEEN

Sarah had just stepped out of St Joseph's and was about to lock the front doors when Philippe pulled up in his old pickup truck. She turned around and frowned when she saw him waiting on the street at the bottom of the steps. She came down the steps to greet him. "Hello, Philippe, what brings you back at this time of day?" She checked her watch. It was just after six.

"Andre and Ed have captured a creature," he told her.

Sarah's eyes widened. "When?"

"I am sure they will answer all your questions when you get to where they have taken it," Philippe said, passing her a piece of paper. "Here is the address. You should go out there as soon as you can."

"I'll leave right away."

The pair headed to the vestry garage and Philippe opened the door. Sarah thanked him, climbed into the four-wheel drive and backed out of the driveway. She glanced into the rear view mirror and saw Philippe closing the garage door. He'd been part of her congregation for several years and also had a secret.

He knew about the creatures roaming the world at night while people slept. Vampires, Lycanthropes, Demons and a multitude of otherworldly inhabitants had discovered a way to cross the supernatural threshold into the real world and had become a serious threat. One afternoon, he had overheard Sarah's telephone conversation with Reece and decided to tell his story. Now he worked with the group on a part-time basis, helping to eradicate the world of such creatures in remembrance of his daughter, who had been taken ten years ago. There had been no trace of her in that time, and her body was never found. He prayed she had come to a quick end, because he didn't want to consider the horror of what had been her fate.

Sarah keyed the address into her navigation device and headed for the highway.

This find was incredible. They had been trying to capture a werewolf for the past couple of months. The creatures had always managed to keep one step ahead of them. Now they had one—a living, breathing Lycanthrope. Could it be one of the missing teens? Time would tell.

‎＼： ∂CƠ

Reece sped toward Beverly Hills to see Adrian. When he caught sight of the digital clock on the dash he remembered Charlotte and their dinner date at seven. It was already 6:47. "Dammit! I can't stand Charlotte up." He pulled into the curb, grabbed his cell phone and hit speed dial. Adrian's number appeared on the screen. Reece asked him to come out to the containment facility around ten.

He did a U-turn and headed for Yang Chow's in China Town. He looked forward to dinner with Charlotte. He knew it wasn't an official date, but he could dream. Something he hadn't allowed himself to do in a long time. He'd come to realize his feelings for Charlotte had grown. They were a good team, and he got along well with her son. Tommy was a great kid. Reece hoped the chemistry between them worked just as well off the job. He was certain it would and tonight would be the deal-breaker.

His thoughts strayed from Charlotte to the monster Ed and Andre had captured. How did it turn before the full moon? If those things could change at will the city was in serious trouble.

Yang Chow's came into view. Reece did a U-turn, parked the van in the parking lot behind the restaurant and walked down the alley to the street. It was a busy night and he was glad he'd booked ahead.

Charlotte was outside the restaurant. She looked different, more feminine. Maybe it was the floral dress she'd chosen to wear. At work, she wore a two-piece pants suit. Practical? Yes. Feminine? No. She was five feet, seven inches tall with short, brunette hair, expressive hazel eyes and a smile to die for. Reece's heart did a happy dance. He couldn't wait to spend the evening with her.

Charlotte noticed him coming toward her and smiled. "Hi."

"Hi. Shall we go in?" Reece opened the door and gestured for her to enter the restaurant ahead of him.

Charlotte waited for him then linked her arm through his.

The man at the counter asked for the reservation name.

"Daniels," Reece replied.

"Follow me, please," he said, collecting two menus and ushering them to their table. "Someone will take your order soon. Enjoy." He placed the menus on the table and returned to front of house.

Charlotte opened hers to peruse the selection of dishes. She was nervous. Tonight, she and Reece would spend time together as regular people, not work colleagues. She felt her face grow warm and hoped it didn't show.

Reece glanced at her over his menu. He wasn't sure what to say to kickstart the conversation. He didn't want to begin the evening talking shop, but they couldn't sit and stare at the menus all night. He cleared his throat. "They have a great selection, don't they?"

Charlotte kept her eyes on the menu. "Yes, they do. I'm not sure what to try. I usually order the slippery shrimp. It's really good. I think I mentioned that earlier, didn't I?"

On impulse, Reece plucked the menu from her hand. "Why not let me order?" He sat the menus on the table.

"All right," Charlotte agreed, smiling. Butterflies flitted in her stomach. It felt strange and nice.

Reece knew he should pay Charlotte a compliment. He wanted her to know he appreciated the effort she'd made to dress up. "You look lovely."

"Thank you. I didn't think you'd notice," she replied, feeling the heat return to her cheeks.

"I noticed," he said, smiling. He spotted a waitress. "Excuse me." The waitress came to their table. "Could we order a couple of drinks?"

"What would you like?"

Reece looked at Charlotte.

"Water's good."

He turned to the waitress. "An Evian and a Budweiser thanks."

"Are you ready to order?"

"Not yet."

"I'll be right back with the drinks." The waitress headed to the kitchen.

"You drink a lot of water, don't you?" Reece said.

"It's good for you, better than sugar-filled sodas or beer."

"I guess. But I don't mind a beer once in a while."

"Oh, I didn't mean…"

"I know." He reached across and rested his hand on hers.

Charlotte's heart fluttered. Reece's gentle touch sent a tingle through her body and she liked it.

℘℧℘

Andre and Ed arrived at the containment facility at the same time as Sarah. She had just pulled the four-wheel drive onto the gravel run off as Ed stopped the van in front of the main entrance.

At the gate, Sarah gazed around the compound through the high wire fence. Impressive. She knew they'd found a secure location to confine the wolves, she had no idea it was the old State Prison. This facility had been the prison of all prisons in its day. She acknowledged the pair as they approached. "Hello, how are you this evening?"

"Good. You?" Ed asked.

"I'm intrigued," Sarah said. "How did you manage to capture one of those monsters?"

"Tranquilizer rifle," Ed told her. "Remember we used it on Jacques' adherents?"

"Yes, but I didn't think you still had it."

"Don't throw anything useful away. That's my motto. You never know when it might come in handy."

"Too true." Sarah stepped up to the gate.

Ed unlocked the padlock and swung one gate back, gestured to the opening and said, "Ladies first."

Sarah stepped into the compound, Andre followed. Ed locked the gates before moving ahead of them. "This place is perfect for holding those furballs. And I'm sure we'll get more of 'em, once we know the location of the lair," he said, leading the way to the security entrance of the two-story building.

When they reached the building, Ed continued his commentary while he unlocked the heavy metal door. "We've made a few necessary improvements. The bars on the cells and windows have been coated with pure silver. If those suckers even attempt to escape they'll get fried."

"Do you know anything about the one you caught?" Sarah asked.

"It hasn't regained consciousness yet," Andre told her.

"Do you know its gender?"

"Male," Ed said with confidence.

Sarah frowned at him. "You're sure?"

"Of course I'm sure. I think I know a di…"

"We're sure," Andre gave Ed a disapproving stare.

"What?" Ed shrugged. "All I was gonna say…"

"Yes, Ed, I understand. Thanks," Sarah said.

"After you," Ed offered, holding the door for her.

The corridor led to the maximum security cell block. Ed had explored the main building and found a functioning gas chamber which, to his mind, could prove useful.

CHAPTER FOURTEEN

Melinda sat by the center window of the small room and looked out at the surrounding dense woods. A tear slid down her cheek as she wondered why this had happened to her. Patrick had explained that each one of them, after embracing their new existence, could return to their lives and no one would be any the wiser.

How was that possible? Wouldn't someone notice a difference? Melinda heard footsteps behind her and eyed Claire's ghostlike reflection in the window pane.

"How're you doing?" Claire sat beside her. "I know it's a lot to take in. Once you've been through it, things will get easier. Promise." She gave Melinda's hand a reassuring squeeze.

Claire was nice and Melinda needed an ally. She had no idea what would happen, even though Patrick had been very explicit in his explanation of the process. He also told her they had another leader. The way he'd explained it, *the* leader and Alpha of the pack. Melinda had the sudden urge to laugh hysterically. She couldn't believe she'd been pulled into this nightmare world, and that it was real.

A quote by Pablo Picasso popped into her head, one she had read while doing an art assignment for school: *'Everything you can imagine is real'*. She shivered as the words echoed through her mind. She had always thought how stupid it was for kids to be afraid of the Boogie Man and other nightmarish monsters. Now she understood why.

Claire leaned in to her, a concerned frown on her face. "You all right?"

Melinda gave a wry smile. "Yeah. I'm fine." Although she knew she never would be again.

CHAPTER FIFTEEN

Ed Borenko paced the corridor sweating on Reece's whereabouts. He'd said he wouldn't be long, so where was he? They were running out of time. The thing in the infirmary was waking up.

When Reece and Adrian entered the Maximum Security block Ed jumped on the PI. "Where the hell have you been, Daniels? You said you wouldn't take too long."

"Remember I made dinner plans with Charlotte? I couldn't just leave her sitting at the restaurant, could I?"

Ed locked the door and led the way along the corridor. "Yeah, ok, you're right, wouldn't be a good move. Missing Persons have anything new?"

"No. And Jamieson is trying to undermine Charlotte's investigation. She's already been grilled by their boss."

"So, what's she gonna do about it?" Ed asked. "Does she need someone to straighten Jamieson out?"

Reece stared at him. "You know someone who can do that?"

"Sure. I have certain contacts when I need 'em."

The PI frowned. This was a side of his ex-boss he never knew existed and wasn't sure he liked.

Sarah and Andre stepped into the corridor as the men approached the windowed office. They'd been waiting a long time for Reece to arrive. Sarah was surprised to see Adrian and it showed on her face.

"Hello, Sarah," Adrian said. "I'm here at Reece's request."

She gave him a bewildered frown.

"That is what you were about to ask me, isn't it?"

"How did you … never mind." She realized he'd read her thoughts.

"I wanted to find out more about these creatures," Reece told her. "I was under the impression they changed on the full moon. Now it seems they're morphing much sooner." He turned to Adrian. "Why is that?"

"Well, not all werewolves change on the full moon. Some can do it at will," Adrian explained. "It depends on whether they were bitten or cursed, or bitten by someone who was cursed."

Reece frowned. "So these things can change whenever they friggin' want?"

"Most packs have an Alpha male and, in some cases, an Alpha female to keep the wolves in line. They monitor the pack's movements and won't allow the members to hunt at random. Set timeframes would be implemented to prevent detection."

Reece paced. "The abducted kids were taken around the full moon, so maybe it's an indication of when that wolf pack changes."

"They are unpredictable creatures. I wouldn't hold to that theory."

Ed opened the connecting door. The creature was strapped to a gurney in the infirmary. This new insight made him more determined to get whatever they could out of their captive, before someone else was taken. "What are we waitin' for? Let's get in there."

The group followed him in.

They stood in a circle around the creature, studying it. Sarah, in particular, watched it with concern. The information Adrian had given threw a whole new light on the subject of how and when these creatures attacked.

"So how are we supposed to know when the next attack will be, if we can't follow some kind of pattern for the pack?" Sarah asked.

"I'm sure if we sit down and check the dates of the abductions there will be a pattern," Adrian told her. "As I mentioned, the Alphas would have some kind of schedule in place. The abductions will be linked in that way."

"What if they aren't?" Ed asked.

"I'm sorry, Ed, I don't have all the answers."

Reece watched the drowsy wolf. Would it talk once it returned to human form? He didn't think so. There had to be a Lycan code of some kind, similar to the saying: Death before dishonor.

The creature opened its eyes, lifted its massive head, and moved its groggy gaze around the room and the people in it. If it wanted to break free it could. It had no intention of doing so. Not yet. Timing was everything.

CHAPTER SIXTEEN

The next morning, Charlotte pulled into the precinct parking lot and before she could get out of her car Ned Bowers cornered her. He tapped on the driver's window, startling her. When she saw it was him she groaned inwardly. Couldn't she start one morning without his pompous monologue? Her finger hovered over the button in the armrest. Should she or shouldn't she? She pressed the button and gave a silent sigh as the window glided into the door. "Morning, Ned," she said, giving him a thin smile.

The disgruntled DA was not in the mood for pleasantries. "Any developments on the Grahame case yet?"

"I did say you'd be the first to know when I had something," she told him, her voice tight. "Why are you so concerned with this particular case? Your line of work is murder investigations."

"Richard Grahame is a prominent businessman, Charlotte. It's imperative we get this case wrapped up as soon as possible." He glanced at his watch.

"Why should this case be any more important than the hundreds of others we have?"

Ned didn't respond to her question. "I have a meeting to attend. Keep me informed." He marched across the car park and into the building.

Charlotte expelled an exasperated huff. That man infuriated her. She gathered her belongings, opened the car door, and stepped out. Gazing around the parking lot, she noticed Josh pulling into a space a few cars along. She closed the door, pressed the remote and hurried over to the doorway before he had a chance to catch up to her. *One asshole in the morning is quite enough.*

When she entered the lobby Reece was there. She was pleased to see him. "Good morning," she said cheerfully, and meant it.

"Morning. I thought we could discuss the case as we didn't get around to it last night."

Charlotte felt her face grow warm. "Ok. Let's head upstairs." They had enjoyed the food and getting to know each other the previous evening. It had been a great night, after the nervous tension had dissipated, and Charlotte realized her feelings for Reece had grown.

"Sure." Reece followed her to the open elevator.

Josh came into view and Charlotte jabbed at the button, hoping the doors would close before he reached them. They didn't.

"Morning, Charlotte, Reece."

"How are you, Josh?" Reece attempted civility despite his dislike for the man.

"I'm excellent. You?"

"I'm good." Reece glanced at Charlotte. She remained silent.

Josh was curious. "To what do we owe the pleasure?"

"Charlotte has asked me to assist with the investigation."

"Is that so?" Josh shot Charlotte a dour look. "Yes, I heard you've helped with previous cases."

"Anything that pushes the investigation forward is a good thing, don't you agree?"

"Of course."

The elevator doors opened, both men waited for Charlotte to step out.

"What's your theory?" Josh was intrigued. He knew Charlotte was losing ground and he was pleased.

"Right now, I don't have one. I plan to go through what the department has with fresh eyes and see where that takes me." Reece didn't want to give the detective the upper hand. The less he knew the better.

Josh wanted to laugh in Reece's face. It appeared the private detective was clueless. When the time came, their boss would listen to him rather than some jaded ex-cop with nothing to go on.

Once out of the elevator, Charlotte made her excuses, grabbed Reece by the arm, and headed to her desk. She wanted to talk to him about the planned meeting with the caller without Josh's involvement. She dropped her bag onto the desk, pulled up a nearby chair and asked Reece to sit down.

"I wanted to talk to you alone about the meeting with the kid." Charlotte slumped into her chair and sighed.

"You know the old saying, Charlotte, 'keep your enemies closer.' He knows you're up to something." Reece directed her gaze across the room. Josh was by the water cooler watching them.

"I don't care. He's causing too many problems with the investigation. If I can keep him at a distance, I'll be a happy woman … or detective … or both." She smiled.

"I want to go with you." Reece was adamant.

"He made it clear to come alone," she told him. "I can't take a chance on him seeing you." She folded her arms across her chest. "Besides, we decided on an out-of-town bus depot so it won't be that risky."

"What if I wait in the car? You could wear a wire and if anything happens…"

"No. This is my one chance to find out where Melinda is and I can't screw it up. I appreciate your concern, but I do know what I'm doing."

"I don't doubt that, it's just … I don't want anything happening to you."

Charlotte rested her hand on his. "Nothing will. I promise." She squeezed his hand. "Besides, you owe me another dinner, remember?"

Reece smiled. "I did say that, didn't I?"

"Yes, and I'm holding you to it."

He tried to convince her again. "What if I park on the outskirts of the town? If anything goes wrong you can call me. I'd be close enough to get to you."

"He asked me to turn off my phone."

"And you think that's wise?" Reece shifted in his seat. "That leaves you vulnerable from where I'm sitting."

"I'll have my gun. If he tries anything, which I don't think he will, I'll be prepared."

"What time?"

"Tonight at nine."

"You'll call me when you're done?"

"Of course I will." She patted his hand.

Reece grabbed hers. "Please be careful, Charlotte."

୫ଠଓ

After leaving the precinct, Charlotte made her way home, stopping to pick up a few necessities on the way. When she entered her apartment she could hear Mrs. Jenkins and Tommy playing UNO™ in the living room. Tommy's cheeky giggle told her he was winning, as usual. Charlotte didn't get much time to play games with her son these days, something she loved to do. So tonight before she left she planned to do just that.

Charlotte walked along the hallway and into the living room. The minute Tommy saw her he jumped up and ran across the room. "Hi, Mom, can I help you with one of those," he offered, pointing to the bulging shopping bags in her arms.

"Thanks honey." She handed him the lighter of the two.

Tommy took the bag into the kitchen, emptied it and put the groceries in the pantry. Charlotte realized she'd trained him well. He would make a great husband one day. She entered the kitchen, pushed the heavy bag onto the counter and unpacked it.

Mrs. Jenkins was ready to leave by the time Charlotte and Tommy finished with the groceries.

"I have a work meeting later and I don't want to leave Tommy home alone. Could you come back around seven thirty?" Charlotte asked.

Mrs. Jenkins expression softened, she was a gentle-looking woman with a kind face. "You work too hard, dear. Of course I'm happy to come back, if you need me."

"I have some distance to travel and want to head off early so I don't get caught in traffic. This meeting is very important and I have to be on time."

"All right," Mrs. Jenkins said as she walked along the hall and picked up her bag and jacket. She turned to Charlotte. "You could do with a vacation, dear. It would be good for you and Tommy to spend some time together." She opened the door and stepped into the hallway. "I'll be back at seven thirty on the dot."

Charlotte scooted Tommy along the hallway into the living room. "Hey, bud, what would you like for dinner? I got two of your favorites —macaroni cheese and hotdogs." She smiled. "And after dinner we can play a game before I have to leave."

Tommy plonked himself onto the sofa. "That's great, Mom! Could we have macaroni cheese pleeeeease? I love that stuff."

"Macaroni and cheese it is. Why don't you go wash up for dinner, while I get started?

"Okay." He sprang off the sofa and padded along the hallway in his socks.

It felt good to be home with him, preparing his favorite dinner. She missed it. The recent abductions had kept her away from home far too often, and although she knew her job was important, Tommy was more important. Tonight would be a fresh start. She would make a conscious effort to spend some mother and son quality time with him from now on.

While she prepared a small green salad to accompany their dinner, the phone rang. Charlotte wiped her hands on her apron and plucked the cordless phone from the wall. "Hello?"

"Hi, it's me," the familiar male voice said.

"Hi, you, what's up?" Charlotte positioned the phone between her ear and shoulder and continued slicing the cucumber.

"I just wanted to give you a call before you left."

"I appreciate that," she said, smiling. The idea of someone being concerned about her well-being was comforting.

"You'll call me once you're done, right?"

"Yes. Promise."

"Watch your back out there. You don't know if this guy is legit or if it's some kind of trap," Reece said. His gut told him she should have back up.

Charlotte kissed Tommy goodnight and tucked him in before closing the bedroom door and heading to her room. She unlocked the small cabinet, took out her pistol and two clips of bullets. She slipped on her shoulder holster and pulled on her jacket, then snapped the clip in place and pushed the weapon into its holster.

Reece's call had troubled her. She had no idea who the kid was or if it was a setup. A chill crawled over her skin and she shivered. Maybe she should have accepted Reece's offer. No. She was a cop and knew how to handle the situation. Charlotte glanced at her watch. It was time to go.

She came out of her room and closed the door. Mrs. Jenkins was at the end of the small hallway with a cup of tea in her hand. "Do be careful, dear. Tommy needs you," she said, as if she suspected the 'meeting' could be dangerous.

"I will. I should be back around 11.30." Charlotte stepped into the hallway and closed the door. An uneasy feeling washed over her and she tried to shrug it off as she made her way down the stairs.

When she left her apartment building she had the distinct feeling she was being watched. She checked her car, which was parked right in front of her, and scanned the street. No suspicious-looking characters lurking nearby or unfamiliar cars. "Don't imagine what's not there," she muttered.

Charlotte climbed into her car and checked the rear view mirror. Her cop instincts were always on the ball and she didn't understand why she felt spooked. She was about to turn the key in the ignition, when she heard a tap on the passenger-side window. Charlotte swung her anxious gaze toward the glass. Breathing a sigh of relief, she pressed the button and the electric window glided halfway. "What are you doing here?"

"I wasn't convinced you didn't need back up," Reece told her, opening the door and settling into the passenger seat. "No matter how good a cop you are there's always room for back up."

Charlotte sighed and smiled. "You know something?"

"What?"

"I was just thinking the same thing."

"Something bothering you?" Reece frowned at her.

"Kind of. Of all things, what you said on the phone made sense. I realized I shouldn't be going out there alone. I don't know this kid from Adam. How do I know he's legit? I could have been setting myself up for … God knows what."

"I'm glad you changed your mind," Reece told her. "I didn't want to have to tail you."

She looked at him, incredulous. "You'd have done that?"

"You bet."

Charlotte had mixed feelings. She didn't know whether to be offended or pleased. Reece was an honest man and he cared about her. She should be pleased. "So, are you going to follow me or hide in back?"

Reece kept his eyes on hers. "I think I'll come with, if that's ok?" He clipped in his seatbelt and Charlotte started the engine.

Neither of them noticed the dark sedan pulling away from the curb only seconds after they did.

CHAPTER SEVENTEEN

Patrick and the other members of the pack led Melinda out to the barn. She was naked and vulnerable beneath the blue cotton robe wrapped around her tiny frame. There wasn't any point to her being clothed as the change would destroy anything she wore. A cage had been constructed in the center of the huge space, its bars two inches thick, with heavy-gauge chains and shackles awaiting Melinda inside. She pulled back when she saw the cage and knew why she had been brought here. "I'm not going in there!" she said, her voice shrill as she backed away.

Claire moved up behind her and rested a reassuring hand in the center of Melinda's back. "It's for your own protection. We don't want you to hurt yourself or anyone else the first time. We've all been in there."

Melinda ran her eyes over the other members of the pack.

"You did say you'd cooperate." Patrick's glare was fierce.

"I – I know…"

"Either you will or you won't. Which is it?" Patrick strutted over to her, hands on his hips. "Well?"

"I'm scared, okay! I don't know what's going to happen to me."

Patrick grabbed Melinda's face. "That's why we're here. To *help* you," he said, his grin sadistic. "The first time is unbearable and exhilarating at the same time." He released her face and gestured toward the gate. "Now get in."

Melinda turned to Claire. The young woman nodded, walked over and opened the gate. "Go on," she said. "It'll be ok."

The full moon would soon be high in the sky, and everyone in the barn knew what would happen, except Melinda. Claire and Patrick led her into the cage and cuffed her wrists, ankles, and neck. The chains and shackles had withstood the change of many new wolves. Patrick bolted the gate then he, Claire, and the others waited outside its perimeter. It wouldn't be much longer.

"Won't you all change too?" Melinda asked, her voice quivering.

Patrick gave Claire a sideward glance and walked over to the bars. "No, Melinda, we're different. We have the ability to change whenever we want. We're not at the moon's mercy." He paced in front of the gate. "You, on the other hand, were bitten by a neophyte wolf. He, in turn, was bitten by our Alpha female who changed on the full moon. They're no longer part of our pack." He smirked, remembering how they died. A pack kill.

"I don't understand." Melinda frowned at him.

"There are different ways a werewolf can be initiated. We were bitten by the Alpha. He was cursed by a warlock. He can change at will. Neither the moon or any other element controls him."

Adrenalin rushed through Melinda's terrified body and she pulled and tugged at the shackles. "I don't believe you. Let me out of here, you're all crazy!" she screamed.

"You'd better believe me because your life depends on it," Patrick told her before turning around and stalking back to the others.

As the night shadows crept into the barn, covering the cage in darkness, four overhead floodlights snapped on one at a time. The stark white light spotlighted Melinda's naked body chained in the center. The pack remained in the shadows. The Alpha's arrival was imminent: to make his presence felt among the pack, and to initiate his new recruit.

When the full moon reached its peak a peculiar sensation coursed through Melinda's veins. Her vision altered and her heartbeat quickened. She stared at the group in a haze of altered color. Her hearing became even more acute and she could hear the others discussing her and the Alpha, who would arrive at any minute.

A surge of heat traveled all the way from her feet to the top of her head. Beads of perspiration dotted her forehead and trickled down her face and neck. Her body spasmed and her knees buckled, her weight supported only by the shackles. The metal cuffs bit into the flesh on her wrists and neck. She tried to stand, her knees wouldn't lock. Melinda panted. She sniffed the air and smelt blood. Her mouth salivated at the thought of raw bloody flesh.

Fine hair sprouted from every pore on her skin and grew thicker as she watched in horror. She heard cracking and squelching sounds as her body contorted into wolf form and she screamed—one, continuous agonizing scream of pain. Her fingers and toes elongated, black claws pushing through the tips. Her legs stretched and grew muscular, her backbone lengthened and a bushy tail forced its way from her coccyx. Through the blood red eyes of a werewolf she saw him. The Alpha. His virile scent wafted into her nostrils and she wanted him.

The group parted as he moved through them and approached the cage. He peered beyond the bars at Melinda's evolving wolf form and smiled. Observing the change always aroused his primal urges, and he couldn't wait to mate with her. Once her change was complete, he would enter the cage and they would copulate as only Lycan can. Her initiation into his pack would be fulfilled.

CHAPTER EIGHTEEN

Charlotte pulled off the road just outside of town and turned off the headlights and engine. She gazed at Reece sitting beside her in the passenger seat. They sat in silence looking into each other's eyes until Reece leaned across and kissed her. She pulled back, staring at him, not sure what she hoped to see in his eyes. After a brief moment, she grabbed his shirt, pulled him to her and pressed her mouth to his.

When the kiss ended, Charlotte moved away, brushed her hair from her face, and gazed out the windshield. Her heart beat so fast she thought Reece would hear it in the silence.

Reece was elated. "Charlotte?"

"Yes?" She kept her gaze straight ahead. She could feel heat in her face. Thank God it was dark.

"I've wanted to kiss you for a long time."

Charlotte let out a sigh. "I – I'm glad because ... I have feelings for you." At last, she admitted it to herself and to him.

Reece was surprised she felt the same and it took a few seconds for the information to process.

Charlotte interpreted his silence as rejection. "I shouldn't have said anything," she blurted, shaking her head. "I should've…"

Before she could finish, Reece pulled her to him and kissed her. When he let her go he smiled and said, "I feel the same. I care for you very much."

Charlotte wanted to continue their intimate tête-à-tête, but she had a job to do. She checked the dashboard clock. 8.55 pm. "Reece, you need to get in the back. It's almost nine."

He looked at her, sighed, then climbed between the front seats and hunkered down on the floor. "We'll finish this conversation later."

Charlotte peered between the seats and smiled. "I hope so."

She started the engine and eased her way along the main street. The place was quiet, no one on the street. The business center had closed for the night, except for a seedy-looking, twenty four hour convenience store adjacent to the bus depot.

Charlotte pulled up in front of the convenience store, turned off the engine, and sucked in a slow, steady breath. She wanted to look over at Reece for reassurance, but decided against it in case she was being watched. She patted her gun holster for comfort, opened the car door and got out. Charlotte stood behind the open door and checked both sidewalks. No one. The place had an eerie feel to it and she wondered why she had agreed to meet here.

Reece whispered, "Be careful." He wished he could go with her.

Charlotte closed the door and crossed the street, relieved she wasn't alone. She stepped onto the sidewalk outside and scanned the interior of the bus depot through the front window. The ticket clerk was behind the counter munching on a greasy burger and reading a magazine. Probably Playboy. As she moved closer to the double glass doors, she glanced around the seats and spotted a young man sitting in the far right corner, near the rest rooms. Charlotte pulled the door open and went in.

The driver in the car tailing them pulled into the curb not far from where Charlotte had parked and turned off the engine. He had already cut the headlights before entering the town because he knew the PI was cloistered in the back of the sedan. He picked up the night vision binoculars from off the passenger seat and aimed them across the street. He searched the depot, moving his sight around the room until it rested on Charlotte.

The detective sat in the far corner talking to a young man the driver recognized. He breathed a heavy sigh and picked up his cell phone. There would be consequences for his betrayal.

Charlotte waited for the young man to speak. He was anxious and kept checking the street through the front window. What was he afraid of? She glanced out of the same window. The town was deserted. Her eyes moved back to him. He was jittery and gnawed on his thumb nail. She reached across and placed a reassuring hand on his shoulder. "It's all right. There's no one here."

The young man shook his head. "They could be anywhere, you'd never know," he said, fear obvious in his voice and his eyes.

"Do you want to tell me why you brought me here? If it would make you feel safer, we can take you into protective custody."

"No, I can't be gone too long it's the night of the full moon."

"What does that have to do with Melinda's disappearance?" Charlotte twisted in her seat.

"Everything!" He jumped to his feet. "You have no idea what's going on, do you?" He stared into her eyes, anxious.

"Why don't you explain it to me?" She gestured for him to take his seat. The young guy perched on the edge of his chair like a skittish cat.

He jumped up. "Because you're going to think I'm crazy!"

"I won't. Whatever it is … look, why don't we start with names. Do you want to give me your first name?"

"There are far more important issues here than names."

"You know my name, won't you tell me yours?" she said in a calm tone.

"All right." He plonked himself down on the seat. "It's Dom."

"It's nice to meet you Dom."

"Yeah, whatever." He glanced at her sideways.

"So why don't you tell me what this is all about?"

Dominic jerked toward her and blurted, "Werewolves!"

Charlotte pulled back. "I don't understand…"

"I told you you'd think I was crazy, but I'm not! Melinda was bitten. That's why she was taken. She's on the property. Tonight she'll change for the first time. The Alpha will initiate her and…"

Charlotte reached up to him. "Dom, slow down." She stood up to meet his gaze. "Do you have proof?"

"Would I be proof enough?"

Charlotte's blood felt like ice water in her veins. Did he really believe that he was a werewolf? He had to be on something. She stared into his eyes, they appeared clear. "How can you prove what you're telling me?"

"Right now, I can't. Not here." He gazed outside. "I need to be confined somewhere I can't attack anybody."

Charlotte shivered as something cold slithered up her spine. She had heard some wild stories during her time on the force but this kid scared the shit out of her. If he believed he was a werewolf, maybe he was the abductor—the killer.

A dark sedan cruised past the bus depot and Dominic spotted it through the front window. "Oh shit, they've found me," he shouted. "They'll kill me for this, I've betrayed the pack."

Charlotte dashed to the window. Could she get the license plate? She spotted the red taillights of the indistinct vehicle disappearing into the distance. When she turned around, Dominic was gone.

She bolted out of the depot, calling to Reece as she rushed across the street. Reece threw the back door open and met her in the middle of the road.

"What happened? Reece asked.

"The young guy took off. He spotted a dark sedan and got spooked. We need to follow that car."

Reece frowned at her. "You don't want to go after the kid?"

"If we can get the license plate of that vehicle, we'll know who's behind all of this."

They jumped into the car, Reece behind the wheel, and sped off after the sedan. They were bound to catch up to it any minute as it hadn't been that far ahead. The road heading out of town was unlit, and as Reece and Charlotte drove on they were puzzled. Although the road stretched for miles they couldn't see any car lights in the distance.

"Maybe it turned off somewhere." He peered through the windshield, only the headlights of their vehicle stretched along the deserted road.

"There are no turnoffs," Charlotte told him.

"Where the hell did it go?" Reece pulled onto the gravel edge, turned off the engine and stepped out of the car. He looked along the moonlit road as far as he could see. There were no lights anywhere.

Charlotte opened her door and got out. "I don't get it. We weren't that far behind."

"Well I think we've lost them. We should've gone after the kid."

"Maybe." She climbed into the car and closed the door. She knew he was right.

Reece sighed. He knew she wasn't happy. He got back in behind the wheel. "Look, I just meant…"

"I know what you meant." Charlotte folded her arms and stared out of the windshield.

"The kid would've been the answer to who's behind all of this."

Charlotte turned to him. "I know you're right, but he freaked me out."

Reece frowned. "How?"

"You're not going to believe me," Charlotte said, feeling uneasy about having to explain.

"Try me. I was a cop, remember. I saw and heard a lot of strange things while I was on the force." Reece had seen and heard it all, and now he was fighting creatures that no one else knew about.

"Dominic told me he's …" Charlotte shook her head. "I can't."

Reece turned her to face him. "Yes, you can. The kid told you he's what?"

"A werewolf. The kid told me he's a werewolf."

"Shit!" He pulled away from her.

Charlotte stared at him. "Reece?" The feeling of suspicion curled through her body.

Reece hoped this day would never come. He wanted to protect Charlotte from the horrors that lurked in the dead of night. A stupid notion, he knew. How long would it have taken her to figure it out for herself, once there was more evidence? As Sarah said, Charlotte was an intelligent girl. And a good cop. He couldn't keep the horrible facts from her any longer.

CHAPTER NINETEEN

The Alpha opened the padlock and swung the gate back. Melinda's change was complete and she hung limp in the shackles, panting. He entered the cage and pulled the gate to, not taking his eyes off her. She was a beauty—her fur golden brown, not gray like the others. He could feel his wolf attraction growing as he moved toward her.

During the final moments of her transformation, he had removed his clothing and shrouded his body in a dark blue robe. Once he stood before her and she looked on him, craving him, he would change into his wolf form and they would join as one. His breathing quickened. He enjoyed this form of sex far more than human lovemaking. It was unbridled and satisfied his primal urges.

He stood before the neophyte wolf and lifted her face to meet his gaze. She was still disoriented. He smiled, knowing she would be worth the wait. He walked over to the bars and reached a hand through the staves. "Patrick, give me the key to the shackles."

Patrick stared at him. "Do you think it's wise to unlock her?"

"I don't intend unlocking them all. I want to remove the shackle from her neck." He preferred his conquests restrained. It made him feel in control, which he was—always. "Hand me the key. Now!"

The Alpha unlocked the shackle and hung it on a hook suspended from a beam above. He ran his hand down the center of her back to her buttocks/tail, grabbed one cheek in his hand and savored the feeling: firm and furry. He smiled as he inhaled her scent. She was untouched, a virgin, very rare these days. Her initiation was more than Lycan copulation, it was her first time and he would enjoy the pleasure.

Melinda opened her eyes again, her focus clear now, and gazed around the cage. She could feel something gripping her buttock and swung around, coming face to face with the Alpha. When their eyes met he transformed, and the primal hunger deep in her loins forced its way to the surface. The teenaged girl no longer existed.

Melinda came to dazed and disoriented. Her eyes darted around the subdued surroundings and she realized she was in a bedroom in the cabin. When her mind grasped what had happened to her, a sudden burst of adrenalin made her jump off the bed. She had been raped by the Alpha in front of everyone. Her skin crawled at the thought of his touch.

A chill spread over her body and when she glanced down at herself she was standing naked in the middle of the room. Her breathing quickened. She wanted to scream at the top of her lungs. She was trapped in a suffocating nightmare. One she couldn't escape.

Out of the darkness, a male voice commanded, "Come back to bed. I'm not finished with you yet."

Melinda spun around and saw the Alpha in naked human form getting off the bed and stalking toward her. She backed away until the bare skin of her back touched the cold wooden door. She gasped and jerked forward into the arms of the man that terrified her.

"Now, that's more like it. You might as well come back to bed. There's nowhere you can go way out here." He gripped her wrist and pulled her toward the king-sized bed.

Melinda dug her toes into the charcoal shag-pile rug and stood firm. "I don't want to."

The Alpha swung around and slapped her hard across the face. "You will do as you are told, if you want to live." He hoisted her into his arms, walked across the room and tossed her onto the bed.

☙❧

Reece pulled Charlotte's car into the curb outside her apartment building and turned off the engine. The drive back had been silent. Reece wasn't sure how to explain about what the kid had told her. He had wanted to spare her, keep her out of harm's way, but now she was part of it all.

He turned to look at her, his heart heavy. Their relationship had just begun, and he wondered if it would continue once he told her what he'd known for so long. Charlotte's look of suspicion was apparent and he wondered what was going through her mind.

"Charlotte, I want to ex…"

She raised a dismissive hand. "Don't, Reece. Don't try to sell me some bullshit." She glared at him. "You know something … and it's obvious you've known for some time by your reaction back there." She sat with her arms folded across her chest, braced for a confrontation. "Werewolves? Are there really creatures like that out there? And have you known all this time?" She looked away from him and sighed. She couldn't believe he'd lied to her.

"Look, will you just let me explain?" he asked, reaching across to touch her arm. She pulled away from him. "All right, if that's how you want to play this. Yes, I've known about werewolves and far worse for a long time now. There are things out there that aren't even in our worst nightmares. I wanted to protect you from it. I didn't want you involved."

"Why? I'm a cop trying to head a futile investigation. Why wouldn't you tell me, so I had some idea of what I was up against? You can't protect me from everything, Reece. I need to do my job."

"I understand that. I wasn't trying to stop you from doing your job."

"Weren't you? By not telling me about those creatures, you were. I've been looking for a human perpetrator. How was I to know any different?"

"And what would you have done, if you'd known?" Reece frowned at her. "Gone after them? Where would you have looked? We don't even know where the lair is yet."

"I – I could've done something." Charlotte knew Reece was right.

"What?" he asked. "We have no clue where they are or how many of the kids have been infected. What could you have done?"

Charlotte threw up her hands, her voice shaky. "Something. Anything!"

Reece pulled her into his arms. "That's exactly how I feel."

It had all been too much for her. Overwhelmed, Charlotte burst into tears and sobbed against his chest.

CHAPTER TWENTY

Tommy was dressed and sitting at the table eating a bowl of cereal when Charlotte padded down the hallway, still in her pajamas.

"Morning, Mom," he greeted with a frown. "Aren't you going to work today?"

Charlotte walked over to him, kissed the top of his head and ruffled his hair. "Yes. I'm just going in late for once." She headed to the kitchen and was about to make coffee when she noticed the coffee maker was already on. She looked at her son. "Did you do this?"

He glanced over the back of his chair and smiled. "Yep, I thought you'd want some when you got up. Told you I was old enough to do stuff."

"I'm beginning to see that," Charlotte replied. She picked up the mug sitting on the counter waiting for her and poured herself some freshly brewed coffee, made by her son. She walked into the living room and sat down at the table. "So what other tricks do you have up your sleeve, young man?" she asked, ruffling his hair again.

Tommy jerked his head away. "Gee, Mom, I wish you wouldn't do that. I'm not a baby anymore."

Charlotte was taken aback by her son's reaction. She hadn't realized it bothered him so much. "I'm sorry, honey. I'll try to remember next time." She sipped her coffee.

He gave her a sheepish look. "I didn't mean..."

"I know. You're growing up and I have to get used to that." She leaned forward and kissed his forehead. "You're becoming the man of house."

Tommy beamed. "Am I?"

"Uh huh." Her heart felt heavy. She knew her son was growing into a young man. Soon he would be a teenager. The thought concerned her. Life was different for the teens of today.

Charlotte glanced at the digital clock on the kitchen counter. It was 8.12 am. "Why don't you grab your lunch from the refrigerator, Jessie and his mom will be here any minute."

Tommy picked up his bowl, went into the kitchen and put it in the sink, then grabbed his lunch from out of the refrigerator. The doorbell rang. "I'll get it," he said, sliding his lunch into his bag and running for the door.

"Hey, bud, how about a kiss?" Charlotte called after him.

"See ya, Mom. Have a great day." Tommy slipped outside and closed the door.

Charlotte sighed. She had missed so much of him growing up and now she was paying the price. Soon he would be busy with high school, sports, girls and so much more. Would there be room in his life for her? Her quiet reflection was interrupted by the phone. Charlotte wanted to let it ring. In fact, she wanted to call in sick and not go into the precinct at all. The caller was insistent. She got up from the table, walked into the kitchen and plucked the phone from its cradle. "Hello."

"Detective Delaney, it's Dom."

CHAPTER TWENTY ONE

Reece was at his desk when the phone rang. He snatched up the receiver and gave the usual spiel. "Double D Investigations, Reece Daniels speaking." The double D stood for Daniels and Delacroix.

"Reece, it's me. Can you meet me at Sarah's church at one o'clock today? It's urgent," Charlotte told him.

"Is everything all right?" Reece was surprised to hear from her. After they'd returned to her apartment a couple of nights before, she had said she wasn't sure she wanted to see him again. She was angry that he'd lied to her. He hadn't lied, not unless lying by omission was actually considered lying.

"No. I had another phone call from Dom. He wants to meet me again. I want you to be there as back up."

"Okay, so why do you want to meet at St. Joseph's?" Reece was confused.

"He wants to meet me there."

"What?"

"He said he wanted to meet me in a sanctified place. I don't know why, he didn't explain. Perhaps he wants immunity or protection from whoever followed him the other night. All I know is this time we need to hold on to him."

"Yeah, for all our sakes." Reece glanced at his watch. "It's a quarter after twelve. I'd better get a move on. See you at one."

Andre crossed the office. "What was that about?"

"Charlotte got another call from the kid. He wants to meet at Sarah's church. The curious thing is why St. Joseph's? Could this all be some kind of setup?" Reece leaned back in his chair and frowned.

"It's strange he would suggest there, of all places." Andre sat down. "What do you want to do?"

"Good question."

"Do you want us along for back up?"

Reece considered it for a moment. "Yeah. Can you arrange it?"

"Sure. We won't be far behind you." Andre picked up the phone.

Reece grabbed his keys from the desk and made a beeline for the door. As he opened it, he turned around. "By the way, bring ammo, silver … just in case."

"Already one step ahead of you."

Reece nodded and walked out the door. He knew Andre had their backs.

Adrian and Ed arrived at the office twenty minutes after Reece walked out the door. Andre had the ammunition and extra weapons ready to go. He hadn't explained the situation on the phone; he wanted to do it face to face. The whole thing was too close to home now. Why did the kid want to meet Charlotte at Sarah's church? How did he know about it?

Once Ed and Adrian were seated, Andre began. "Reece had a call from Charlotte and that's where he is now. The young guy, Dominic, called and asked her to meet him again."

"So you want us along as back up." Ed knew before Andre answered.

"Yes. Dominic asked Charlotte to meet him at St. Joseph's."

Ed lurched forward in his chair. "Jesus, Andre, how did he know about that?"

"We don't know. That's why Reece wants back up, in case something goes down over there. If he knows about us the Alpha does too." He glanced at the wall clock. 12.40 pm. "We'd better get over there."

℘)Cℜ

When the trio pulled up outside St. Joseph's, Reece was already on his way down the steps. He'd been waiting at the front doors with Charlotte and Sarah. He opened the van's passenger doors and Ed and Adrian stepped out. "I'm glad you're here."

Andre came around the vehicle and joined them.

"An anonymous note arrived by courier about ten minutes ago. There's no way to trace it back to anyone."

"What does it say?" Ed asked.

"Come inside. We need to talk."

The trio followed Reece up the steps and they entered the building.

Sarah and Charlotte sat in a back pew while the men stood in the nave.

"I guess the best way to start is to read you the note. Do you want to take a seat?" Reece gestured to the pew in front of the women.

"Sure why not." Ed moved into the row and sat down.

Adrian sat in the opposite pew on the other side of the nave. Andre joined him.

Reece remained standing. "The note is from the kid." He cleared his throat. "It says, "'If you get this note I'm dead. I betrayed the pack. They don't like that. Death for disloyalty is their motto. What I told the detective is true. We are werewolves. Some of the missing kids are part of the pack now.

They'll stay hidden, just like they did before. No one will find them. That's why I'm telling you where they are, because I want it to stop. The killing, I mean. Too many people have died, including me. You have to stop them!'"

"The rest is directions to the lair." Reece folded the note and pushed it into the pocket of his shirt.

"Are we going out there?" Sarah asked, standing up and sidling out of the row.

Reece sighed. "Of course we are. But until we know this note is legit we're going to take it one step at a time. This could be part of some elaborate trap set up by the Alpha to get us out there where we can be killed."

"What do we do in the meantime?" Charlotte stood up and moved into the nave.

"Let's head back to the office." He turned to Charlotte. "Can you find out if the kid had a record? Might give us some insight into who he was, if he does."

"Sure. I'll need to go into the precinct though." Charlotte had already performed a preliminary check on Dom and came up with nothing. She'd planned to dig deeper.

Reece nodded. "Ok. Give me a call if you find anything."

The others followed Reece back to his office. It was time to devise the perfect plan.

∞⚬⚭

Tommy was in front of the television playing an Xbox game when the doorbell rang. He pressed the pause button, got up off the floor and raced along the hall. Thinking it was Mrs. Jenkins with the laundry he unlocked the door and swung it open. "Do you need any help with the…?" A man dressed in a dark blue suit stood in the hallway. "Oh, I thought…" What his mom had told him about not telling strangers he was alone popped into his head.

"Hi, Tommy, I'm someone who knows your mom. Is she here?" He peered past the boy as he spoke, then returned his gaze to him and smiled.

"Mom's at work." Tommy frowned. "Do you work with her?"

"She wasn't there today, that's why I'm here." He glanced past Tommy again. "Is someone with you?"

Tommy felt his stomach do a nervous flip. His mom didn't talk about the people she worked with, and Tommy had a feeling something was wrong about the guy. "Mrs. Jenkins minds me."

"Can I talk to her? Maybe she knows where your mom is."

Mrs. Jenkins waddled along the hallway with the overladen laundry basket, huffing and puffing. When she reached the front door, she stopped and frowned at it. Why was it ajar? Her heart palpitated as she dropped the washing and threw the door open. "Tommy? Tommy where are you?" she called, rushing along the small hallway to the living room. The game he had been playing was on pause, the television screen in fade mode. She hurried back along the hall and burst into his bedroom. He wasn't there.

"Oh, my God, where is he?" she gasped, stumbling into the kitchen, grabbing the phone and almost yanking it off the wall.

A police woman was questioning Mrs. Jenkins when Charlotte and Reece rushed into the living room. The older woman was on the sofa sobbing into a handkerchief and trying to relay what she could remember. Her face was flushed from crying as she explained that she had gone downstairs to the laundry room to collect the washing and bring it back to fold. Tommy wanted to help her. He's such a sweet boy. She was gone only a few minutes. He had been in front of the television playing a game when she left. And the door was locked.

Charlotte rushed across to her. "Mrs. Jenkins, how did this happen?" she asked, breathless.

The policewoman stood up and stepped between them. "Ma'am, if you just wait over there until I've finished questioning the lady, I'll be right with you."

"I'm Detective Charlotte Delaney. Tommy's my son."

"I know who you are ma'am. You need to wait over there and let me do my job so we can get your son back safe and sound."

Charlotte opened her mouth, but before she could say another word Reece took her by the arm and led her into the kitchen.

"What are you doing?" She shrugged out of his grasp.

"Doing the only logical thing I can think of right now. The cop's trying to do her job, Charlotte. Let her do it." He rubbed her arm.

"Who would do this, Reece? Who would take my little boy?" Tears welled in her eyes.

Reece shook his head. "I don't know."

Charlotte gazed up at him, a sudden look of awareness on her face. "What if *they* took him?" She raised a hand to her mouth. "Oh, God, Reece, what if the pack took him because they know we know?"

Reece stared into Charlotte's eyes, not wanting to say that he suspected the same thing. He wanted to console her, to allay her fears, not add to them.

Charlotte searched his eyes. "You think so too. You think they've taken him, don't you?" She burst into tears.

Reece pulled her into his arms and held her tight. They needed to step up their plans—and fast!

ಬಿಐಞ

Tommy regained consciousness in the trunk of a car. He was gagged and his hands were tied behind his back. His nostrils flared as he tried to breathe through his nose, the air felt thick and suffocating in the tiny dark space. And something on his clothes reminded him of the hospital.

Tears stung his eyes when he thought about his mom and Mrs. Jenkins, and how worried they'd be. His head felt woozy. How did he get here? He tried to make his brain think. He remembered the man at their door. The man who said he worked with his mom. The man in the dark blue suit. Was he driving? Where were they going?

Tommy wriggled forward and tried to turn over. He remembered the stranger danger video at school about kicking out the taillight if you were ever locked in someone's trunk. His feet faced the back seat and it was difficult to move without the use of his hands.

The car jerked to a stop. A door opened and closed. Tommy's heart thumped against his ribs. He heard footsteps crunching gravel as they moved around the car. His breathing quickened even more, his head spun. He remembered what his mom told him: 'When you feel nervous, honey, take slow deep breaths.' Tommy breathed in and out through his nostrils and could feel it working, until the trunk popped open.

CHAPTER TWENTY TWO

Ed Borenko opened the door to Reece's office and charged into the room, leaving the door open. "Daniels, we're goin' out there to get Charlotte's kid back, right?" he said, breathless, hurrying over to Reece's desk.

"As much as I want to, we can't go bursting into the lair without a better strategy. If we go out there half-cocked, we could all end up dead. Or worse, Tommy could."

"Okay, okay, but we have to get the kid back." Ed paced in front of the desk. "So how are we gonna do it?"

Sarah appeared in the doorway. "God, Reece, how did this happen?" She rushed across the room and stood beside Ed.

"The babysitter said she left Tommy playing an Xbox game while she went down to collect the laundry. She was gone a few minutes and when she got back the apartment door was open and the boy was gone."

"And you think someone from the pack took him, don't you?" Sarah asked.

"Yeah, I do. They know we know about them and this could be their way of putting a lid on the whole take them out deal." Something occurred to Reece. "Maybe it's a tradeoff."

Ed looked at him with instant awareness. "For the fucker we've got out at the facility?"

"Maybe. Until we hear from them, and I suspect we will, we'll just have to sit tight. The police are investigating Tommy's disappearance, so we'll let them do their job. For now."

Sarah came around the desk to Reece. "What if they…?"

"They won't!" Reece didn't want to believe the pack would kill Charlotte's son. He was a bargaining tool.

Adrian was the next one to arrive. "How is Charlotte coping?" He gazed around the office. "Where is she?"

"She wanted to wait by the phone, in case she gets a call from the kidnappers. And she said she needed some time alone. I had to respect that."

"Is it wise?" Adrian joined Sarah and Ed, giving them a brief nod. "What if they go back to the apartment?"

Reece hadn't considered that possibility. He grabbed the phone.

ℴ℧

Charlotte stood at Tommy's doorway staring into the empty room, tears spilling down her face. She hugged his favorite teddy to her chest and rocked back and forth. She wondered if she would ever see her little boy again, her oh so grown up ten year old. Did the pack take him? The noisy jangle of the telephone interrupted her thoughts and jolted her into the present. Startled, she dropped Tommy's teddy on the floor. Realizing what the sound was, she rushed along the hallway into the kitchen and snatched the receiver from the wall. "Hello?"

"Hi, it's me," Reece announced.

"Heard anything?" Charlotte asked, anxious.

"Nothing yet." He wished he had good news for her.

"Me neither. I'm beginning to think…" Beeps alerted Charlotte to another call. "Can I call you back, I've got another call?"

"Sure. Go."

Charlotte pressed the button to answer the second call. "Hello?"

"Charlotte Delaney?"

"Who's this?" An icy chill wrapped itself around the base of Charlotte's spine, and her heart shriveled into a tiny ball.

"Never mind who I am," the gruff male voice said. "We have your son. I want you to listen carefully to what I have to say, if you ever want to see him again."

ଽଠଓଃ

Reece thought about driving over to Charlotte's, just to be on the safe side. Adrian's suggestion that they could go back for her too bothered him. If the Alpha had taken Tommy, and Reece's gut told him he had, what would stop the pack from going back for Charlotte? It could be the Alpha's way of picking them off one at a time.

"Is Charlotte all right?" Adrian asked.

Reece looked up at him. "Yeah, I think so. She had another call. She'll call me back as soon as she's done."

"You're concerned about her safety, aren't you?"

"Yeah, well you made a valid point. We have no idea what those things are planning. For all we know they could come after all of us." He frowned at Adrian. "Is there a reason for the visit?"

"Does there have to be?"

"No." Reece shook his head. "Of course not."

"As a matter of fact there is," Adrian told him. "I've been doing some in-depth research on Lycan packs and discovered some interesting facts."

Reece raised a curious eyebrow. "What kind of interesting facts?"

"It appears the wolf curse can be reversed. There is a catch though. It can only occur if the victims haven't partaken of human flesh."

Ed frowned at Adrian. "What does that do for us?"

"It means that if Melinda and the other young people haven't fed, and someone can kill the alpha before they do, she and the other new wolves will be released from the curse."

"How would we know if they've fed or not?" Sarah asked.

"By the next full moon they'll be ravenous and will do anything to consume human flesh. If we can confine them then we'll know for sure."

The three turned to Reece. He seemed preoccupied with his thoughts as he stared at the phone.

"Reece, did you hear what I said?" Adrian asked.

"I heard." He rubbed a hand across the stubble on his chin. "That's good news. I hope for their sakes they haven't fed. It would be good to see the kids go home to their families. Charlotte's worked long and hard on this case. It'd be a great outcome for everyone."

The phone interrupted their discussion. Reece scooped it up. "Charlotte?"

"No, it's me. I take it Charlotte's not with you."

"You do know her son's been kidnapped, right?"

"Yes, an unfortunate situation."

"What do you want with Charlotte, Jamieson?"

"Look, I know you don't care too much for me, and I can say the same for you. That aside, the reason I'm calling is I've been to Charlotte's apartment and no one's there."

"Maybe she doesn't want to talk to you."

"I'm a detective I have access to crime scenes. Charlotte's not at her apartment. That's why I called you. I know you two have a *thing*."

"Where are you now?"

"I'm in my car outside her building."

"Stay put. I'm on my way." Reece slammed the receiver down and looked at the bewildered faces staring at him. "Charlotte's missing."

CHAPTER TWENTY THREE

Melinda watched the suit shove the boy through the front door, the force causing him to stumble on the threadbare rug. He was blindfolded, gagged and had his hands tied behind him. Melinda sprang from her chair and threw her arms out to stop his fall. The boy recoiled, his breathing ragged.

"It's ok. Don't be scared." What else could she say?

The suit glared at her and Melinda backed away and sat down. She didn't want to be hit again by anyone. The pale blue bruise on her cheek, covered with makeup Claire had applied, was a reminder of where she was and what could happen if she didn't do what she was told.

Patrick stalked across the room, grabbed the boy and dragged him along the hallway to one of the rooms. The suit waited until the pair was inside and the door closed before he spoke to the rest of the pack.

"The boy is to remain in the room. Understood?" He focused his serious gaze on Melinda and smirked. "He's our insurance policy, at least for now. Patrick has authority to deal with him, orders of the Alpha." With that said he turned on his heel and headed down the hall.

Melinda shivered, remembering when she'd woken up in the shed and her initiation in the barn. She straightened. Had the boy been bitten? Would the Alpha allow someone that young to be turned? He looked about nine or ten. She felt the sickening feeling in the pit of her stomach rise into her throat. No, she told herself. The Alpha wasn't that depraved ... was he?

Claire noticed Melinda's concern for the boy and crossed the room. "Everything ok?" She sat on the floor in front of Melinda's chair.

"What's going to happen to the little boy?"

Claire shrugged. "He's our insurance policy."

Melinda stared into her eyes. "What does that mean?"

"It's not for us to question. That could be dangerous." Claire rested a comforting hand on hers.

"But he's just a kid," Melinda told her. She frowned. "Has he been bitten?"

Claire's voice thinned. "No, of course not." She wasn't at all sure. How could she be? The Alpha and his cronies did whatever they wanted. She climbed to her feet and walked away, hoping she was right.

Melinda gazed along the hall. What could be taking so long?

CHAPTER TWENTY FOUR

When Reece arrived at Charlotte's apartment building, he parked his Mustang on the opposite side of the street, got out of the car and scanned both directions for Josh. He wasn't sure what kind of car the detective drove, so he crossed the road and peered inside every nearby parked car. All empty.

"Dammit!" he said. "Where are you, Jamieson? Why didn't you wait?"

Reece headed up to Charlotte's apartment to take a look around. He had been a detective too and knew the tricks of the trade. He'd be inside the apartment in seconds.

He climbed the stairs to the second landing and walked along the small corridor to number 24. A middle-aged couple passed him so he waited until they were gone before sliding the lock-picking tool from his wallet and fiddling with the lock. After a few seconds, he felt the click and pushed the door open and walked along the short hallway to the living room.

The last time he'd spoken to Charlotte was on the phone when the other call came through. Reece walked into the kitchen and scooped the notepad off the counter. He moved over to the window and studied the page. Charlotte had scribbled something down on the torn off sheet. He went back to the counter and plucked a pencil from a jar of assorted writing implements and ran the lead over the surface.

"Shit!" Reece tore off the page and pushed it into his pocket. He rushed out of the apartment, raced down the two flights of stairs and onto the street. When he hit the sidewalk he searched for Charlotte's car, hoping he was wrong. It wasn't there.

"Shit, shit, shit!" He rushed across the road, jumped into his Mustang and pushed the key into the ignition. The tires squealed away from the curb.

Reece pulled his cell phone out of his jacket pocket and pressed the number into the keypad. "Andre, get everyone together and meet me at St. Joseph's. Don't ask questions just do it!" He rang off and threw the phone onto the passenger seat. Pushing the accelerator to the floor, he stuck his old police siren onto the hood and sped toward Sarah's church.

As he approached the stop sign at the end of Charlotte's street, he spotted Josh Jamieson's car in the opposite lane. Reece screeched the Mustang to a stop in the middle of the road, got out and marched across to the stationary vehicle. "Where the hell have you been, Jamieson? I asked you to wait for me at Charlotte's."

"I had urgent business to attend to, sorry I didn't do as I was told," Josh retorted.

"Look, smartass, I don't have time for your shit. Charlotte's in trouble and we need to work together to help her." Reece stood with hands on hips.

Josh sighed. "I'll do what you ask only because I don't want Charlotte to get hurt, regardless of what she thinks of me."

"Park your car and come with me."

"I'm not leaving my…"

"You want to get into this right now?"

"All right." Josh pulled his Mercedes into the curb, got out and pushed the button on the remote. "You'd better hope nothing happens to my car."

Reece headed back to his Mustang. Josh followed. "Or what, Jamieson?" He stopped beside his car and glared at the detective. "This is an ok neighborhood. Your precious car will be fine. Get in."

CHAPTER TWENTY FIVE

The suit had left some time ago, leaving strict instructions that no one was to go near the boy. Patrick had seen him off and had gone back to his duties in the vegetable garden with the other guys. Some of the girls were in the kitchen cooking, and Claire had gone to her room, leaving Melinda to contemplate her next move. She wanted to find out if the boy was ok. Could she help him? How?

Melinda eased herself out of the chair and moved into the hallway. She glanced over her shoulder and scanned the living room before checking the other kitchen doorway that led into the hall. It was closed. She sneaked along the threadbare carpet to the room, leaned in and whispered, "Hello?" No answer. "Hey, kid, can you hear me?" Nothing.

She wondered if they had drugged him to keep him quiet. No. She remembered he was gagged. They wouldn't have removed it just in case he called out. Not that anyone would hear him out here.

Patrick had the keys. How could she get her hands on them? A sudden epiphany told her what she had to do. Melinda wandered back along the hall and opened the front door. Patrick had made it clear he had a thing for her and now she could use his weakness to her advantage.

Charlotte's senses were on high alert. She pushed through the trees until she came to a clearing and a rundown homestead. Drawing her weapon, she continued to move closer. She heard voices and ducked down behind some thick scrub. The voices were adolescent male. One ordered the others around, telling them to get on with the job and to hurry up about it. And don't give him attitude. *What a little punk.*

She realized she'd have to lay low for a while. When the sun set, she'd move in and find a way to get inside. Charlotte was determined to wait out nightfall and get her son back.

Melinda wandered out to the yard where the guys were working and stood nearby. She waited for Patrick to notice her. When he did, he told the others to keep working and walked over to her. "What do you want?" he asked, noticing the short skirt. She knew she had him right where she wanted him—compelled by his overactive hormones.

"I need to get some wood from the barn for the stove. Would you help me carry it into the house?" She played coy, biting her bottom lip.

Patrick's attraction for her moaned deep in his groin. His eyes moved from Melinda to the others working in the vegetable garden. "Garry," he called. "Take over till I get back." The young man dropped his hoe and moved into a position of authority.

Melinda turned and walked ahead of Patrick making sure he could view her long legs under the short skirt he'd already noticed. She was prepared to let him grope her to get the keys. She'd bear it to help the boy. Patrick was a good-looking guy, that wasn't the problem. He was arrogant and cruel and Melinda found that a turn off. Once she got her hands on the keys, she would feign feeling sick and make a hasty retreat.

The pair reached the barn and walked into the sun-streaked interior. Patrick pulled the large door shut and before Melinda knew what had happened, he pushed her into the pile of hay beside the closed entrance and climbed on top of her. Covering her mouth with his hand he said, "Don't scream, I'm not going to hurt you." She nodded, and he removed his hand.

"Why would I scream?" she asked, pulling him closer.

Patrick frowned in bewilderment. "Why'd you bring me in here?"

"Why do you think?" Melinda replied, her smile seductive.

He could feel his need growing inside his jeans. "Don't play with me, Melinda. You made it clear you didn't want anything to do with me. Why the sudden turn around?"

"Maybe because there aren't any guys here I'm interested in. You're different." She snaked an arm around his neck, pulled him to her and kissed him hard on the mouth, feeling around his jeans.

Patrick liked Melinda touching him and responded by running his hands over her body to her breasts, her slender thighs, and her most vulnerable spot. It was warm and moist. He pulled back and looked at her with lust in his eyes. "I'm going to enjoy this," he told her, pushing a hand over her mouth, reaching under her skirt, and pulling her skimpy lace underwear down to her ankles.

CHAPTER TWENTY SIX

By the time Reece and Josh arrived at St. Joseph's the whole group was gathered inside. Andre had also realized they might need some extra vampire muscle when they attacked the lair, so he asked Nathaniel to join them for the briefing.

Nathaniel still operated Decadent Desire, the night club once owned by Andre's brother Jacques, and had a small entourage of trusted immortals working for him. Whenever Reece needed assistance he and his team would be available.

Reece and Josh walked down the nave to the first row of pews. Everyone was surprised to see the detective with him, and Reece was equally surprised to see Nathaniel.

He walked over to him, hand extended. "I didn't expect to see you here, but I'm glad you are. We could use all the help we can get right now."

"I am pleased to offer assistance." Nathaniel's intense gaze fell on Josh.

Reece glanced over his shoulder. "That's Josh Jamieson. Works missing persons with Charlotte. He offered to help."

Sarah stood up and walked over to the pair. "Does he know?"

"Uh, no, not yet, there hasn't been enough time."

Ed joined them. "He needs to know what's goin' on, Daniels. He may not want in once he does."

Josh ran his gaze around everyone, then back to Reece. "What should I know and why wouldn't I help?" He tugged at the cuffs of his expensive suit and squared his shoulders.

Reece took him by the arm. "I think you'd better sit down, Jamieson."

He pulled free. "I'll stand, if you don't mind."

"Have it your way." Reece stepped into the center of the carpet beneath the pulpit and stood with his hands on his hips. "We have a problem in this city. There are things happening that no one's aware of. Things of a supernatural nature."

The detective chuckled. "Supernatural?"

"Look, Jamieson, just hear me out before running off at the mouth, ok?"

The detective pursed his lips and glared at Reece. He would much prefer to be somewhere else. "Fine. Get on with it." He glanced at his watch. "I have somewhere else to be soon."

Reece glowered at him. "We need you here. Where else do you have to be?"

"That's my business. If you need help, I'll help. Don't tell me where I should or shouldn't be. I do have other official duties to attend to."

Ed walked over to him. "Yeah? Well, once you hear what Daniels has to say you may change your mind about that."

"We've come upon a wolf pack. We believe they're responsible for the abductions," Reece told him.

"What are you talking about?" Josh looked skeptical.

"We're dealing with werewolves." Reece folded his arms across his chest.

Josh scoffed. "You can't be serious."

"We have one contained out at the old state prison."

"So what you're saying is you've captured a *real* werewolf?"

"Yeah." Reece's intense gaze met the detective's. "Got the balls to see for yourself?"

Steal fingers gripped Josh's insides and squeezed the air from his lungs.

The team made preparations to head to the lair. They planned to tranquilize the teenagers and transport them to the facility. Reece wanted to keep the Alpha alive long enough to find out if there were more Lycan packs in the state, or the country for that matter. If there was one lair there was bound to be more, the same as vampire covens.

Nathaniel's team would meet them out there in one hour. By that time, the sun would have set and Reece's group would be inconspicuous shadows amongst the dense army of trees.

In the meantime, Reece and Ed had taken the detective out to the prison. If he needed proof they'd show him proof. Up close and personal proof. Josh could shelve his attitude until the war was won. After that, the two of them would deal.

The van skidded to a stop at the fence. Ed and Reece climbed out of the vehicle and motioned for the detective to follow them over to the gate. Josh took his time. Once on the ground, he straightened his tie and brushed off his suit before joining them.

"This isn't a beauty pageant, Jamieson," Ed told him. "Let's move it, we have to get out to the lair."

ℰ〇ℛ

Melinda sat on a window seat in the empty living room gazing out at the thick, shadowed woods. Everyone else was in the kitchen eating dinner. She wasn't hungry. She was still trying to process what had happened in the barn. Why had her well-laid plan gone so horribly wrong?

How stupid she'd been not to think Patrick wouldn't take advantage of her. Tears welled in her eyes and her body trembled as she remembered how forceful he'd been. There had been nothing gentle about the way he'd used her. It had been the third time she'd been assaulted against her will. She had to get away, but she wouldn't leave without the boy.

Despite Patrick's quick release, which she'd been grateful for, she had managed to find the keys in a side pocket of his jeans after he'd pulled them off and thrown them beside her. Too engrossed in his own satisfaction, he hadn't noticed her feeling the pockets. Now she would bide her time—wait until they were all asleep—snatch the boy and get away, before they could do any harm to him.

ℰ〇ℛ

When they left the facility and climbed into the van Josh remained silent. Reece wondered if seeing the creature had been too much for him to deal with. He came to the conclusion Josh was an arrogant sonofabitch who didn't like to be proved wrong. Reece sat in the passenger seat watching him in the rear view mirror. *Could he be in shock or is something else going on inside that devious mind of his?*

Ed glanced at Reece sideways. "What's the matter, Daniels?"

"Nothing. I'm good." He peered into the rear view mirror. "What about you, Josh? You all right?"

The detective's dark gaze stared back at Reece through the mirror. "I'm fine."

"You don't sound fine." Ed noticed the pallor on his face.

"I said I'm fine." He turned away from the pair, folding his arms across his chest.

"Hey, Jamieson, there's no shame in being shocked by what you saw back there," Ed told him. "It's a lot to get your head around, ya know?"

Josh didn't respond. He had other things on his mind.

CHAPTER TWENTY SEVEN

As the sun slid into the distant hills, Charlotte thought she'd made a huge mistake not calling Reece before coming out to the lair. She wasn't sure what she could do alone against so many. *How many?* From what she remembered about the horror stories she'd heard as a teenager, silver bullets were the only weapon against werewolves and she didn't have any.

She heard a sound behind her. A twig snapped. She swung around, pulled her pistol and aimed. "Show yourself," she ordered in a loud whisper, her body trembling.

A familiar voice came out of the shadows. "You plan to shoot me, do you?" Andre appeared from the trees, his hands raised.

Charlotte breathed a relieved sigh and holstered her weapon. "Am I glad to see you."

"I come with reinforcements." He glanced over his shoulder. Sarah, Adrian, and a couple of men Charlotte didn't recognize emerged from the woods.

"You're not kidding," she said. "Where's Reece and Ed?" Her eyes moved past the group.

"They'll be here soon. Josh is with them."

"Why?" Charlotte didn't want him involved in her son's rescue.

"He offered." Andre shrugged. "So what's happening?"

"Nothing, so far. A group of young guys were out here earlier working in the garden. That's about it."

"Where are they now?" Adrian asked.

"I think they're all in the house. I haven't seen any movement outside for the past hour." Charlotte's gaze rested on the two unknown men. "Who are they?"

"Oh, sorry. The big guy is Nathaniel and the other is Philippe. He helps out at St. Joseph's," Andre explained.

"Okay." Something about Nathaniel unsettled her. She took Andre by the arm and moved away. "Why is Nathaniel here?"

Andre knew he would have to tell Charlotte what he was at some point and, as she was asking about Nathaniel, now was as good a time as any. "Charlotte, there's something you need to know about me, Adrian and Nathaniel."

"What is it?" Charlotte frowned. "Don't tell me you're werewolves too."

"No … we're immortals. Vampires."

Charlotte stood in silence, allowing the information to settle into the processing center of her brain. "Right. Vampires. Why not?" She shook her head. "Reece *is* human, isn't he?"

Andre smiled. "Yes, he's human."

"Are vampires and Lycan enemies?"

"They were once the daylight servants of vampires but now they have a deep-seated hatred for us, and with good reason. Ancient vampires abused and used them."

"Unbelievable!" Charlotte shook her head again. "You're going to capture them and kill them, aren't you?" She glanced at the rundown house.

"Yes, otherwise they'll continue to infect humans."

"What about Tommy? We have to get him out of there."

"And we will," a voice said from behind Charlotte.

Charlotte rushed over to Reece and threw her arms around him. "I'm so happy to see you. Where's Josh?"

Reece held her close. "He said he'd follow us out here. He had something to do at the precinct first."

He took Charlotte by the hand and led her to a small break in between the trees. Andre and the others followed.

"We need to survey the property, find out where everyone is, focus on a couple of entry points, get inside and do what we came here to do." He looked at Nathaniel. "Where's your team?"

"They are here." Nathaniel eyes moved to the woods.

Reece gazed around the trees. "Where?"

Nathaniel turned around. "Show yourselves."

Four immortals, two males and two females, materialized from the shadows as if by magic.

"Let's move in," Reece ordered.

They had to get to Tommy before it was too late.

CHAPTER TWENTY EIGHT

After he informed his boss about the raid, Josh decided he'd better keep his word and head out and join the swoop on the lair. Teaming up with Daniels and Charlotte to rescue her snotty-nosed brat would be a huge contribution to his list of achievements. The safe return of a colleague's child, and the other abducted teens, would be a step in progressing up the department's food chain.

When he left the building and crossed the well-lit parking lot, he noticed the Chief of Detectives' vehicle pulling out of a space a few cars down. Josh walked over to his Mercedes and was about to get in when he noticed another car leaving the lot. If he didn't know better, he'd suspect the second car was tailing his boss. He craned his neck to see if he recognized it. Was it Ned Bowers? He scanned the lot. The DA's car was not in its usual place. Was he following MacKinnon?

Josh decided to let it go. He had more important matters to attend to. It would take about forty minutes to get out to the cabin, so he had better step on it or he'd miss the action and wouldn't be able to extract some form of credit for the bust. Working with Reece Daniels left a bitter taste in his mouth. The ex-detective had been his nemesis for far too long.

ঞৎ

Both teams were prepared to seize the cabin and Reece wondered why Josh hadn't made an appearance. He'd given his word he would be here when they went in. *Where had he gone in such a hurry, and why was it so important?* Reece glanced at Charlotte. The terrifying situation had taken its toll on her and he recognized the signs of emotional strain on her face. He took her by the hand and walked away from the others.

"Charlotte, listen to me," he said. "We're going to get Tommy back safe and sound. You can trust me on that."

She sighed. "I hope so, Reece. What if…"

"Don't." Reece pulled her into his arms. "He'll be fine. They need him. They wouldn't jeopardize their chance for a tradeoff. Not yet."

Charlotte stared into his eyes, looking for reassurance. "You believe that?"

"Yes, I do."

She gave him a half-hearted smile. "Ok. I'll believe it too."

Reece rubbed her arm and smiled. "That's my girl."

Andre marched over to the pair. "We're ready to go."

Charlotte gave Reece an anxious look.

"You all right?" he asked.

"Sure. Let's get this done. I want my son back." She headed over to join the group.

Andre stared at Reece. "She's worried they've turned Tommy, isn't she?"

"Yeah."

"What did you tell her?"

"I told her he'll be all right." There was doubt in his eyes.

"Do you believe that?"

"Yes." He tried to sound convincing.

"Reece?" Andre stepped closer. "Do you believe it?"

He gave a heavy sigh. "I want to. I need to."

"Then be honest with her."

Reece frowned at his friend. "I'm trying to keep Charlotte together and focused. The last thing we need is for her to go off half-cocked and do something stupid."

Andre glanced over his shoulder and frowned. "Where is she?"

Reece threaded his way through the group searching for her.

Ed noticed. "Lost somethin'?"

Reece glared at him. "Yeah. Charlotte."

"She was just…" He glanced around. "Where the hell did she go?"

"Shit!" Reece pushed to the front of the group. "Everyone, listen up. Charlotte's gone in alone. We have to move now!"

℘℃Ω

Josh sped along the freeway, heading toward the location on his SAT Nav. He considered the possible scenarios as he drove. Maybe Reece would get injured in the crossfire. Maybe one of those things would tear him in two. Anything could happen. A smirk of satisfaction spread across his handsome, arrogant face. Could he be that lucky?

He took the off ramp and continued driving until he came to an isolated stretch of road that turned onto a dirt track. He switched to high beam and traveled into the dark woods. The musical tone of his cell phone broke the silence, startling him, and Josh swerved off the road. Gaining control of the vehicle, he hit the Bluetooth control on the console. "Jamieson," he snapped, flustered by the near miss.

"Where the hell are you?" Reece snapped.

"Good to hear from you too." Josh rolled his eyes.

"How long before you get here. We need to move *now*."

Josh was pleased the PI was agitated. "Something happen?"

Reece wasn't about to explain over the phone. "Just get your ass out here as soon as you can, otherwise you'll miss the action. And you wouldn't want to do that, would you?"

The detective was annoyed at the PI's accurate assessment. "Look, we can argue all night, it still won't get the result you want. So why don't you let me get off the phone and we can continue this later."

"You bet we will!" Reece rang off.

Josh growled and jabbed the Bluetooth button on the console. He was pissed. Reece Daniels was more perceptive than he gave him credit for. That was not a good thing.

He took the bend too fast and spotted the parked cars just in time to avoid a collision. "Shit!" He swerved around the van and pulled off the road in front of it. "Why did I offer to help these morons?" Josh reached into the back and pulled his Kevlar jacket over to the front seat. He got out of the car, shrugged into the vest, tightened the Velcro straps and checked his weapon. He popped the trunk, grabbed a flashlight, and headed into the pitch black woods.

CHAPTER TWENTY NINE

Melinda ran her hand down her thigh and fingered the keys in the pocket of her jeans. She was glad Patrick hadn't noticed them missing. Not yet, anyhow. She glanced down the hallway and focused on the locked door that held the little boy. Once everyone was asleep, she'd sneak along the hall, unlock the door and slip inside.

She had to get him out before something terrible happened. Her hands were clammy and her heart shuddered in her chest. She didn't care, she had to do it. She had to get them both far, far away from this terrible place.

Claire wandered across the room. "Heading to bed?"

Melinda gazed up at her. "Not yet, I just want to sit here in the quiet for a while."

The other young woman studied her. "There's no way out of here, you know. All the windows and doors are locked."

Melinda frowned. "I wasn't planning on going anywhere. Where would I go?"

Claire's serious expression broke into a slight smile. "Good. Patrick can be a hard task master sometimes and I wouldn't want to see you on the receiving end of his rage."

Melinda forced a smile. "Me neither."

"Well, don't stay up too late." Claire walked to the hallway and glanced back at her before heading to her room.

Goosebumps traveled up Melinda's arms and she shivered. She sucked in a deep breath and told herself 'I can do this.' There was no other choice.

Melinda noticed movement outside the window. She sprang to her feet and peered through the dirty pane of glass. Had she imagined it?

She glimpsed someone edging along the side of the house. A woman. Who was she? The boy's mother? Melinda's heart thudded in her chest and she gasped. What should she do? She swung around and glanced along the hall. All quiet. Everyone had gone to bed.

When Melinda returned her gaze to the window, the woman popped up in front of her giving her a start. She had something in her hand. What was it? A gun. Melinda darted away from the glass. The woman waved her hands and mouthed 'I'm here to help you.'

Charlotte recognized Melinda Grahame from the photos at the precinct. The sudden realization hit her. *Melinda is a werewolf.* What had she been thinking coming in alone? There was a pack of dangerous werewolves in that house!

She backed away from the window, shoving her gun in its holster. A sudden surge of adrenalin pushed her forward. Tommy was inside and she had to get to him before the others broke in. She peered through the glass. No sign of Melinda.

Charlotte prayed the girl hadn't gone to alert the pack. She crouched at windowsill height and continued watching the living room. What did she hope to see? Tommy? Melinda appeared on the other side of the glass. She pushed a piece of paper against the pane.

All the doors and windows are locked. I have a set of keys.

Her eyes exuded fear.

Charlotte pulled her notepad from her jacket pocket and scribbled.

How many inside? Where are they?

Melinda turned the paper over and scribbled. She smacked the note against the pane.

Ten. They're asleep in the back of the house.

Charlotte scrawled *What about the boy?*

Melinda's eyes widened. She scribbled again.

Second room on the right along the hall.

Charlotte nodded.

A noise caused her to swing around. Her eyes widened when she saw the dark shape behind her. Before she could react, she was whacked in the face and slipped into a black void.

Nathaniel and his team went in first. They would deal with the wolves before Reece's team moved in. The group moved closer to the cabin. Reece lagged behind, waiting for Josh.

He checked his watch and made the decision to follow the others in. It was late, and now that Charlotte had gone in solo it was imperative that they move fast. A horrible thought jumped into his head and he pushed it aside. Two hostages were better than one, and a cop was the perfect bargaining tool.

He caught up to Ed and Andre. "Is Nathaniel's team in place?"

"Yeah. They're just waiting for the go ahead."

"Good. The sooner we get this done the better." Reece was worried about Charlotte. Was she in the house? He hoped she'd used her head and kept a low profile. The situation had turned into an assault team's worst nightmare.

Charlotte came to in a dark room. She was gagged and her hands were bound behind her. What happened? Where was she? Someone had knocked her out. Although her mind was fuzzy, she thought there had been something familiar about her assailant. What was it? She gazed through the gloom. Was she alone? She strained to listen. Breathing? Tommy?

A single shot ripped through the silence of the woods. It had come from inside the cabin. Reece rushed forward. "Ed, send Nathaniel's team in *now*," he ordered, panic in his voice. He paced outside as the other members of his team waited to move in.

All of a sudden, a static response came over the handset. "Cabin is secure." It was Nathaniel.

"Copy that," Ed confirmed. "Come on, let's go." He drew his weapon, waved the others forward and marched up to the front door.

Nathaniel met them. "All wolves have been secured in a back room. Charlotte is inside with her son. He appears unharmed although unconscious. The girl shot a young man with Charlotte's weapon. He is dead."

Reece pushed past the huge vampire and rushed across the living room. Charlotte was perched on the threadbare sofa in the middle of the room with her son in her arms. "What the hell were you thinking? Did you want to get yourself killed?" he said, relieved to see she and Tommy were all right.

She looked up at him, tears streaking her bruised face. "I didn't plan on getting knocked out and dragged in here. I was careful."

Reece crouched in front of her. He brushed her bruised cheek with trembling fingers, his anxious heartbeat slowing. "I thought…"

Charlotte touched his hand. "I know." She forced a thin smile.

Reece crossed the room to Melinda. She was at the window where she always sat to look outside. "How are you feeling? I believe you assisted the team by killing one of the pack."

Melinda glanced up at him, her eyes vague. "Pardon?"

"You shot one of them." Reece crouched in front of her. "Who was he?"

"He … raped me. He wanted to kill the little boy. He deserved to die." She swiped at a solitary tear sliding down her cheek, sniffled, and blinked back more tears threatening to spill. "Patrick." Bile rose in her throat when she said his name and her chin quivered.

Reece frowned. He knew she'd turned, Dom had told them that, and he needed to hear it from her. "Were you attacked by anyone living here?"

She looked at him blankly, her thoughts disjointed and anxious—she had killed someone. "What did you say?"

"Were you attacked?"

"I – I…" She glanced down at her trembling hands.

"It's not a difficult question." Reece stood up and towered over her on purpose.

Melinda's gaze remained on her hands. "I don't know what you mean."

"You're a smart girl, I'm sure you know what I'm asking." Reece kept his serious gaze on her. She didn't look up. "Think about the consequences." He walked over to Sarah. "Have a talk to the girl and see if you can get anything out of her."

Sarah eyes rested on the young woman. "I can't promise anything."

"Do your best. We need to know if she's been infected." Reece wandered back to Charlotte. She had folded her jacket, pushed it under her son's head and gotten up off the sofa. "Do you think Melinda's infected?" She glanced across the room.

"Yeah, I do. She's not about to admit to anything, apart from killing the kid." He watched the two women seated at the window.

Charlotte looked up at him. "There's something I have to tell you."

Reece eyes returned to her. "What is it?"

She lowered her voice. "I think the Alpha is the one that hit me." Her fingers touched the purple bruise on her cheek.

Reece's intense gaze settled on her. "Did you get a look at him?"

"No, it was too dark. There was something familiar about him though."

"Who do you think it is?"

Their conversation was interrupted when a pair of paramedics entered the room and headed over to Charlotte and her son.

Josh Jamieson stalked toward the ambulance. He knew the PI would be pissed with his no show and ready for a confrontation. Testosterone was overrated. He'd been close enough to witness the whole break and enter. The team had everything under control, so why interfere?

Reece was talking to a paramedic when he spotted Josh. He cut his conversation short, stormed across the yard and grabbed the detective by his Kevlar vest. "Where the hell were you, Jamieson? You were meant to be here when the team went in." He shoved the detective backwards. "Haven't got the balls to take on a man, but you can weasel your way around a woman, can't you?"

Josh straightened his vest. "I *was* here. I thought someone should scope out the exterior, in case there were more of them in the barn or coming back from…"

"You're gutless. You know it, I know it. I'll bet you cowered in the bushes waiting for the whole thing to be over." He scowled at the detective, turned on his heel and marched back to the ambulance before Josh had a chance to respond.

The paramedics were loading Tommy and Charlotte inside.

"Reece, I need to talk to you," Charlotte told him as the paramedics lifted her gurney into the back of the ambulance.

"I'll follow you to the hospital. We can talk later." He took her hand. "Just make sure you and Tommy are ok first."

As the ambulance drove off, Reece scanned the crime scene. Josh Jamieson was once again nowhere to be found. That bothered Reece. A lot.

CHAPTER THIRTY

The ride to the hospital was super-fast as the ambulance hurtled along the highway, siren screaming, the red and blue strobe lights flashing like Christmas tree bulbs. After they took the off ramp, Reece got caught up at an intersection and almost lost sight of it. He managed to maneuver his way through the traffic and pulled in behind again. Although he knew which hospital they were going to, he wanted to stay close to Charlotte and Tommy until they got there safe and sound.

Once they arrived, Charlotte unclipped the safety belt, jumped off the gurney and hurried through the double doors behind the ER staff wheeling Tommy inside. She was afraid for her unconscious little boy. Afraid he wouldn't wake up.

A doctor stopped her in the corridor and asked to have a look at the bruise on her face. He took a penlight from his coat pocket and checked her pupils to determine if she had a concussion. She didn't.

Tommy was wheeled to x-ray, and while he was gone a nurse escorted Charlotte to a cubicle. Reece followed.

Charlotte sat down in the only chair. Reece crouched in front of her. "Are you sure you're ok?"

She nodded, rubbed her cheek and sighed. "I think so."

He reached out and touched her cheek with careful fingers. "Wait till I get my hands on that sonofa…"

"Reece, please. I'm ok." She gave a thin reassuring smile.

"I'm not. No man should ever hit a woman!"

Charlotte leaned forward and rested a hand on his shoulder. "You're one in a million. Where were you when I...?"

A nurse slid back the curtain and Tommy was wheeled in. Charlotte jumped up from the chair and rushed to his side, taking his hand in hers. She looked at the nurse. "Any news?"

The matronly woman in blue uniform shook her head. "Not yet. Doctor's looking at the x-rays now. Shouldn't be too long." She stepped out of the cubicle and pulled the curtains together.

Charlotte gave Reece a distressed frown. "Why doesn't he wake up? What happened out there?"

Reece wrapped a comforting arm around her shoulders. "I wish I knew. He's a strong kid, he'll be fine."

"I hope so." She gazed at her unconscious son with tears in her eyes. He was all she had.

ஏ௸

Ed Borenko drove the van full throttle along the dark road, transporting their captives out to the containment facility. There were three of them, two males and one female. The kids were with Nathaniel, who was right behind them. Sarah sat in the passenger seat, riding shotgun, facing the belly of the van, tranquilizer rifle aimed at the sleeping wolves.

"How much longer?" she asked, her nerves tingling. If one of them woke up, it would be a bloodbath—hers and Ed's.

He glanced at her sideways. "About fifteen minutes. You ok?"

Sarah shook her head.

Ed reached across and patted her knee. He knew it was inappropriate, her being a priest and all, but he just wanted to reassure her. "We'll be fine. Nathaniel's behind us. If anything happens, he'll take care of it. But nothing's gonna to happen, so don't worry."

The African-American priest gave a heavy sigh and scowled at him. "That's supposed to make me feel better?"

"Well, yeah."

"Didn't work."

He shrugged and gave her a crooked half smile. "I tried."

"Mm."

One of the creatures moved in the back, its huge leg banged against the sidewall causing the van to skew across the center line.

"Pull over, Ed. Pull over now!" Sarah's heart lurched in her chest.

The van screeched to a stop on the dirt shoulder of the dark narrow road.

Ed swung around and snatched the rifle out of Sarah's hands. "Which one?"

She pointed to a big brown male near the back doors.

The deep rumbling growl shivered through the van. The beast's red eyes snapped open. "Rrraaahhh." Heavy silver cuffs were searing its fur and skin. A pungent burnt hair smell permeated the van and prodded Sarah's nostrils.

"Shoot it, Ed, shoot it!"

The metallic ping of the tranquilizer rifle echoed around the interior as the drug-filled torpedo hurtled toward the beast, hitting it in the chest with a solid thud. Another horrendous loud "Rrraaahhh" echoed around the van and dissolved into a slurred "Rrr" as the beast slid into unconsciousness.

Ed looked at Sarah. "You drive. I got this." They switched seats.

Nathaniel appeared at the passenger window, startling the pair.

Ed wound the window down. "Jesus, Nathaniel, you scared the sh…" He shot Sarah a sideways glance, "…bejeepers out of me, could you let us know you're there next time?"

"I am sorry, my concern was that you were in danger and I did not want to alert the beasts to my presence."

"Well you accomplished that." Sarah was shaken; the caustic taste of scorched fur lay thickly on her tongue.

"I apologize," Nathaniel said. "Shall we continue? The sooner we have these dogs contained the better for us all."

"No kiddin'?" Ed turned to Sarah. "You right to go?"

She shivered and nodded.

When Ed turned to the window, Nathaniel was gone. "I wish he'd stop doin' that."

Sarah gave him a wry smile, started the engine, eased the van off the dirt shoulder and continued along the pitch black road.

ഇൗരു

Reece left Charlotte at the hospital while he headed out to the old state prison to help the others with the lock down. He also wanted to question Melinda further. She would remain at the facility until Reece had the answers he needed. He knew she'd been infected, but didn't know if she had fed. As soon as the next full moon came up she would turn and…

And what?

There were too many unanswered questions about how to reverse the 'curse', despite Adrian's knowledge and further research. If they could find a cure maybe the kids could go back to their families. Resume their lives. The big question was what if they couldn't find one?

Reece didn't want to think about that. All he wanted to do was prevent anyone else from being infected. They had the pack. The Alpha was next.

CHAPTER THIRTY ONE

The doctor's grave expression caused Charlotte's blood to chill in her veins. What would he tell her about her son's condition? She stood up and braced herself for the news she knew would not be good.

"Hello, I'm Dr. Sherman. I apologize for the long wait. I wanted to be thorough before I came to see you." He gestured for her to take a seat. She remained standing. "It appears your son is in a coma. We're not sure why because there's no head trauma, which is a good thing. The x-rays haven't provided any clues, I'm afraid. I am confident, though, that it's only a matter of time before he wakes up."

Charlotte folded her arms across her chest, more for comfort than anything else. "How can you be sure he'll wake up at all? Why is he in a coma?"

"We don't know."

"What *do* you know?" She brushed her son's hair off his forehead. His skin felt hot and clammy.

"I'm sorry I can't tell you more right now. We will continue to investigate. We may have to do a bone marrow biopsy."

"Why? What will that tell you?"

The doctor picked up Tommy's chart and scanned the front page. "I hope it will give us some kind of answer."

Charlotte was not impressed with Doctor Sherman. She signed the papers for the spinal tap, hoping it would provide the answers they needed. Tommy was taken away once again.

While Charlotte waited for her son's return, she settled into the armchair, closed her eyes and sighed. She was exhausted. As the soothing warmth of sleep wrapped its welcoming embrace around her, Charlotte drifted into a restless dream…

∽)(∾

…Reece's Mustang screeched to a halt outside the old prison. He flung open the door, jumped out of the convertible and raced to the gate. He unlocked the padlock, entered the compound, and reattached the lock. No one would get in uninvited.

Nathaniel met him at the door. "We have secured the do…, the wolves."

"Where's Melinda?"

Nathaniel bolted the door behind them. "She is with Andre and the priest. Why?"

"Because I need answers. Charlotte's son is still unconscious and she's worried he might've been bitten."

"And what will happen if he has?"

The pair walked down the long passage to the office.

"If Adrian's right about breaking the curse then we have to find the Alpha ASAP."

They continued through the office to the infirmary. Reece hoped to get information from the creature, but it hadn't changed to human form.

Nathaniel knocked on the door and Ed opened from inside.

"Any luck?" Reece asked.

"Nope. And there isn't much hope of him talkin' while he's a wolf."

"There has to be a way to get him to change." He looked at the vampire.

"Perhaps some form of distress would cause it to turn." Nathaniel stepped up to the gurney and stared at the beast.

Ed and Reece frowned at each other.

"What do ya mean?" Ed asked.

"Sear its skin with silver or jolt it with a laser gun." He continued to stare into the creature's red eyes.

"You think we should torture it?" Reece asked.

Nathaniel turned to him. "I believe you should do whatever is necessary to save Charlotte's son and the other young ones."

"I'll go get the stunners and silver chains." Ed hurried out of the room.

Nathaniel ordered the other members of his team to move out of the infirmary, leaving him and Reece alone with the creature. He locked the door.

While they waited for Ed's return, Reece circled the gurney studying the werewolf. Something about him seemed familiar. When he'd stared into its eyes earlier, he thought he saw a glimmer of the human beneath the fur.

Nathaniel stood by the door watching Reece, arms folded across his muscular chest, his back against the wall. It was necessary to take every precaution. Although the wolf was chained to the bed, it was no guarantee.

"I would not get too close, if I were you. These creatures are cunning."

Reece's eyes moved from the creature to Nathaniel. "I know what I'm doing."

Ed appeared at the door and Nathaniel opened it.

Before anyone could react, the creature snapped its restraints and propelled its huge body off the gurney. It grabbed Reece by the throat, sank its sharp canines into his shoulder and hurled him across the room into a glass medical cabinet.

Ed thrust his large body across the room and jabbed the monster over and over with the stunner. The beast roared and made a swipe at him with its large claws.

Nathaniel transformed into his vampire state, hissing at the creature. He wrenched at its arm and bent it backwards with a loud snap. The beast roared again, its arm hanging limp at its side.

The chief continued to jab at the creature with the electrical current until it fell back onto the gurney, out cold. He tossed the stunner on the floor and rushed to Reece's side.

Nathaniel followed.

The PI lay unconscious in a spreading pool of blood and glass fragments.

Ed felt for a pulse. "Come on, come on, where is it?" He prodded the vein in Reece's neck with his fingers. He stared up at the vampire. "I'm not gettin' anything."

Nathaniel got down on one knee. No heartbeat. He pounded his huge fist into Reece's chest twice and listened again. The heartbeat was shallow and unsteady. "He is alive, but barely."

Ed jumped to his feet, rushed across the room and slammed the duress button with his hand. The shrill sound of the lock down siren echoed along the corridors of the huge vacant building, alerting the other members.

℘℧℆

Josh decided not to go into the precinct, instead, he figured he should make an appearance at the facility otherwise the PI would wonder where he was and give him the third degree the minute he arrived.

He got into his car, backed out of the parking space and headed for the street. Just as he was about to ease into the traffic, he spotted Ned in the rear view mirror standing in the middle of the lot, watching him leave. Josh's suspicious mind went into overdrive. Why would the DA watch him? As he drove toward the freeway, he checked his mirror for Ned's dark blue sedan.

When he took the off ramp, he realized his suspicions had been unfounded. There were no headlights pursuing him. He breathed a relieved sigh.

Driving along the dark narrow road toward the old prison, Josh thought he could hear something other than the radio. He pressed the button and cut off the commentator mid-sentence. By the time he reached the facility it seemed all hell had broken loose. The shrill bursts of the lock down siren echoed into the night and orange strobe lights flashed from every angle of the old prison.

Josh pulled off the road, jumped out of the car and rushed to the gates. They were locked. What the hell had happened in there?

The electronic scream continued as Andre and Sarah raced into the infirmary. When Andre spotted Reece lying in a pool of blood he flew across the room, shoved Ed aside, fell to his knees and lifted Reece into his arms. There was little life force. He looked up at Ed; his face strained, and shouted, "What happened?"

Ed knelt beside him and pointed at the unconscious wolf. "That monster did it."

Sarah slid to the floor beside Ed, tears welling in her eyes. "Will he…" she shouted, the siren died and she lowered her voice, "…be all right?"

Andre stared at Reece's ashen face, blood trickling from the corner of his mouth. He checked his friend's eyes. Dilated pupils. "I don't think so."

Ed grabbed Sarah's hand, his face almost the same color as Reece's, his voice jagged and anxious. "What do you mean you don't think so? You're a goddamn vampire with supernatural powers, and a friggin' doctor, do something!"

Andre frowned at Ed. "There's nothing I can do. If I tried to help him I'd kill him."

"Try Goddammit!"

"Ed, if I give him my blood, which under any other circumstance would save him, I'll *kill* him. Lycan and vampire blood are not compatible."

Ed frowned at him. "You mean you're not even gonna try? You're just gonna let him die? What kind of friend are you?"

Sarah squeezed his hand. "Ed, don't."

"Don't tell me not to. He could save Daniels. He could. But he won't even try."

Nathaniel spoke up. "While we debate his life is slipping away. We may have more time if we give him a blood transfusion. Once that is done we can decide what to do."

Andre's intense gaze locked onto him. "You know that won't work. Why suggest it? Don't give hope where there is none. You know Reece is dying."

"No, I do not know that and neither do you. You are concerned that if he survives he will become unnatural."

Ed and Sarah turned their confused gazes to Andre. "Is that why you won't help him because he'll become a werewolf?" Sarah asked.

Andre picked up his friend without effort, carried him to a gurney and eased his broken body onto the thin mattress. He turned around to face the others. "Reece wouldn't want to be a monster."

"That doesn't answer the question." Sarah stood up. "Is that why you won't try to save him?"

Ed got to his feet. "You can't let him die. I won't let you. Nathaniel, can you give him your blood? Would that help him?"

Nathaniel's eyes moved to Andre, then his gaze returned to Ed. "It is not without risk, Lycan and vampire blood are incompatible. If he were to survive he would be *different*. He would become a hybrid. I don't know what that would do to him."

Andre rushed across the room. "You can't! No one has survived."

Nathaniel frowned at him. He knew otherwise. "Yes, they have."

"Who has survived this kind of treatment?"
The black vampire gave him a knowing look.
Andre stared at him in disbelief. "Jacques."

CHAPTER THIRTY TWO

Charlotte awoke from the frightening dream and was momentarily startled when a uniformed cop peered through the cubicle curtain. It took a few seconds for her dazed senses to realize it was Dan McCredie and she popped up out of her chair. He must have heard about Tommy through the department grapevine. She felt a small pang of guilt for not calling him. He rushed over to her.

"What the hell happened? Is he going to be all right?" He rested a hand on her arm. "How are you holding up?"

Charlotte tried to smile. Tears stung the back of her eyes. "I'm ok. When we stormed the cabin we found him unconscious in a locked room."

Dan pulled her into his arms. "God, how'd this happen? Why would anyone take our son?"

Exhausted, Charlotte let herself be held by her ex-husband. She wished it was Reece holding her in his arms. She needed him. Why hadn't he called?

She eased herself out of Dan's embrace. "It's classified. I can't tell you anything. I wish I could."

He stared into her eyes. "Has this got something to do with the investigation? Did the person who took those kids take Tommy?"

Charlotte did her best to remain poker faced, but her emotions got the better of her.

Dan ran a hand over his face. "Jesus, Charlotte, why let me find out like this?"

"I couldn't tell you. What was the point of calling?" She folded her arms across her chest, a scowl forming on her tired face. Whenever they were in the same room *this* happened.

"Because he's my son too." Dan walked over to Tommy and took his hand. "Hey, buddy, it's dad. How're you doin'?" He turned to Charlotte. "What did the doctor say?"

"They don't know why he hasn't come out of it. They're still running tests."

He let go of his son's hand and mirrored her movements. "So, we just wait?"

Charlotte signed. "No, I do. You need to go."

"What makes you think I'm going anywhere? I want to be here when my son wakes up."

"I'll call you." Charlotte could feel the tension building in her body and knew they would have an all-out argument if he stayed.

"You haven't so far and you won't have to if I'm right here."

They glared at each other.

The curtain slid back and a nurse stood at the opening. "Is there a problem in here?" she said, her voice low. "Everyone can hear your conversation. Perhaps you could continue it outside."

Dan glared at the nurse. "Don't worry, I'm leaving." He returned his serious gaze to his ex-wife. "Call me when he's awake. Okay?"

She nodded. "You know I will."

He stared at his son, then stalked over to the open curtain and punched it as he pushed past the nurse and stormed out of the cubicle.

"Are you all right?" the nurse asked.

"He's just anxious about our son."

The nurse glanced over her shoulder. "That's Tommy's dad? Oh, I thought…"

Charlotte smiled. "No, Reece isn't his dad. I know it seems that way…"

"Sorry. I didn't mean to pry."

"You didn't."

"Can I get you anything? Coffee? Something to eat?"

"No, thanks, I'm fine."

"Well, if you want something, you know where I am." She pulled the curtains together and went back to the nurses' station.

Charlotte sat down and gave a heavy sigh. She gazed at her sleeping boy and wished he was Reece's son. She knew she was in love with Reece and wanted to spend the rest of her life with him. Charlotte hoped he would walk through those curtains any minute. For some reason she couldn't explain, she was worried about him. She rested her head against the headrest of the armchair and once again drifted into the same dream…

℠℞

…Josh snatched his cell phone from the inner pocket of his jacket. He keyed in Reece's number and raised the phone to his ear. Standing outside the facility was a huge inconvenience. He could have been at home with a bottle of Dom Perignon and a high-class hooker in his bed.

The phone went to voicemail.

The detective sighed and ended the call. He wasn't about to leave a message that could incriminate him later. Why didn't Reece answer his phone? He checked his cell's address book. Did he have Ed Borenko's number? Yes. The line rang and continued to ring. No voicemail kicked in. He was about to ring off when he heard a voice. A female one.

"Hel …lo?" She said, breathless.

The detective pulled the phone from his ear and stared at the number. It was Borenko's.

"Detective Jamieson, can I speak to Lieutenant Borenko?"

"Just a minute." He heard. "Ed, it's Josh. He wants to talk to you."

Ed got on the phone. "Where the hell are you, Jamieson, you were meant to be here an hour ago. All hell's broken loose in here. Reece…"

"Reece is what?" Josh pressed the phone to his ear, straining to listen. He could hear the muffled conversation although he couldn't make out what was being said. "Hello?"

"Nathaniel's coming out. Be at the gate."

The hairs on the back of Josh's neck stood erect. Something was wrong, he could feel it. "What's going on?"

"You'll find out when you get in here."

The line went dead. "Shit!"

Josh dropped the phone into his pocket and strutted over to the gates.

Nathaniel arrived and unlocked them. He swung one back, allowing Josh just enough room to enter, then secured the lock. "Follow me."

The detective was suspicious of the huge black man and walked a few paces behind.

Nathaniel glanced over his shoulder. "It would serve you well to keep up. There has been an attack."

Josh's ears pricked up. "An attack? On who?"

"You will find out once we are inside.

Could he be free of that meddling, moronic PI once and for all?

When Reece's team took over the old prison, the infirmary had been set up to be fully operational. It had been their only option, because if anyone was attacked they couldn't explain it to hospital staff. And the police would be called in.

Reece had been moved to another room, cleaned up and hooked up to a blood bag.

The creature was now secured in the treatment room, and the team waited in the Warden's office so Josh wouldn't find out what had happened.

When he entered the office and gazed around the room his instincts supported his theory. Reece wasn't there. He would wait for confirmation.

"So, what happened?" Josh walked over to a chair in front of the desk, dusted it off with his hand and sat down.

"The wolf in the infirmary got loose." Ed rested an elbow on the desk.

"Who was attacked?" Josh clasped his hands in his lap and crossed one leg over the other, waiting for the welcome news.

Ed cleared his throat and tried to sound convincing. "The wolf. We zapped it with lasers."

The detective shifted in his seat. He didn't believe him. "You're telling me you attacked it with lasers and they worked?"

Andre stepped into the detective's view. "Yes. It's unconscious in another room. Want to take a look?"

Josh's top lip twitched. "I'll take your word for it. So where's Reece?"

Nathaniel spoke. "Questioning the girl. He is determined to get the answers he needs because of Charlotte's son."

The detective's expression darkened. "Is he? Why didn't he answer his phone?"

Ed reached across the desk, picked up a phone lying on it and checked the screen. "Because it's here. Call if you want."

"If everything's fine, as you say, what was all that babble about getting in here fast?"

"We were still trying to contain the creature and I thought we'd need your help." Ed stared him down.

Josh broke eye contact first. "Well it seems you have everything under control. Perhaps I should go."

Sarah and Ed's eyes met. "I want you to go to the hospital and tell Charlotte to call me. I know she won't have her phone on. Not allowed in the ER," Ed told him.

"Is that it?" Josh looked incredulous. He sighed and stood up.

"Yeah. We need to keep incommunicado with her; she's part of the team now. Besides, we want to know if there's any word on her boy. You got a problem with that?"

Josh crossed the office, then turned around. "Tell Daniels I want to talk to him. Soon."

Nathaniel opened the door.

Ed gave him a crooked grin. "Sure, I'll tell him. Nathaniel, see Jamieson to his car. Wouldn't want anything to happen to him on the way."

Josh glanced up at the hulk. Something about him seemed off, not that he could put his finger on what it was. "No need. Just see me to the gate and I'll be fine."

"Very well. Follow me." Nathaniel stalked along the corridor. Josh followed at a distance.

The detective wondered if he could extract any information about the PI from the large black man. "Do you have any idea when Reece will be leaving? Maybe I can wait for him."

"The team is staying here tonight."

"Well, then, perhaps I should stay too."

Nathaniel stopped and turned around. Josh jolted to a stop a couple of feet away. "You have a task to perform, do you not?"

"I could do that first thing in the morning. I'm sure not much has changed, otherwise Daniels or Borenko would've heard."

Nathaniel could read the detective's thoughts and knew he was stalling. "We have several Lycan contained here. That could prove dangerous, if another one gets loose."

"You're right. I should go and complete my assignment." As soon as they reached the gates Josh made a beeline for his car.

Nathaniel stood at the fence and watched the detective drive away before returning to the team. Something about Josh Jamieson disturbed him.

Andre unhooked the empty blood bag from the stand and replaced it. Although Reece was still unconscious, his vital signs had stabilized and his complexion had regained a tinge of color. Enough to assure he was no longer on death's door. He checked his friend's pulse. Weak and steady.

What happened now was in the lap of the Gods.

He remembered what Nathaniel had said about his brother Jacques. Had he been a hybrid? Would Reece become something dark and uncontrollable too?

Ed entered the room. "How's he doin'?"

Andre turned around. "Weak but stable. That's all we can hope for right now. He's lucky to be alive at all."

The chief crossed the room and stood beside him, a worried frown on his unshaven face. "Do you think he'll make it?"

Andre checked Reece's blood pressure. "He's holding his own and he has a strong will."

Ed rested his hand on Andre's shoulder. "Thank you."

"For what?"

"Doing this." Ed directed his gaze to the blood bag. "I know you were worried about what could happen, and I get that, but I couldn't let Daniels die. We've been through too much together, you know?"

"Do you think I want him to die? We've been through a lot too. He's my friend, my brother, my partner in all this madness. I know if he does come out of it he'd rather die than become something unnatural."

"Maybe he'll be grateful he's alive." Ed frowned at Reece and hoped he was right.

Andre had given blood, along with Sarah and Ed. They were using a technique that hadn't been tried before, infusions of vampire blood followed by human. No time to cross-match. If Reece survived the infection raging through his body he would become a whole new breed, and a dangerous one.

CHAPTER THIRTY THREE

Nathaniel walked over to the gurney and studied the unconscious PI. The blood therapy appeared to be keeping him alive, but for how long? He knew if Reece died, the only way to bring him back was with vampire venom, something Andre would never allow.

The blood bag was almost empty. How long could the humans continue to give blood before they became too weak? How long could Andre, before he would need to feed?

Nathaniel sat in the armchair, unwrapped a sixteen gauge needle and pushed it into the large vein in the crevice of his elbow. He cut a strip of medical tape to secure the needle and attached the tube to a new bag. When he released the valve blood began to flow. The more vampire blood Reece could take the better his chances.

Andre entered the room to check on Reece. When he saw Nathaniel he stalked over to him, an angry scowl on his face. "What are you doing?"

"Is it not obvious?"

"All right. Why are you doing it?"

Nathaniel gaze moved to the detective. "He once saved my life, something no one has done for me before. And the humans will not be able to give blood for much longer."

Andre crouched beside his chair and checked the line. "He said you were even, remember?"

Nathaniel shook his head. "It does not matter. It is vital we help each other now."

Andre stood up and rested his hand on Nathaniel's shoulder. "Thank you."

"There is no need. You would do the same for me."

After checking Reece's vitals and replacing the blood bag, Andre headed back to the Warden's office. As he walked along the corridor, he wondered if his friend would make it. What would he do if Reece died? Would he be prepared to take drastic measures to bring him back?

℘ℂℛ

Dan McCredie parked his motorcycle in the hospital parking lot and strode toward the ambulance entrance of the Emergency Room. Charlotte had left a short voicemail message on his cell phone for him to come to the hospital as soon as he got it. She needed to talk to him. Had Tommy woken up? Had the worst happened?

With his heart hammering in his chest, he rushed into the ER and headed for his son's cubicle. He flung the curtain back. Tommy's trolley wasn't there.

"Where's Tommy?"

Charlotte had been crying, her face red and blotchy. She had spoken to Ed and had been given the horrible news.

"Charlotte, what is it?" Dan's expression paled and beads of cold sweat formed on his brow. "Is he...?"

She stood up and rushed into his arms. "He's all right, Dan. They took him for another CT scan. He'll be back soon." Charlotte could feel the tension in his chest dissolve beneath her as he let out the breath he'd been holding.

Dan eased her away from him and stared at her. "You've been crying. I thought..."

"I'm sorry I worried you. I didn't mean to. Something else has happened. I need you to stay with Tommy." She looked into his eyes, tears threatening to spill. "Will you?"

"Of course I will. Where are you going?"

"It's Reece. He's been injured." She knew Dan wouldn't understand why she had to go. Leave their son and rush to a man she hardly knew, but she was in love with.

Dan walked her to the armchair and sat her down. "How bad is it?"

Charlotte was surprised at how calm he was, given the circumstances. "Bad. He … he could die."

He sighed and brushed the tears from her cheeks with his thumbs. "Then you should go. I'll call in and let Simpson know I'm here."

She nodded, sniffing back the urge to sob.

Dan walked out of the cubicle, pulling his phone from his uniform shirt pocket. He was back within minutes, saying he had all the time he needed.

Charlotte waited until Tommy returned to the ER. She kissed his forehead, told him she loved him, and walked out of the cubicle. Dan followed.

"I hope Daniels'll be ok."

"Me too. I won't be gone for long. I just need to make sure he'll be all right. Once I know for sure, I'll come back."

Charlotte gazed through the curtain at her son, her heart torn. Before she could change her mind, she rushed out of the ER. She had to get to Reece before it was too late.

❧❦

The sedan screeched to halt at the gates of the old prison, stirring up a whirlwind of roadside gravel and dry grass. Charlotte flung the door open, jumped from the vehicle and rushed to the gate. Nathaniel was there to take her inside.

"Will he live?" she asked, breathless. Tears stung her eyes and she blinked them back. She had to stay strong.

Nathaniel could sense the panic inside her. "He is stable for the moment. We are transfusing him with human and vampire blood to strengthen him."

She scurried alongside him, trying to keep up with the huge vampire's stride as they crossed the compound. "What does that mean? He was attacked by a werewolf, aren't you concerned about what will happen to him?"

The vampire stopped and turned to her. "Right now we are more concerned with keeping him alive."

Nathaniel followed her into the building and secured the door, then they walked along the stark corridor together.

Ed rushed out of the office to meet her. "Sorry to bring you out here like this."

When they entered the office, Charlotte hugged Andre. Her body twitched, her nerves a tangle of anxiety. "Can I see him?"

"Sure you can," Ed said, his voice sympathetic. He rested a hand on her arm. "We're doin' everything we can. My gut tells me he's gonna make it."

Charlotte's heart pounded against her ribs, she felt giddy. She frowned at Ed. "Can you guarantee it?"

Andre walked over to comfort her, and when she looked into his pale, strained features she fell into his arms and sobbed. He helped her to a chair and sat her down. Her mind was a jumble of confused thoughts and conflicting emotions. It occurred to him that the two most important people in her life were lying unconscious, their lives in jeopardy. How much longer could she hold it together? Would she be able to cope? Andre hoped so, because they needed her investigative expertise to find the Alpha before anyone else was bitten.

Charlotte stopped at the closed doorway and took a deep breath to steel herself before facing Reece lying at death's door. Andre, Ed and Sarah were behind her. She glanced over her shoulder at the solemn faces. Could she go through with it? Could she stand at Reece's bedside and pretend everything would be all right?

Andre touched her arm. "You don't have to go through with this, you know. If it's going to be too much for you don't do it. At least for now."

Charlotte covered his hand with hers. "I know you mean well, but I have to."

"Why?" Andre frowned.

She sighed and stifled a sob. "Because I do."

Ed stepped up and opened the door. "Ready to go in?"

Charlotte hesitated, then nodded. "Ready as I'll ever be."

Andre took her hand and walked her across the room to an adjoining door. He stopped and gave her a concerned frown. "Are you sure about this?"

"I don't have a choice, Andre."

He opened the door and motioned for her to go in ahead of him. Ed and Sarah followed them in.

Charlotte gasped. Seeing Reece so pale and still, hooked up to blood bags, and a bloodied bandage covering a huge wound on his shoulder was too much for her. Her ears rang, her legs buckled, and the last thing she heard was Andre's anxious voice calling her name as his strong arms closed around her to prevent her from hitting the floor...

CHAPTER THIRTY FOUR

…Sucking in a deep breath, Charlotte jolted awake. She blinked the hazy film of sleep from her vision and realized someone had called her name. She opened her eyes and her body stiffened. Reece loomed over her, his cold, blood red gaze locked onto her face.

She let out a shrill scream and punched at his chest, trying to fight him off. He was too strong. His face altered as he moved closer. Shoots of charcoal gray fur sprouted from his skin and his jawline elongated into a muzzle with a sickening crunch, his body shape followed. Why wasn't he on the floor writhing in agony?

Charlotte threw herself at him and continued to pummel his chest with her fists. She hoped to force him far enough away to make a run for it, but the power in his broad muscular body was too much for her to struggle against.

Reece's threatening form pressed in on her.

His hot, fetid breath made her stomach swirl. Charlotte turned her face away so she couldn't look into his wolf eyes. Never look into the eyes of a predator. Her heart hammered so fast she thought it would shatter in her chest. She sucked in a sharp breath and her head spun. Before she had a chance to grab for her gun, her terrified senses unraveled and a black wave slammed into her.

Charlotte jolted awake, sprang to her feet and punched the air. She had to get free. Had to escape.

"Everything's ok." Reece wrapped his arms around her trembling body. Disoriented, she struggled against him. "Let me go. Let me go!"

"Charlotte," he said, grabbing her hands. "Listen to me. You're all right. You're safe."

She continued to struggle, until logic prevailed. She stopped struggling. It had all been a horrible dream, triggered by her anxiety of what could happen to him. She pulled him to her and held him tight, tears sliding down her face.

A nurse whisked the curtains apart and frowned at them. "Everything all right in here?"

"Yeah, everything's fine. She had a bad dream. She'll be ok in a minute or two."

The nurse studied the pair for a moment before pulling the curtains together.

Reece backed Charlotte into the armchair and crouched in front of her. "What's wrong?"

Charlotte shook her head, unable to speak, the painful lump of words stuck in her throat. Tears continued to spill.

"Hey." Reece wiped the tears from her cheeks with his fingers.

Charlotte threw herself into his arms and kissed him.

When the kiss ended, he stared into her tear-filled eyes. "Ok, what's going on? It's obvious the dream has upset you, so tell me what happened?" He brushed her cheek with the back of his hand. "And don't say 'Nothing.'"

Her chin quivered and she sniffed back the urge to sob. Reece was all right, he hadn't been bitten. He was still the same wonderful man she fell in love with. "I was worried about you."

"And?" His right eyebrow rose.

"And that's it. I'm glad you're here." She leaned in and wrapped her arms around him, never wanting to let him go.

Reece wasn't convinced. He eased himself out of her embrace. "Charlotte?"

She glanced across at Tommy. She didn't want to tell him about her horrifying dream.

He reached out and turned her face to him. "Tell me what happened."

Charlotte knew he wouldn't let it go. "I had a bad dream. It freaked me out."

"I got that. What happened?" Reece stood up and gazed down at her.

"It was … it was about you. It was so real, I thought…"

Reece folded his arms across his chest. "Stop stalling."

She shook her head. "I really don't want to vocalize it. It could still happen."

"Come on, Charlotte, you don't believe that. Tell me."

She stood up and gazed into his sincere green-gray eyes. "You were attacked by the werewolf you've got restrained in the infirmary and…" Tears started to spill again.

"Hey, come here." He held her close, stroking her hair. "Don't worry about me. I know what I'm doing. I won't let anything happen to me." He lifted her chin and looked into her glistening eyes. "Promise."

"You can't make that kind of promise."

He sighed. "Yes I can, because I know me. And I thought you did too. You have to trust me."

She rested her head against his chest. "I do trust you. I told you that before. It's just…"

"Let it go, Charlotte," he said, his voice gentle. "Nothing's going to happen to me."

Charlotte stepped away from him and gave him a weak smile. "I'll try."

"Good." Reece walked over and took Tommy's hand. "Hey, buddy, how's it going? I got you something today." He reached into his jacket pocket, pulled out a colorful packet and laid the Xbox game on the boy's pillow. "When you wake up we'll play this together. You'll probably beat the socks off me, and that's ok."

Charlotte squeezed his hand. "Thank you."

His face flushed. "No problem."

They stood staring into each other's eyes, and it wasn't until a nurse stepped into the cubicle to check on Tommy that they broke the connection.

"Don't let me interrupt," she said, poking the electronic thermometer into Tommy's ear and watching the monitor.

The pair stepped away from each other.

The nurse walked over to the curtain. "Oh, by the way, your husband phoned, he'll be in as soon as he can. He's been delayed."

Charlotte frowned. "Thanks."

The nurse stepped out of the cubicle and closed the curtains.

"I wish people would stop calling Dan my husband. We've been divorced for over eight years. Tommy was a baby when our marriage ended." She gave a huffy sigh and scowled. "And of course he's been delayed. Everything is always more important than his son." She folded her arms. "It's been hours since I left the message on his voicemail."

Reece pulled her to him. "Don't let him get to you, Charlotte. I know that's easy for me to say. You've done a fantastic job of raising Tommy on your own. Your ex doesn't even come into the equation."

Charlotte looked into his honest eyes. "Thanks. I just wish he wasn't my son's father. He's a token dad. Only there when it suits him and makes him look good." She remembered how he'd acted in her dream – understanding and ready to help. She sighed. *Why couldn't he be like that in the real world?*

Dan McCredie pushed back the curtain and stepped into the cubicle. "Well, doesn't this look cozy?"

Reece moved away from Charlotte and locked his serious gaze onto the cop. He wanted to say something, but thought it best to keep his opinions to himself and let Charlotte handle her ex-husband.

Charlotte glared at him. "Reece was comforting me. Is there something wrong with that?"

"All depends." He closed the curtains, walked over to the gurney and looked at his comatose son.

Charlotte swung around and folded her arms across her chest. "On what exactly?"

Dan glanced over his shoulder. "On his agenda." He turned his gaze to the PI. "So, Daniels, what is it?"

Charlotte stepped between them. "That's none of your business. You're not my husband anymore, or have you forgotten that?"

Reece touched her arm, keeping his gaze on her ex. "It's all right, Charlotte, I'm more than happy to answer his question."

"You don't have to."

He gave a thin smile and said, "I know that." He looked Dan in the eye. "I'm in love with Charlotte."

Dan looked surprised. He didn't expect the PI to be honest with him.

"I would've liked to tell her over a candlelit dinner but as you want to force the issue, there it is."

Charlotte turned around, a smile spreading across her face. "You are?"

Reece smiled and his voice softened. "Yes, I am."

"Mm-m-o-m?"

Shocked by the unexpected sound, the three turned around and stared at the boy.

CHAPTER THIRTY FIVE

"We need to get this situation under control," Josh Jamieson said into his cell phone as he sat behind Ned Bowers' desk, gazing out of the high-rise office window at the city's glittering nightscape. He swung around in the deluxe, high-backed chair and glanced across the room. Something caught his eye.

Josh popped out of the chair and walked over to Ned's briefcase, his cell phone still pressed to his ear. He unclipped the bag with one hand, fingered through the folders, pulled out a file and frowned at it. He carried the manila folder back to the desk and sat down. "What happened should never have happened. You know there'll be serious consequences if we don't step in now." He rang off and slid his phone onto the desk with a huff. Josh flipped open Charlotte's personnel file and her department photo stared back at him from inside the blue folder.

Why does Ned have Charlotte's file in his briefcase? Is she under investigation?

Josh scrutinized her unsmiling face and felt a pang of guilt. Even though he detested the woman, he was sorry her son had been involved in all of this. He was an innocent. Josh hoped the boy would wake up soon.

All of a sudden, it occurred to him that the DA was not in the building. *Where is Ned?*

Josh put Charlotte's file back into the District Attorney's briefcase and walked out of the office. It was not like Ned to leave the precinct without it. He was pedantic when it came to his personal possessions, especially his briefcase. Not that there was anything incriminating or worthwhile inside, the DA was a control freak, nothing more.

The detective continued along the corridor to the elevator. He pushed the button and gazed up at the numbers lighting up and dimming as the elevator made its ascent. The number for his floor lit up and the doors hissed open. Ned stormed out of the elevator almost colliding with him.

"What's the hurry? I wasted my time waiting, as you requested. Where have you been?"

Ned was red-faced. "Get out of my way!" He maneuvered past the detective and stalked along the corridor.

Josh studied the DA as he strode to his office, disappeared inside, and slammed the door.

What's his problem? Didn't get his moment of release, perhaps. He smirked, still believing Ned left the office in the evening to visit a stress relief therapist, better known as a prostitute.

He sauntered back along the corridor and stood outside Ned's office. Should he make an effort to find out what had happened or leave the DA in the company of his dark mood?

Josh sighed and knocked.

No answer.

He glanced at his watch. 7.00 p.m. He knocked again.

He tried the handle.

Locked.

He frowned. "Ned?" He leaned close to the door. "Are you all right?" Not that he cared. He was more intrigued with what had put the DA in such a rage. Josh sighed again. Playing the concerned colleague was tedious. If Ned wanted to be left alone, so be it. He turned, strutted to the elevator and jabbed the button.

As the doors slid open, the detective glanced along the corridor once more before stepping into the lift and pressing G.

When Josh stepped out of the elevator into the ground floor lobby he was confronted by meddlesome journalist bitch, Sonia Edwards. He groaned inwardly and mustered the best smile he could. "And to what do we owe the pleasure, Ms. Edwards?"

"I'm here to see the District Attorney," she said. "Why, Detective Jamieson, think I'm stalking you?" She smirked.

"There's no reason why you should, and I'm sure we both have far more pressing issues to deal with." He glanced at his watch. "And I'm meant to be somewhere." Josh side-stepped the journalist and headed to the parking lot.

Sonia watched him leave before pressing the elevator call button. The detective had no idea what pressing issues she was here to see the District Attorney about. She smirked as she entered the elevator and pressed the button for Ned Bowers' floor. No idea at all.

CHAPTER THIRTY SIX

Reece and Nathaniel arrived at the old prison at the same time. They entered the building and strode along the corridor to the Warden's office. No one was there. The pair frowned at each other and continued down the corridor to the infirmary. They entered the first room. Still no one.

"Where are they?" Reece said.

Nathaniel closed his eyes and used his immortal hearing. After a few seconds his eyes snapped open. "In the maximum security cell block."

"What the hell? They know better than to go in there without backup." Reece pushed past the black vampire and strutted down the corridor to the solid gray metal door with a square glass panel. He peered inside.

Sarah and Ed were sitting outside the first cell talking to Melinda.

Reece threw the door open and stormed into the block, Nathaniel behind him. "What are you two doing? Don't you know how dangerous this is?"

Sarah tilted her head and looked up at him. "What happened to hello?"

Reece sighed. "Yeah, yeah. Hello. Now, what do you think you're doing?"

Ed stood up. "We thought we were helpin', Daniels. Got a problem with that?"

Reece stood with his hands on his hips. "When you're putting your lives at risk, I do."

Nathaniel moved closer. "Where are the members of my team?"

Ed shrugged. "Don't know. Somewhere around the prison, I guess."

"You'd better go check on them," Reece said.

Nathaniel nodded and disappeared through a second doorway into the adjoining cell block.

Sarah stood up and walked over to Reece. "How's Charlotte doing?"

Reece had forgotten to give them the good news. When he'd first arrived and found them missing, he'd been more concerned about their safety. "Tommy's awake."

"That's wonderful news, I'm so pleased," Sarah told him.

"Yeah, me too. Can we head back to the office?"

After securing Melinda in her cell, and checking on the other teens, the three left the building.

Once in the secure confines of the Warden's office, Reece closed the door and folded his arms across his chest. "So what did Melinda tell you?"

Nathaniel's senses were on high alert as he walked past each cell and checked the sleeping wolves. The three had been knocked out with heavy-dose tranquilizers which would keep them out for at least another 12 hours. When he reached the end of the block he whisked across to the last cell. The door hung askew on one hinge, the wolf gone. All that remained of his two team members was blood spatter and scattered smoldering ash on the floor. The solid steel door at the back of the block had been ripped from the wall.

Nathaniel hit the alarm and the shrill squeal echoed through the prison.

CHAPTER THIRTY SEVEN

Charlotte held her son in her arms, her heart elated. She had feared the worst, thinking he would never wake up again. He was weak, his usual bubbly voice quiet, but he was back in the land of the living. The doctor had no answers. None of the extensive tests had shown anything adverse, and her son's bloodwork had come back clear. So why had he been unconscious for so long?

"Mom," Tommy whispered into his mother's chest. "Can I have some water, please?"

"Of course, honey." Charlotte didn't want to disengage herself from him for fear it was another dream. She eased him out of her arms, walked over to the tray on the equipment trolley and poured some water into a capped blue plastic cup with a straw.

Tommy leaned on one elbow and took a couple of sips, then dropped back onto the pillow. His face was pale with dark circles around his eyes. "Thanks, Mom."

She brushed his hair off his forehead. "That's ok, sweetie." She gave his hand a gentle squeeze. "I love you."

Tommy heaved a sigh and closed his eyes. "Love you too, mo...m," he whispered and drifted off to sleep.

Charlotte heard a sound behind her and turned around.

"How is he?" Josh asked.

"He's awake. That's something." She motioned for him to step outside. "Why are you here?"

"I was wondering how your son was. Is that a problem?" He folded his arms across his designer jacket.

Charlotte was exhausted. It had been a very long couple of days. She didn't want to play Josh's games. "It is if you're up to something."

"I'm not up to anything, Charlotte. I was concerned about your son." He stared into her eyes. "He didn't deserve what happened to him."

Should she believe him? His concern seemed genuine. She decided to be charitable. "Then I appreciate you coming by. He's still weak, but the doctor says he'll make a full recovery."

Josh glanced through the open curtains. "That's good."

"How's the investigation going? Has Reece located the Alpha? I've been out of the loop being here, but I couldn't be anywhere else."

"They snatched another young woman off the street in broad daylight. I'd say the Alpha is desperate, now that he doesn't have the support of his pack."

Charlotte raised a curious eyebrow.

Josh noticed. "Yes, Charlotte, I've been reading up on those creatures. No point in remaining naïve."

"Did the team get all of the pack?" She folded her arms across her chest.

"As far as I'm aware. Why? Think there's still some strays out there somewhere?"

She frowned. "It's possible. Anything is."

"That's true. Have you spoken to Daniels lately?"

"Why?"

"Shouldn't he be warned? If the Alpha discovers where the pack is he might decide to launch an attack to retrieve them."

Charlotte snorted. "Fat chance anyone could get into that place. It's a lockdown."

Josh frowned at her. "Yes. Well, stranger things have happened. I think I'll take a drive out there and see how it's going."

"Would you ask Reece to call me?" She walked back to the curtain.

"I'm not..." He caught himself, realizing he should continue to play good cop for a while longer. "Of course." He turned on his heel and headed for the door.

Charlotte made sure he was gone before rushing to the nurses' station and picking up the phone.

ॐ ○ ∾

Reece was at the gate when the detective arrived. He unlocked the chain and swung one gate back. Josh took his time getting out of his Mercedes. He wasn't in the mood for tiresome repartee with the PI. He just wanted a heads up in case the shit hit the fan, because he wasn't taking the rap for any of what had gone down so far. Not unless it involved a commendation.

He got out of his deluxe sedan and strutted over to the gate. "Daniels."

"What are you doing here, Jamieson?" Reece locked the gates, turned and stalked off ahead of him.

The detective gave a grunt and followed him over to the door. "I am a part of this team. Any of the wolves awake yet?"

"No. We dosed them to keep them out of action for another 10 hours or so. Why?"

"No reason." He gave Reece a wry smile.

Reece pushed the door open and gestured for the detective to step in ahead of him. "Oh, there is one thing you might want to know."

Josh's eyes narrowed. "What's that?"

"One of the wolves escaped."

Josh stopped in his tracks. "What?"

"One got away." He locked the door and turned around. "A couple of Nathaniel's team was taken out too."

"So what happens now?"

"That's what we're about to discuss. Coming?" Reece headed along the corridor.

The recent events had everyone shaken up. They believed this particular facility would be the perfect place to contain the massive beasts. They'd been proved wrong.

Josh walked into the office behind Reece and took a seat in the corner.

Reece crossed the room to the desk and sat on the edge. "Look, I know this has spooked all of us, but we have to keep our heads and make sure this doesn't happen again. If we don't keep one step ahead of the Alpha we won't have a chance in hell. He's out there somewhere creating a new Lycan army, and we have to find a way to stop him."

Ed cleared his throat. "How? We've done everything we could to keep the creatures locked up and now one's escaped. You know what that means. The Alpha will be pissed and lookin' for payback."

Adrian stood up and walked over to Reece. "Perhaps a natural remedy is in order."

Reece lifted a curious eyebrow. "What do you mean?"

"There's one thing that can put a Lycan out of action. And it's permanent."

Ed frowned. "It'll kill 'em?"

Adrian nodded. "Yes."

Reece shook his head. "No. We have to try to save those kids. What's the point of all this if we don't?"

"They're gonna die anyway, if we don't find the Alpha soon," Ed said. "We can't have those things runnin' around the city ripping people to shreds, can we?"

"What if we can't find the Alpha?" Sarah asked.

Reece folded his arms across his chest and sighed. "I don't have all the answers. If I did this situation would be under control and the Alpha would be history." He turned to Adrian. "So what's this natural remedy you're talking about?"

Adrian reached into a pocket of his cardigan and pulled out a handful of small shriveled purple flowers.

Sarah walked over to him and studied the flowers in the palm of his hand. "Is that what I think it is?"

"Yes."

Reece frowned at it. "What does it do?"

"Wolfsbane is toxic to werewolves." Sarah picked up a flower by its tiny stem, brought up to her face and twirled it back and forth in her fingers. "It's a slow painful death. Not something we should inflict on those kids."

Adrian turned to her. "In the end it might be our only option. One wolf *has* managed to kill two immortals and escape. And they are far worse predators than we are. Savage."

Josh sat back taking everything in. Would they resort to killing the teenagers? He didn't think the PI had it in him. Although drastic times did call for drastic measures and Daniels could always prove him wrong.

CHAPTER THIRTY EIGHT

The continuous musical tone woke the Alpha from a sound sleep. His eyes snapped open and he groaned deep in his throat, his inner wolf agitated. He grabbed for the cell phone vibrating across his bedside table, frowned at the luminous display and jabbed the button with his thumb. "Do you have any idea what time it is?"

"There's a way into the prison," the cool voice announced.

The Alpha sat up, threw back the covers and swung his legs over the side of the bed. "How? That place is a fortress. I've had someone look it over."

"I just broke out of there, so now there is. They won't have time to do anything about it if we move tonight."

A smug smile spread across the Alpha's face. It was more than time for payback. Those meddling PIs and their crew were a serious problem. And when he finished with them there wouldn't be much left.

"Are you up for it?" He wanted to know if the wolf had been injured.

"Yeah, I'm ok. Nothing a little trans ... *mutt* ... ation won't cure." He chuckled at his own joke.

The Alpha sighed. "What about the new wolves? They haven't had time to adjust. Think they can handle it?"

"Sure. They'll be hungry for blood." The thought of fresh meat made his gut rumble.

"Round them up and get out there."

"Will do. Can't wait."

The Alpha ended the call, slid his cell phone onto the table and stood up. Tonight he would retrieve his pack and eliminate the one obstacle standing in his way.

ഓരു

The team had secured the damaged door the best they could for the time being. Ed would make a call first thing in the morning and organize having it reinforced. Until then, the wolves had been moved to another secure block.

Nathaniel had contacted the remaining members of his task force and they were on standby. He had a feeling about the Alpha, although he chose not to share it. He knew the Lycan psyche. He'd had many dealings with the creatures during his long existence, and his immortal instincts never failed him where the dogs were concerned. They were, and would always be, a threat.

Only he, Reece, Ed and Sarah were on site. Andre and Adrian had left to follow up a lead, and Josh, well, Josh did whatever he wanted. No-one knew where he was at any given moment.

It was almost midnight, and Nathaniel was on watch while the humans slept. He stood in the compound, eyes closed and his acute hearing alert. To his mind, it was a given the Alpha had been warned about the security breach and would plan an assault to retrieve his wolves. If he did, Nathaniel's team would be ready.

No matter how hard he tried, Ed couldn't sleep. He had a feeling the Alpha might try something. Tonight. He'd contacted some cops … ones that owed him a favor. He'd done a lot to help out many on the force and knew that one day it would come back to him ten-fold. Tonight was that day. He got up off the cot and wandered into the corridor. Nathaniel was on watch so he decided to go out to talk to him for a while. Better than tossing and turning.

He walked out into the compound and stopped beneath a stark, white security light. No Nathaniel. Ed frowned. *Where is he?*

Something massive and dark hurtled toward him. "Get inside now!" Nathaniel swooped in, picked him up and flew into the building.

Ed struggled. "Put me down you big oaf! What do ya think…?"

Nathaniel dropped him on his feet, slammed the door, and turned around, his dark eyes intense. "Alert the others. We have company."

The older man nodded and raced down the corridor.

Nathaniel wrenched his cell phone from a pocket in his pants and hit speed dial. "I need you here now!" His team would take to the air and be there in a matter of minutes.

He flicked off the light and strode along the dark corridor. When he reached the office he did the same. Lights out.

Everyone was up.

Reece rushed over to him. "Are you sure?" he asked, snapping the clip of silver bullets into his weapon.

"I am sure."

"How many?"

"At least six. But more will come."

"Where?"

"A mile up the road. They must be waiting for the Alpha or other dogs to join them." His lip twisted into a grimace.

Sarah strutted over to the pair, her high-powered, double chamber crossbow gripped in her hand. "How many are there?" Her words were sharp, breathy, anxious.

Reece turned to her. "At least six. Nathaniel thinks more are coming."

Her face paled. "We're outnumbered."

"My team is on its way. They will arrive at any minute," Nathaniel said.

Ed joined them. "Ok. I've got two pistols loaded with silver. We've also got the rocket launcher with silver-tipped stakes, the big gun, the tranquilizer rifle, and I've got a little surprise of my own." He smiled crookedly.

Reece's eyebrow rose. "What kind of surprise?"

"I got some markers comin' in. They'll be here soon. Can't be too careful, ya know."

"Who's coming?"

Ed shoved one pistol into the waistband of his pants. "Some cops who owe me, that's who. They're on their way." He glanced at his watch. "Should be arrivin' in the next thirty minutes."

Sarah breathed a sigh of relief. "I was beginning to worry."

Ed's forehead wrinkled. "You? Worry? No way. You're the toughest female I know." He gave her a wink.

"What about Andre and Adrian? Shouldn't we get them back here?" Sarah asked Reece.

"Already on their way. I called them as soon as Ed woke me."

Nathaniel turned and looked along the dark corridor. "My team has arrived."

Everyone turned and followed his gaze.

Four darkly-clad figures emerged from the shadows.

Ed shivered. "Geez, I hate the way they do that." He looked over at Nathaniel. "No offence."

"None taken."

Adrian and Andre entered the infirmary about thirty minutes later. "We brought reinforcements."

When the pair stepped out of the doorway, six hulking, muscular, uniformed cops entered the room. "So where's the party?" one asked.

Ed walked over to them. "Don't worry. It'll liven up pretty soon. I need to brief you." He turned to Reece. "You comin'?"

"Yeah."

The group disappeared into the dark corridor.

The cops took the information surprisingly well. Ed thought they would think he was a nutcase, turned out they were very receptive. Should he be worried about that? No one could speculate what was coming. Each and every person in that cell block knew the outcome would mean serious injury—or death, if they weren't prepared.

"I think the dogs will attack through the breached door," Nathaniel informed them.

Reece stood with his arms folded across his chest. "Let's get set up. The other wolves shouldn't be a problem, they're still out."

"Don't be so sure of that," Adrian said. "When the Alpha calls them it's quite possible they'll snap out of it."

Sarah paled. "He's that powerful?"

"Yes. We need to be on our guard at all times."

"What about the kids?" she asked.

"They could turn the minute they know he's here."

Sarah trembled. She couldn't imagine having to fight the kids. "Wouldn't the tranquilizer darts work on them again?"

"I don't believe so," Adrian said. "Once the sedative has been through their system they'll be more resistant to its effects. Their circulatory system is altered when they're in wolf form; it pumps harder and faster and can eliminate toxins in a shorter period of time."

Ed frowned at him. "So, what you're sayin' is they could already be awake and fakin' it?" The implications of that thought disturbed him.

Adrian gave him an earnest look. "It's possible."

Reece joined them. "Then we could be in deep shit if your suspicions are correct." He turned to Nathaniel. "Get your team in there to make sure."

Nathaniel nodded and motioned for his team to move fast.

"Let's go." Reece stalked through the door and disappeared into the corridor.

CHAPTER THIRTY NINE

The doctor told Charlotte Tommy could go home tomorrow, but she wanted to get him out of the ER and into familiar surroundings where he could recuperate. She wanted to pamper him, tuck him into his own bed, curl up on the spare bed next to him and watch him sleep. Listen to those soft snores she loved so much. And know he was safe.

She signed the release forms at the objection of hospital staff and waited for Dan to pick them up. As soon as her ex-husband arrived, they would be on their way back to some kind of normality, for the rest of the night at least.

The curtain jerked open and Dan stepped into the cubicle. He didn't look at all happy. "Ready?"

Charlotte sighed, picked up the travel bag and passed it to him. "We are now."

She wrapped a protective arm around their son and helped him off the high gurney. "Ready to go home, honey?"

Tommy smiled and nodded. "Yep."

She took his hand.

Dan strutted along the corridor ahead of them, out through the automatic doors and into the parking lot. His sedan was parked in an authorized parking zone near the entrance. He tossed the bag into the trunk and opened the back passenger door for his son. "Climb in, buddy."

Tommy glanced up at his mom. She nodded. He climbed in and his dad closed the door, then marched around the car to the driver's side and got in.

Charlotte shook her head. Did she really expect him to open the door for her? He used to once. She opened the car door, slid into the passenger seat and clipped in her seatbelt.

Dan started the engine. "I have one stop to make before I take you home. Hope you don't mind." It wasn't a question he expected her to answer. He pushed the automatic shift into reverse and backed out of the parking space.

"Can't it wait? Tommy needs to get home to bed. He is still recovering or have you forgotten that?" She folded her arms across her chest.

"No, I haven't forgotten. This can't wait. You'll understand when we get there."

Charlotte gave a heavy sigh and gazed at her grim reflection in the window, wondering where they were going.

When Dan took the freeway heading out of town, Charlotte sprang up in her seat and peered through the windshield. She watched the road for a while, trying to ascertain in which direction they were travelling. They were heading toward the old prison. Had Dan found out about it somehow? Why would he take her and Tommy out there?

"Where are we going?" She frowned at him, doing her best not to show fear, although she was afraid.

He didn't respond.

"Dan?" Her voice sounded thin, strained, even to her.

His unsure eyes met hers for a brief moment before he averted them back to the road. Still no answer.

"Answer me!"

He kept driving.

Charlotte unclipped her seatbelt. "Pull over. Pull over right now!"

Tommy's anxious voice resonated from the back seat. "What's wrong, Mom?"

Dan gave his son a quick glance over his shoulder. "Your mom's tired, buddy, that's all. Don't worry about it. Everything's fine." His dark eyes met hers. "Right?"

Charlotte peered around the seat at her son. "Your dad's right. It's ok, honey." She turned her worried gaze on her ex-husband.

"All sorted. Just sit back and relax, we'll be there before you know it."

Charlotte's stomach shrank into a tight tangle of nerves as she re-clipped her seatbelt. She hoped she was wrong about their destination.

CHAPTER FORTY

Reece knew the Alpha would launch an attack, he just hoped they'd have more time to prepare. They had no idea how many wolves would be in the attacking pack, all they could do was plan their strategy around who they had on board and the skills they could contribute to the fight, human and supernatural. His team amounted to fourteen now, which were better odds than six.

He knew he could count on the people he trusted, but what about the cops Ed had wrangled in to help them? Would they bail out or step up when the going got rough? They seemed keen and weren't disturbed about fighting werewolves. Why was that?

It had taken him some time to get his head around that fact—otherworldly creatures breaching the boundary between hell and earth and infiltrating the human world. He'd quit the force to make sure there was someone out there taking a stand against those things. He knew a lot more now than he had back then, and was still learning, and he would use what he knew to his best advantage in the fight to save humanity against the dark forces.

Nathaniel joined him. "Everything is in place. Now we wait."

Reece rested a hand on the black vampire's arm. "Thank you."

Nathaniel's gaze locked onto his. "There is no need. I made a promise to you when you saved my life and I will honor that promise."

"You know you don't have to."

Nathaniel nodded.

"I appreciate you being here. We couldn't do this without you."

"It is my privilege." He turned and walked back to the others.

Ed came up behind Reece. "Hey, Daniels, what was that all about," he asked, pointing along the corridor at Nathaniel.

"Just an understanding between comrades."

"You trust him?"

Reece frowned at his ex-boss. Where had that come from? "You don't?"

"I'll reserve judgment until after this thing's over." He turned to leave and Reece grabbed his arm.

"Wait. What's on your mind? You haven't doubted him before."

Ed sighed. "He's a creature, ya know? Who knows when he might decide the other team's a better choice. They both deal in blood, don't they?"

Reece sighed. "There's too much at stake here. First the whole Charlotte and Tommy thing, and now this. I don't want to be suspicious of anyone in our crew."

"Sorry. It's how I see it." He shrugged, strutted along the corridor and disappeared into the cell block.

Reece frowned at the open doorway. Ed was wrong. He had to be.

When the Alpha's heavy arrived, the small pack of unruly teen males bayed at the moon. "Aooooo, ow, ow, Aooooo." He wasn't impressed. He stepped out of his sedan, closed the door and stalked over to them.

"Enough," he ordered. "We don't want them to know we're here. The bats have acute hearing. Remember what you were told about them." He wondered if his boss had made a big mistake. These guys were young, raw … and stupid. Would they perform when the time arrived? It didn't matter, his boss was prepared. He always had a backup plan.

He knew the other reliable members of the pack *would* perform, to the death, and they were prepped and waiting for the order. He briefed the six wolves while they undressed and sent them on their way, watching their human form shift as they disappeared into the tall grass.

The show was about to begin. There would be no survivors. Tonight would be a bloodbath.

Nathaniel's acute hearing located the pack. The dogs were closer than he had first thought, their stench pungent. He stalked along the semi-lit cell block and out to the corridor to the PI. "They are almost upon us."

Reece frowned into Nathaniel's face. The seed of doubt Ed had planted taking root. "You're sure about that?"

"Yes, I am sure."

Reece picked up the cache of weapons and followed the black vampire into the cell block. He dropped the crate near the first cell and turned to the others. "Listen up. The wolves are on their way. Let's be ready for them."

Each member of the team was prepared: riot gear on and weapons in hand loaded with silver bullets. The picture painted an impending war zone.

Ed strutted over to the pair. "I gotta go back to the infirmary. I forgot somethin'."

"Can't it wait?"

He squinted at Reece and barked, "No. It can't wait. It's important."

The PI sucked air in through his nostrils and gave his ex-boss a serious stare. "Well make it snappy. We all need to be in the same place at the same time. Who knows where those things plan to break in. For all we know, they could rip the door clean off its hinges at the other end of that corridor and swarm the place."

Ed's right eyebrow twitched. He hadn't thought of that. "Sure. No problem. Won't be more than a couple minutes, tops." He swallowed hard as he stepped through the door into the dark corridor alone.

Walking its length, he heard every sound: an owl hooted in the distance, and a metal clang somewhere outside. His body jumped and he picked up his pace.

When he reached the infirmary's outer door, Ed stopped and gazed along the length of the corridor toward the door he couldn't see in the dark. Those things could probably do what Reece had said. They were strong enough. Cold beads of sweat erupted across his forehead and the knot of nerves hovering in his gut sank into a pit of fear.

He stumbled through the office and the first ward with only the dull beam of his flashlight to guide him. Small comfort. His senses were on extreme alert, the hair on the back of his neck static, as the encompassing darkness wrapped itself around him. When he reached the second doorway he stopped short. "What the hell are you doin' in here? And how'd you get in?"

CHAPTER FORTY ONE

Charlotte berated herself inwardly. She was a cop for God sake, why hadn't she notice Dan's strange behavior? She sat rigid in her seat. Would he really go to these lengths and take her and their son out to the facility? Was he part of it all?

The sedan took an off ramp and Charlotte breathed a huge sigh of relief. She knew where they were going.

They pulled up outside Mrs. Jenkins house and Dan got out of the car. He opened the back passenger door. "Jump out, buddy."

Tommy's eyes widened and he looked at his mother for confirmation.

Charlotte nodded. "It's ok, honey. Do what your dad says."

Tommy unclipped his belt and slid across the seat. When he got out of the car he squinted up at his father's six feet three inch frame. He was worried about his mom. Why was his dad dropping him at Mrs. Jenkins's? Would his mom be ok? Where was his dad taking her?

The door to the house opened and Mrs. Jenkins rushed out to the street, arms wide. "How's my little man?" she asked, wrapping her arms around him and giving him a big squeeze.

Tommy tried to wriggle free, but she had him in a firm grasp. "I'm ok, Mrs. J," he whined into her cardigan.

Dan opened the front passenger door. "Hey, give your mom a kiss. We have to go."

Tommy was relieved to be free of the older woman's hold. His nostrils were filling up with that odd smell Mrs. Jenkins had: a mixture of mothballs and lavender. He rushed across to the open door and hugged his mom, tears welled in his eyes.

Charlotte held him tight. "Listen, everything's going to be ok. You trust me, don't you?" She moved him to arm's length and looked into his eyes. Tommy nodded. "Stay here with Mrs. J, rest up, and I'll be back before you know it." She smiled and hoped it was convincing.

Dan thanked the older woman, ruffled his son's hair and walked around the car to the driver's door. He opened it and said, "Hey, bud, don't worry about your mom, she'll be safe with me. Promise." He got in and drove away.

Charlotte clipped in her belt and glanced at her ex-husband sideways. Would she really be safe with him?

As if Dan could read her thoughts, he turned to look at her. "There are things you don't know about me, Char, things I couldn't tell you before." Should he tell her? He had no choice. She'd find out soon enough. "Now I need to."

"What things?" Charlotte asked in a quiet, shaky voice. She was afraid of him for the first time in her life. "What do you mean?"

"You remember that time I got bit, when we were first married? I told you it was a German Shepherd? You do remember, don't you?"

Charlotte's gut twisted and a wave of nausea rolled around her stomach. The conversation had taken an ugly turn. She stared at him with apprehensive understanding and nodded.

"It wasn't a dog."

Oh, my God! Dan's a wolf. Charlotte's heartbeat accelerated and she couldn't take a breath. She tried to push her voice out, it was a whisper. "So you're saying...?"

"I think you know what I'm saying." He pulled the car off the road. "I thought we'd be ok, until you got pregnant. Then I knew I had to leave. That's the reason I couldn't be around you and Tommy. That's why I've been such an asshole, to keep you two at a distance and keep you safe. I didn't want anyone doing what they've just done to you or our son. I thought it would protect you. But it hasn't."

Charlotte stared out the windshield at the dark night. Would she wake up and find out it was just another bad dream? She knew better. It was real. A living nightmare. *And Tommy has Dan's genes.*

"Is that why Tommy was unconscious?"

"Yeah, it's a wolf thing. He's too young to change. That won't happen until he's sixteen. It was his body's way of protecting him."

"He's never done that before."

"He was in a pack environment. A pack his underdeveloped wolf genes didn't recognize. It's a subconscious form of protective hibernation."

She glowered at him. "Why didn't you tell me this at the hospital? Why have me out of my mind with worry?"

"I wasn't sure if you knew about us. Would you have wanted to know? I wish I could have spared you both but it's too late for that now."

Charlotte's eyes filled with tears. Could this situation get any worse? Her ex-husband was a werewolf, and so was her son. Or would be when he turned sixteen.

Dan rested a hand on her shoulder and snapped her out of her unbearable contemplation. She jerked free from him before realizing what she'd done. "I'm so sorry this happened to you. I had no idea about any of this until a few days ago." She shook her head. "Why is this happening?"

He touched her bruised cheek with gentle fingers. "I don't know. All I know is we have to do something about it."

"Is that why we're going out to the facility?"

Dan nodded. "Something's going down tonight."

Charlotte frowned at him. "What?"

"A fight to the death."

Charlotte sat bolt upright. "How do you know that? Are you part of the Alpha's pack?"

He shook his head. "I'm part of another pack."

"Another… What do you mean? There's more than one?" Charlotte's heartbeat ratcheted up a notch.

"There's another Alpha. A woman. She wants to shut down the Alpha's operation. It's bad for everyone. She wants to live a normal life without any consequences, and she's prepared to do anything to stop him."

"Do anything? What does that mean?" The nervous knot in Charlotte's stomach unraveled and wrapped itself around her heart.

"She wants the Alpha dead and she's set in motion something that will achieve it. Once he's out of the picture the kids will be released from the curse."

"What has she got planned?"

"I can't tell you. You'll just have to trust me … and her."

Charlotte sighed. She didn't want to know about any of it. The only thing she wanted to be sure of was that the people she loved would be safe. "Will she be there tonight?"

Dan shook his head. "No, but we will."

"Who?" The whole scenario had become more disturbing.

He smiled. "You'll see when we get there." Dan started the engine and headed back toward the highway.

CHAPTER FORTY TWO

Josh gave the older man a glowering look. He had hoped to remain incognito for a while longer. It hadn't been part of his plan to be found yet, and he was angry with himself. He stood with his arms folded across his chest and stared the detective down. A Mexican standoff. What could he say, he'd been caught out?

He inhaled a deep breath through his nostrils and blew it out. "I came here to help. I figured it wouldn't be long before the Alpha planned an attack. He must be pretty pissed. So here I am." He opened his arms wide.

Ed squinted at Josh. "And you expect me to swallow that? You don't *help* anyone except yourself, Jamieson."

"That's not true." He folded his arms again.

"Yeah, it is. And don't give me any of your baloney, 'cos it won't wash with me." Ed thought for a moment. "And don't change the subject. How'd you get in here?"

Josh knew Borenko would ask again when he realized he hadn't given an answer. "I hid my car down the road, walked up and climbed over the fence."

The older man folded his arms and pursed his lips. "So let me get this straight, you walked about a mile up the road, climbed over an eight foot razor wire fence to come to our rescue? Hah, what do you take me for?" Ed shook his head. "Now give me the real version."

"That is the real version." Josh huffed out a frustrated breath. "Look." He snatched his designer jacket off a gurney and pushed it toward the

Lieutenant. "See, my jacket is torn to shreds. I used it to get over the wire. Doesn't that prove it?"

Ed studied the ripped jacket in Josh's hand. "That could've happened anywhere. For all I know, you could've done it yourself. Plenty of sharp implements around here."

Josh's temper rose. "But I didn't," he spat. "Do you want my help or not? The question is simple, even for you."

"Oh, ha ha, very droll. You must think I'm a complete moron." He squeezed an arm out of the fold and poked his finger at the detective. "Well let me tell you somethin', pal. I'm not as asinine as you might think. So let's try this again. How. The. Hell. Did you get in here? The question is simple, so answer it."

Josh gave a heavy sigh. "I climbed over the fence…"

"That doesn't answer the question." He ran his suspicious gaze around the infirmary and back to Josh. "This place is in lockdown. So I'll ask you again, how did you to get inside?"

CHAPTER FORTY THREE

Ned Bowers smiled as he drove along Santa Monica Boulevard. Something he didn't do often. He knew tonight would be the turning point in his miserable existence as District Attorney.

The meeting with that journalist, Sonia Edwards, seemed to have gone well. He believed it was an amicable negotiation and mutual satisfaction.

Everything appeared to be coming together. Charlotte had the current missing teen investigation in a total shambles and would soon be taken off the case, along with her meddling boyfriend, Reece Daniels. What had she been thinking, bringing him in? Hadn't his partner been imprisoned as a suspected serial killer a few years before? Probably guilty as hell and got off on a technicality.

None of that mattered now. That upstart, Josh Jamieson, would be running the show soon enough, and maybe, just maybe the case would be shelved. It made the department look incompetent. There had been no sightings of any of the abducted teens, and there never would be. Sooner rather than later, their boss would pull the plug and the case would be shelved as unsolved like so many others.

He turned down his street and just as he reached his house his cell phone vibrated. He tugged it from his jacket pocket. "Bowers speaking. What? Goddammit, I'll be right there."

§⟩⟨ℛ

When Ned's sedan skidded to a halt at the entrance to the alley, he was furious. He flung the door open, stepped out onto the road and, for the first time ever, slammed it before pressing the remote and charging toward the cordoned off alleyway.

A uniformed cop stepped across his path and the DA glared at him. "Get out of my way. Don't you know who I am?"

One of the investigating detectives, Brendan Caldwell, called out, "It's all right, Spencer, he's the District Attorney. You can let him through." He returned to his conversation with another detective and a member of the forensic team.

Ned eyeballed the cop as he brushed past him and stalked over to Caldwell. "So what have you got here?"

The detective stepped aside. "You tell me."

Two members of the forensic team were pulling pieces of a mutilated body out of the dumpster behind a delicatessen, the clothing and flesh shredded. The body looked as though it had been through a meat grinder.

"Jesus Christ!" Ned paled.

"Yeah. Won't know anything until they get the pieces back to the lab. Looks male, late teens. Haven't found the head yet." Caldwell stopped one of the forensic guys, took the bagged body part and shoved it at the DA. "Looks like chew marks, wouldn't you say, Ned?"

Ned's nostrils flared. "Why are you asking me? You're the detective and they're forensic experts. Don't they have the answer?"

"I'm sure they will once they examine the remains." He handed the arm back. "Could be one of the missing kids, but I sure as hell hope not."

Ned turned on his heel to leave, stopped short and turned around. "When you do have something I want to know about it. Got that?" He continued along the alley and back out to the street.

Caldwell eyed him with distaste. "Sure asshole, whatever you say. Not friggin' likely," he mumbled. He turned to his partner. "What do we know about the almighty acting DA?"

"Why are you asking?" Bryant turned and watched Bowers disappear around the corner of the alley. No one in the department could stand the guy.

"Something doesn't sit right with him and I want to know what it is. He's an asshole, no doubt about that, but there's something else going on there." He frowned at Bryant. "See if we can get our hands on his file."

His partner smiled. "Sure. I know just the person to ask."

When the DA turned the corner a bright light flashed on almost blinding him and a microphone bobbed in front of his face.

"Sonia Edwards, KTLA 5 News. Is the body in the dumpster one of the missing teenagers, District Attorney Bowers?"

The DA tried to contain his annoyance. He thought they had come to an arrangement. He attempted not to glare at her and swallowed his reaction before speaking. "I'm not at liberty to divulge any details at this early stage of the investigation." He pushed past the journalist and her cameraman, heading for his car. They followed.

"Is there anything you can give our viewers, District Attorney?"

"Not at this stage. That's all I have to say." He pressed the button on the remote key tag and climbed into his car, shutting the irritating news reporter out of his life for a while.

Ned reversed onto the road, slammed the automatic shift into drive, gave Sonia Edwards a glowering look and sped off.

As he drove along the highway he thought about the wounds on the remains found in the dumpster and wondered what the coroner's conclusion would be. Would he agree with Caldwell's theory and determine that cause of death was from being ripped apart by an animal?

The DA clenched his teeth and gripped the steering wheel so hard it made indentations in the leather. The situation was out of control.

CHAPTER FORTY FOUR

Ed Borenko's scrutinizing gaze remained on the intruder. Josh Jamieson had managed to get himself inside the prison, without an invite, and Ed wanted an explanation. One he was prepared to believe. From where he stood, Josh had a lot of explaining to do and he wasn't going anywhere until Ed was one hundred percent sure what he'd told him was the truth.

For all he knew, Josh could be one of the Alpha's henchmen, or a more terrifying conclusion, a closet werewolf hiding amongst them waiting to let the other wolves in when they arrived. The thought turned his blood to ice. Why had Josh been hiding in the infirmary? What was he planning to do in here? Ed wished he'd brought a weapon. He didn't trust Jamieson one bit.

"So answer the friggin' question. How did you gain entry? And don't try givin' me any cock and bull story, because I'll know." Ed folded his arms above his pot belly.

Josh reached into a pocket of his jacket, and the older man recoiled, expecting him to pull a pistol. The detective sighed. "I don't have a weapon, if that's what you're thinking. I'm getting these." He tossed his jacket onto the gurney and held up a wad of keys. "Funny what you can acquire when you know who to ask."

"What are they for?" Ed frowned at the tangle of keys.

The detective rolled his eyes. "Are you kidding? They're keys for this place. That's how I got in."

Ed marched over and snatched the keys out of Josh's hand. "You mean to tell me you've had a set of keys for this place all along."

Josh gave him an indignant glare. "No. I collected them yesterday."

"How do I know that?" Ed pocketed the keys.

"Because..."

"What were you plannin'? To let the other monsters in when it was time?"

Josh waved a defensive hand. "Now wait a minute."

Ed poked him in the chest. "No. You wait. We're vulnerable in here. If those things get in we're dead. I don't wanna be worrying about you and your shenanigans so get moving." He motioned for Josh to head for the door.

A voice echoed into the room. "What's going on in here?"

The chief swung around. "This punk's been hidin' in here. He had these." He pulled the wad of keys from his pocket and tossed them to Reece.

Reece held them up. "So, Jamieson, just what were you planning to do with these? Not on the Alpha's payroll, are you?"

Josh folded his arms. "I'm not going to dignify that with a response."

"Well you better, otherwise we'll lock you in a cell with the other wolves." Reece threw the keys back to Ed. He did have a gun.

"You can't be serious?" Josh gave him an incredulous stare.

Reece pointed his weapon at Josh. "You better believe it."

Nathaniel stalked along the cell block to Sarah, Adrian and Andre. The wolves were outside the fence.

"The wolves are outside the perimeter of the compound."

Adrian turned around. "The fence has just been activated, so that should hold them off a while longer."

The black vampire's serious expression turned even darker. "The dogs are resilient. The fence will not keep them out for long. And I suspect there will be more joining them soon."

Sarah glanced over her shoulder at the breached door. "Do you think they'll try to get in there?"

Nathaniel's gaze followed hers. "Yes. We must all be here and ready for them."

"We will be." Reece was adamant as he entered the cell block with Josh Jamieson at gunpoint.

Sarah pointed at Reece's weapon. "Why the gun?"

"Josh didn't give me the answer I needed. He's going in a cell."

"We need all the manpower we can get. Shouldn't he be with us?" Sarah asked.

"Yeah he should be. Problem is I can't trust him." He pushed Josh forward. "Get in." He motioned with his gun at the first empty cell. "And think yourself lucky I didn't keep my promise."

Josh crossed the block, head held high, and stepped into the cell. Ed slammed the door and locked it, chuckling as he removed the key and slid it into his pocket.

The detective wrapped his fingers around the bars and peered out at the group. "You're going to regret this. You *need* me."

"Sure we do. Like a hole in the head." Ed raised his right hand to his temple, stuck out his index finger, cocked his thumb and mouthed the word 'boom.'

Reece walked along the cell block to the adjoining door and everyone followed him. Sarah stopped and glanced over her shoulder. It was a bad idea leaving Josh alone, for a lot of reasons.

CHAPTER FORTY FIVE

Detective Brendan Caldwell sat at his computer skimming through the pages of Ned Bowers' departmental records. Bryant had come through for him. The people you know, huh? Nothing seemed out of place in the DA's file. No reprimands, no misconduct, nothing. Squeaky clean.

Caldwell was pissed. He wanted the DA out of the picture. Bowers was a belligerent piece of work who didn't deserve the important position he held. Everyone on the force couldn't stand him.

After going over and over everything in the electronic file, Brendan decided the only course of action was to call in a favor. Someone he knew who could rake up the dirt on the untouchable District Attorney.

He had a feeling about Bowers. There was something not right with the man, and the detective wanted to know what that something was.

Caldwell plucked his cell phone from his coat pocket. He couldn't make this kind of call on department phone lines. He got up from his chair and took the stairwell up to the roof.

"I need a favor."

The female voice asked, "Who?"

The detective coughed a chuckle. She always knew what he wanted. "You remember our conversation a couple of weeks ago? Him."

"All right. You'll have it before noon tomorrow. Good luck."

"What does that mean?"

"Be careful what you wish for, Brendan." The line went dead.

"Wait…" The detective pulled the phone from his ear and stared at it as though the answer would miraculously appear on the screen. It didn't. *What did she mean by that?*

CHAPTER FORTY SIX

Josh made himself comfortable, what else could he do? He lay back on the cot and tucked his hands behind his head, staring up at the gray concrete ceiling. Daniels left a bitter taste in his mouth and he wished he'd taken care of him a long time ago. He heaved a heavy sigh. What could he do? He was trapped.

His thoughts wandered back to the infirmary, before he was discovered by Borenko...

He'd stumbled upon the drowsy wolf shackled to a metal stretcher and decided to take a closer look. The hairy monster was snoring and he didn't want to disturb it. When he got closer, its eyes snapped open.

Shit! He jumped back, his heart doing the Rumba in his chest.

The thing snorted and inhaled a deep breath, taking in his scent.

Josh moved closer. "Think you're going to have a piece of me, do you?" He smirked and circled the stretcher.

The creature's blood red gaze followed him.

Josh stopped and stared into its eyes. Even though it was a monster, he recognized something human about it.

"I know you, don't I?" He pointed at the beast. "You're a cop, aren't you?" He paced, then swung around and snapped his fingers. "You're Dan McCredie's old partner, Paul ... what's your last name?" He pointed at the wolf again. "Paul ... Rogers. That's it. Is that why you won't turn back to human form?"

A deep growl rumbled in the creature's chest.

Josh stepped back. "How many are there? Twenty? Fifty? A hundred?"
The wolf roared.

"There's an army of you on the force, and probably in other areas of the public sector too." He paced again. "This is fantastic!" …

A smirk spread across Josh's face as he gazed at the ceiling. The others had no idea what they were up against.

A force of wolves. LA could be the inaugural city for a supernatural law enforcement bureau. One that was unstoppable. One that couldn't be corrupted by human thought processes. *One* that was in control.

Everyone in the cell block was ready for whatever was to come. They all bowed their heads and Sarah gave a prayer, closing with Amen.

Everyone echoed "Amen."

Just as the group separated and took up their positions, a loud crack and an electrical buzz echoed through the cell block and everything went black.

Josh jumped off the cot. "Shit." His nervous eyes scanned the dark. The speed of his racing heart pulsed in his neck and a wave of fear crawled over his skin. "Hey," he called out, shuffling toward the cell door with hands outstretched out like a blind man. He found the metal bars and gripped them with both hands, pressing his face against the cold steel. "Hey, can anyone hear me?" His voice echoed around the empty block. He rattled the door hard, hoping it would pop open and set him free. It didn't. "Hey," he yelled louder. "I need to get out of here."

The stark bright beam of a flashlight hit him in the eyes and he raised a hand to shield them from the glare.

"What are you squawkin' about, Jamieson?" Ed Borenko asked. "Afraid the Boogie Man might get you?" His throaty chuckle boomed into the cell.

"No." Josh stepped back. "I thought you might need my help. The wolves are obviously here. An extra pair of hands may be of some use."

Ed squinted at him in disbelief, although Josh couldn't see his expression. "Are you kiddin' me? I wouldn't trust you with a pair of tweezers let alone a gun. I sure as hell don't want a bullet in the back and neither does Daniels."

Josh pushed himself toward the bars. "You think I would stoop that low?"

"You bet your life I do. Now sit down and shut up, otherwise those things will know exactly where we all are, includin' you." He turned to walk away.

Josh was desperate and his words came out in a rush. "I give you my word I won't shoot anyone other than a wolf." He took a breath. "Please don't leave me here." He hated begging, but he didn't want to be locked up in the dark. He valued his life more than his pride.

"Let him out, Ed." Sarah came up beside him.

The chief glanced at her sideways. "Not a chance in hell. He can't be trusted."

Sarah sighed. "He gave his word."

"And you believe him?"

Sarah shone her flashlight at Josh. "Do you give me, a priest, your word? If you break it you'll answer to God."

He nodded. "Yes, yes, I give you and God my word."

Sarah gestured to the door.

Ed sighed, gave her the flashlight and pulled the keys from his pants pocket. "I think we're gonna regret this." He pushed the key into the lock and turned it, knowing in his gut it was a bad move.

Dan pulled the car off the road and hid it amongst a patch of tall, thick trees. He wanted to be sure no one would find it, at least not until they were safe inside the prison. He huffed out a silent sardonic laugh at the thought. Safe? No one was safe tonight.

Charlotte moved around the car. "So, what do we do now?" she asked, gazing at the surrounding dark and feeling a shiver run through her. Like Reece, she knew how to use a weapon to protect herself, but this was way out of her comfort zone.

Dan took Charlotte by the hand and trudged through the brush and tall grass, threading his way toward the compound from the rear so the other wolves wouldn't pick up his scent.

"Wait, Dan. Please, can we stop for a minute?" She tugged his hand.

Her ex-husband swung around. "What? His tone was tight and he realized it. "Sorry, what's wrong?"

"Don't you think we need a plan? We can't just go in there guns blazing and not expect to be injured, or worse."

Dan sighed, let go of her hand and folded his arms. "This is what we'll do. We'll get to the fence, hope it's not working, cut a hole and climb through." He pulled a pair of wire cutters from the back pocket of his pants and held them up.

Charlotte gave him an incredulous frown. "That's it? That's the plan? Where's the rest of your pack? The ones who were coming to help us?"

Dan gave her an odd smile. "Already inside. And no, that's not the plan. Trust me, will you?"

Charlotte glanced off into the distance, examining the massive building in the center of the surrounding dark. "So what if the fence is electric? How do we get in?"

"I'll cross that bridge when I get there. Right now, let's just get there without any complications." He grabbed her hand and continued leading her through the tall grass. It was good cover.

Everyone was in position. The cops Ed had called in were at the forefront. They seemed well prepared and keen to get into the action. Reece wished he felt as confident.

When Sarah and Ed arrived with Josh in tow, Reece moved out of position and stalked toward them. "What's he doing here?" He jabbed a finger at the detective.

Ed raised defensive hands. "Don't look at me. It wasn't my idea." He glanced sideways at Sarah and she gave him a glowering frown.

"No, it was mine," she said, stepping to the front.

"What the hell were you thinking? We don't know what his intentions are, for all we know he could be connected to the Alpha."

Josh tried to refute the PI's accusation. "But..."

Reece raised his hand. "Don't bother. Nothing you could say would convince me to trust you."

Ed gave Sarah a smug smile. "See, what'd I tell ya."

Sarah kept her gaze on Reece. "We need all the manpower we can get. Those creatures are much stronger than we are, the more firepower we have against them the better. Please, Reece, let him help."

Reece eyeballed Josh. "Sarah's right. We do need everyone on board. Your life is at stake here just as much as ours, so you'd better not fuck this up or you're a dead man, one way or the other."

Josh stepped between Ed and Sarah and stared at the PI. "I told you I'd help and I will. I realize I'm at risk here, from both sides it would appear, so I don't intend to *fuck* it up."

Reece kept his intense gaze on the detective, contemplating whether or not to hand him his automatic loaded with silver bullets. After a few seconds he shoved the gun at Josh and told him to suit up.

The group joined the others and waited in anticipation.

Charlotte was almost at a run and out of breath as Dan strode through the tall grass pulling her along behind him. "Can we stop for a second?" she asked, puffing. She'd gotten a stitch and her side had a painful twinge.

Dan stopped short and she crashed into his back.

He whirled, his eyes red, his voice throaty. "We need to get there fast."

Charlotte's breath caught in her throat, she yanked her hand free and stumbled backwards. "Oh my God, you're changing!"

"Don't be afraid, I won't hurt you. I've had years to learn how to control it."

Charlotte stepped back further, panting. "Are … are you sure? I don't want to…"

"Charlotte, I won't hurt you!" He grabbed her hand. His skin was hot and reminded her of whisker stubble. "We have to go. *Now*."

They were only a few hundred feet from the fence and as they moved closer Charlotte could see the building was in total darkness. Where were Reece and the others? Were they safe? Who was inside? Who was outside?

When they reached the perimeter, Dan started to undress.

"What are you doing?" Charlotte asked.

He kicked off his boots and pulled off his socks. "I'll need these when we get over. So you can hold onto them for me."

"What are you going to do?" Dan threw her his shirt and she folded it.

"I'm changing into wolf form so we can get inside." He threw her his pants. She folded them too.

"I don't understand how that's going to help us get over the fence." She plucked his socks off the ground, balled them up and pushed them into his pants pocket.

"When I change you'll get on my back. I'll jump the fence, which is electrified by the way, and we'll be inside. Simple as that."

"Simp… you've got to be joking! You don't think I'm going to climb on your back once you change into a werewolf, do you?"

He threw her his underwear. "That's what I know. Now step back, you don't want to be too close."

As Dan changed into wolf form, Charlotte wondered how painful it was. It looked painful. His body twisted and stretched and snapped and squelched. And his roar sounded agonizing. Once he transformed, she tucked his clothes inside her jacket, buttoned it, and climbed on his back. She leaned her body into his and wrapped her arms around his large, muscular neck. His fur was thick and surprisingly soft. It felt comforting in a way, and Charlotte realized she wasn't afraid of him.

The wolf bounded toward the fence and leaped into the air.

Reece's phone went off and he snatched it from the pocket of his jeans. He'd forgotten to turn it to silent. A mistake he shouldn't have made. He looked at the screen. It was Charlotte. He pushed the button and walked to the end of the cell block away from the others. "Hi, what's up?"

"Dan and I are outside and…"

"Outside? You mean here? What the hell were you thinking?!" He raised his hand to his forehead and paced. "You need to go. You shouldn't be here."

"Dan wants to help and so do I. Will you please let us in? We're at a rear door on the left-hand side of the building."

Reece covered the mouthpiece. "Shit!" He removed his hand. "All right. Stay put and I'll be there as fast as I can." He shoved his phone into his pocket.

Ed stood with hands on hips watching Reece. As he approached him he said, "Who was that?"

Reece gave him a stern look. "Charlotte."

"Everything ok with her?"

"She's here with her ex."

Ed balked. "Jesus! You mean here? Where?"

"The back door of the infirmary. I'm going to let them in. You keep things under control here until I get back." He headed for the door. "And ask Sarah to organize some riot gear for them. There should be some spares in the metal locker in the storage room."

"Will do. Jesus, what a cock up. She shouldn't be here." He shook his head and threw the wad of keys at Reece.

"You think I don't know that?" The PI stalked through the door and headed to the infirmary. He wondered how Charlotte found out about tonight.

When he got to the back door, he knew it would take a few minutes to find the right keys. There were five deadlocks and two large hasps with padlocks. He fumbled through the keys and unlocked one lock, then fumbled through again to find the key for the next lock. "Charlotte? Can you hear me?"

Charlotte's muffled voice echoed through the heavy door. "Only just."

"It's going to take a couple of minutes. Everything ok out there?"

"For now." Charlotte was anxious to get inside. They were vulnerable and she had a bad feeling. "Please hurry."

Reece leaned toward the door and shouted. "I'm doing the best I can. Stay cool, shouldn't be much longer." Continuing through the keys systematically he made it to the last lock and swung the door open. "Come in. I need to get the door secured." He gave Charlotte a brief smile when she stepped through the doorway and eyeballed Dan as he followed her in. "Why did you bring her here?" He noticed something was off as he gave the cop the once over. "And where are your shoes?"

Dan McCredie locked his intense gaze onto the PI and raised his chin. "What's it to you?"

Charlotte stepped between them. "Now, now, boys, let's play nice. There are more important things to do right now." She pushed them apart. "I left Dan's shoes outside the fence. I forgot to pick them up. There's got to be a pair around here somewhere, it is a prison after all."

"An *unused* prison," Reece reminded her. "And don't try to throw me off, why isn't your ex wearing his shoes?"

Dan moved Charlotte out of the way and stepped up to Reece. He stared into the PI's eyes and showed him why. A red glow radiated to the edge of his brown eyes, then shrank back into the pupil.

Reece pushed back. "Fuck! You're a…"

"Werewolf. Yeah." Dan stepped away.

Charlotte rushed over to Reece. "It's ok. He belongs to another pack. One that wants to get rid of the Alpha."

Reece looked at her, his eyes incoherent for a moment. "What?"

She glanced at Dan. "He's here to help."

Another pack? Reece couldn't stretch his mind around that piece of information.

CHAPTER FORTY SEVEN

Ned was not at all pleased about the new turn of events and needed to make sure this murder investigation ran smoothly, without too many questions. He had no time for Detective Brendan Caldwell. They had locked horns before over another investigation and the DA was not happy that Caldwell had been assigned to this particular case.

He had a habit of delving into matters that were of no concern to him, and his unorthodox methods of investigating had landed him in hot water on previous occasions, with a six week suspension at one point. Ned was concerned that the detective would over-step his boundary once again.

Ned checked his watch. 11.30 pm. He pulled his sedan into the driveway of his home, turned off the engine and stepped out. He'd requested a full report of the findings on the latest victim and hoped when he opened his email it would be waiting for him. When he reached his front door a voice came out of the dark.

"Hello, Ned. Long time no see." A man dressed in a black hoodie and jeans materialized out of the shadows on his porch and ambled up to him, hands tucked in the pockets of his jacket. All that was visible was his stubbled pasty face.

Ned balked. "What are you doing here? Shouldn't you be...?"

"In prison? Got paroled last week. I heard you had a serious conversation with Sonia Edwards."

The DA cleared his throat, anxious. His gut tightened. "Yes, yes I did." He had to show no fear. He raised his chin and stared the man in the eyes.

"What concern is it of yours? Why are you here?"

The man sighed, pulled a hand from his pocket and flicked a spot of fluff off the DA's suit coat. "I was sent to give you a *message. You know who* isn't pleased."

Ned's arrogance returned. "Well, you can tell *you know who* there's nothing to worry about. We've come to an understanding."

"You'd better be sure of that, Ned, because if anything goes wrong you know the consequences." He headed down the path of the elegant LA home and as he reached the front fence he turned around. "Some friendly advice, watch your back. If this gets out of hand, your life won't be worth shit. There'll be nowhere you can hide." He opened the gate and stalked along the street.

Ned rushed down the path and peered along the sidewalk. His visitor had evaporated into the night.

෨෬

Detective Caldwell headed to his desk with the take away coffee from the all night café down the street. He and his team were pulling a late night because of the dumpster body. He'd expected the package to be on his desk by midday. It never arrived. As he reached his desk in the corner of the workroom, he hoped what he'd been waiting for would be there, even though it was close to midnight. "Dammit," he cursed under his breath when he saw that the package wasn't there.

Just as he was about to sit down his cell phone vibrated. He sat the cardboard coffee cup on his paper-strewn desk and snatched the phone from his shirt pocket. Not looking at the incoming caller ID he said, "Detective Caldwell…"

"It's me."

"Where's that information I asked you for? It should have been here hours ago." She had never let him down before.

"I need to see you. Can you get away?" She always sounded so aloof, calculating.

He glanced around the office and sighed. "Where are you?"

Her glossy red lips spread into a smile. "I'll meet you. The café down the street in twenty minutes." The line went dead. She had a habit of cutting him off before he could protest and he didn't like it.

Caldwell looked around the workroom for his partner, Eric Bryant. He was over by the candy vending machine. It was late and he needed a sugar hit. The detective stalked across the office.

"Hey, Eric? I have to go out for a while. Can you cover for me?"

His partner turned around and frowned at him, munching on a mouthful of chocolate. When Bryant saw the expression on Caldwell's face he swallowed the wad of gluey candy and coughed as it forced its way down to his stomach. "Where you going?"

"I could tell you but then I'd have to kill you." Caldwell gave him a humorless grin. "Don't make me do something illegal." He knew that's exactly what he *was* doing. Something totally illegal.

Eric didn't know how to take his partner's jibes. He wondered if Brendan was serious and came to the conclusion he didn't want to know. "Sure. How long do you need?"

"Don't know." He shrugged.

"Can you tell me anything?"

"Like I said…"

"Yeah, yeah, if you told me you'd have to kill me." He sighed.

"So we're good?" Caldwell raised an enquiring eyebrow.

Bryant nodded. "Yeah, sure, we're good."

Caldwell slapped his partner on the shoulder, turned and headed to the elevator. This meeting was far too important to miss.

CHAPTER FORTY EIGHT

Ed Borenko watched the doorway. For some reason he couldn't explain, his gut told him something wasn't right. He wondered where Daniels was and why he and the others hadn't returned. They should have been back by now. Ed stood up and walked over to Sarah. "I'm gonna find out what's takin' Daniels so long."

Sarah grabbed his arm. "You should wait, Ed. I'm sure Reece will be back any minute. He probably wanted to brief Charlotte and her husband before bringing them down here. It would be the right thing to do."

Ed frowned at her. "Ex-husband," he corrected. "And he could do that here. No, somethin' doesn't feel right." He patted her hand and removed it from his arm. "I won't be long." He snatched a flashlight off a box nearby and headed for the door.

"Wait. I'm coming with you." She grabbed her weapon and called to Nathaniel. "Keep an eye on Josh."

Nathaniel gave a sharp nod and crossed the cell block.

Sarah caught up to Ed. "Safety in numbers."

Ed gave her a crooked smile. "Aw, I didn't know you cared."

She glowered at him, even though it amused her. "You're incorrigible, you know that?"

"Sweet talkin' me will get you everywhere." He chuckled and headed for the door.

Sarah turned around to make sure Nathaniel was with Josh before following the detective out. "Ed Borenko, are you flirting with a priest?"

She played along, giving him a mock incredulous frown. It was a great stress reliever and she needed the distraction.

"Could be." He stopped and waited for her to catch up to him. "Why? Am I goin' to hell?" He chuckled again.

"Maybe," she said, laughing. "But not for flirting with a woman of the cloth. We're both single, it's not as though we're committing a sin."

He glanced at her sideways. "You really think I'm goin' to hell?"

"I'm kidding. I do have a sense of humor too, you know."

"Good to hear."

They continued along the pitch black corridor, Ed aiming the flashlight as far as it would reach. They didn't need any surprises or to be jumping at shadows.

When the pair was almost at the infirmary Reece stepped into the corridor, startling them. "What are you doing here, you're meant to be keeping an eye on Jamieson?"

Ed shone the light in Reece's face. "We were worried about you, Daniels."

Sarah corrected, "*He* was worried about you. Where's Charlotte and..."

Reece pushed the light out of his face. "Come inside, there's something you need to know."

Ed and Sarah followed Reece in, Ed holding the flashlight up between them so they could see each other.

Sarah mouthed to him "What's going on?"

He shrugged and mouthed back "Beats me."

Reece turned around. "I know what you're doing. So stop it." He opened the infirmary door and waved them through. "After you."

The pair gazed around the room as they stepped inside. Charlotte and Dan were over by some medical cabinets on the opposite side of the infirmary.

Sarah rushed over and hugged Charlotte. "What are you doing here?"

Charlotte eased herself out of Sarah's embrace. "We came to help. From what Reece has said you could use some extra muscle."

"Dan has something to tell you," Reece said.

"What is it?" Sarah asked.

Reece gestured to the cop. "Over to you."

Dan cleared his throat and surveyed everyone's faces in the dim light of the lantern they had found. He sighed. "When Charlotte and I were first married, I was on patrol one night and we got a call to check an alley down town. Someone had heard some kind of altercation and called it in. Paul was driving that night, and when we turned into the alley he stopped the patrol car and got out. He pulled his flashlight and continued on foot, telling me to wait in the car. I was a rookie, so I guess he was just looking out for me.

"Anyhow, he disappeared into the dark and the next thing I know he's screaming. Adrenalin and fear kicked in and I jumped out of the car. I couldn't move at first. After a couple minutes I ran along the alley. I was scared shitless. I didn't know what had happened to him and I was hesitant about pulling a weapon, in case I shot him by mistake.

"When I found him he was lying in a pool of blood with deep gashes all over his body. His uniform was torn to shreds and his breathing was so shallow I couldn't hear it. I thought he was dead. Before I had a chance to call it in, something huge came outta nowhere, hit me like a bulldozer and tackled me to ground then bit my leg and took off."

Sarah and Ed stared at him in disbelief. Sarah was the one to ask, "So you're a..."

"Yeah. Funny how things happen, huh?"

Ed frowned at Reece. "So this guy's part of the pack?"

Reece shook his head. "He's part of another pack."

Sarah and Ed both said, "Another pack?"

"Yeah. It's a long story. He's here to help. And I've just learned who our friend is in there." Reece pointed to the other room.

"Who?" Ed asked, feeling unnerved.

Dan answered. "Paul."

"Your partner?"

"My old partner." He pointed to the door and looked at Reece. "Can I go in? Once he sees me he'll turn back. We could use his help too."

Reece stared at the door for a long time. He knew it wasn't a good idea. "How trustworthy do you think he is? He could be part of the Alpha's pack."

Dan frowned and gave it some thought. "It's been a while, you know? You could be right."

"Ok. I think he can stay where he is. I wouldn't want to give him the benefit of the doubt and have him turn on us when things heated up."

"Can I go in anyway?"

"Sure. Ed can accompany you."

Ed gave him a serious frown. He didn't want to go in there, not if he didn't have to.

Dan walked over to the door, opened it and turned around. "Coming?"

Ed sighed and followed him in.

Sarah gave Reece a look of disapproval.

"What?" he asked.

"Why didn't you go?"

"We're all in this together. If I can't allocate a task and expect it to be done we're in serious trouble."

"Okay, I understand that…"

"Bottom line is you all asked me to head this operation and I'm doing the best I can." He glanced at Charlotte. "Anyway, I wanted to talk to Charlotte while Dan's not here."

Sarah raised her hands. "I won't say another word."

Reece took Charlotte by the arm and led her to the other side of the room.

She gazed into his concerned eyes. "Please don't tell me I shouldn't be here. I need to be here. I love you."

Reece rubbed her arm and smiled. "I love you too, but this isn't the way to show you care. I want you safe. You should be home with Tommy. He needs you right now."

"He's in good hands. Let me help you." Charlotte pushed herself against him and he wrapped his arms around her. When he glanced over at Sarah she had an 'I told you so' look on her face.

"Can Dan be trusted? How do you know he belongs to another pack? Only by what he's told you, right?"

Charlotte moved out of his arms. "Well, yes…"

"Did he say who the other Alpha is?"

"No. He just said it was a woman."

"A woman?" He frowned at her. "He didn't give a name or any kind of clue?"

"I was so shocked I didn't ask. This is all so personal now. But I believe him."

Reece's eyes moved to the closed door. His gut had other ideas. "I hope you're right."

CHAPTER FORTY NINE

Ned stormed into his house and slammed the door. "Who the hell do they think they are, telling me what I can and can't do?" He charged along the hallway and into the kitchen, dumped his briefcase on the counter, pulled off his jacket and flung it over the back of a tall stool.

The latest murder and now this invasion of his personal space was too much. He rushed into the living room and over to the stereo in his entertainment center. He remembered the first line of Act I from the play *The Mourning Bride,* 'Music has charms to soothe the savage breast', and smiled as he hit the play button. Shostakovich's symphony no. 5 pulsed from the speakers. Ned laughed. It invigorated him, not soothed him. Adrenalin pumped through his body. He turned the music up and stood facing the stereo like a maestro, waving his arms to the dark refrain.

Once this murder investigation ceased, he'd be on his way to a different state or maybe a different country. He would decide when the time was right. LA had become uninspiring and he needed a change of scene. The rest of the mess could be cleaned up by some other incompetent fool.

Realizing he hadn't had dinner, despite the late hour, he turned down the volume control and marched back into the kitchen to the refrigerator. He wrenched the door open and peered inside—he was ravenous. Ned ran his eyes over the contents, nothing appealed to his acute hunger. He slammed the door, raced out of the kitchen and up the stairs to change. It may have been late, but he knew exactly where he could get what he wanted.

ಐಂ

Dan and Ed returned to the others. Trying to reason with the creature had been a waste of time. Paul, it seemed, had no intention of turning back to human form. Ed wandered over to Sarah and Charlotte, while Dan walked Reece away from the group to give him his opinion.

"I think you could be right about Paul. Nothing I said made a difference. He's not prepared to even try to turn. He seems messed up. His eyes..." Dan stopped and shook his head, "there's something wrong with them."

"What do you mean?"

"Not sure. Has he been drugged?"

"Well, yeah. There wasn't any other way to capture him." Reece folded his arms across his chest. "You don't think it was the drugs we gave him, do you?"

Dan shook his head. "I think he's been given something to keep him from changing."

Reece sighed. "So you think he's part of the Alpha's pack?"

"Yeah, I do."

"And what do you suggest we do about it?"

Dan stared Reece down. "What do you think?"

The pair returned to the others.

Reece pondered his options. Should they kill the creature on Dan's say so? Or did Paul know something Dan didn't want them to find out?

"Is there something you want to share with the rest of us?" Sarah walked over to Reece.

Pulled from his thoughts, he looked at her. "No. It's something I need to sort out."

Reece decided the creature would remain secured in the ward until he had time to consider the best course of action. He wasn't going to *execute* someone without good reason. And Paul could have the answers he needed.

When he told everyone to head back to the cell block Dan was reluctant to leave. Reece stood his ground. Once he was alone he entered the ward.

The creature appeared to be sleeping. Reece stepped up to the gurney and jabbed at the wolf several times to wake it. It roused and opened its eyes, taking in a long inhalation of the PI's scent. Reece circled the gurney slowly. "We know who you are?" He stopped at the foot. "I know you can understand me and I need to ask you something. Can Dan be trusted?"

The creature's blood red eyes focused on the PI and it snorted.

Reece moved around the gurney. "You're not going anywhere, so why not be useful. When this is all over there might be a cure."

The wolf snorted hot air at Reece through its huge muzzle.

The PI stepped away from the fetid breath. "You don't want to be cured, do you? You like what you've become."

The beast looked like it was smiling.

A shiver ran the length of Reece's spine and he took another step back. "I get it. It's the power. But think about the consequences. You must know you're never leaving here alive if you remain a wolf, right?"

The creature wrenched at the shackle clamped around its left wrist. The metal snapped in two and the chain hit the floor with a loud clang.

Reece balked. He didn't have a weapon. He rushed toward the door and before he reached it the creature spoke.

Ed and Sarah entered the cell block with Charlotte and Dan. Charlotte had been fitted with a flak jacket, goggles and helmet on the way back. She had also replaced her pistol clip with silver bullets.

Sarah called to Nathaniel, waving him over. Before leaving his post, he told Josh to remain seated on the floor and that if he moved he would sustain a permanent injury.

Josh glowered at him, folded his arms and let out a heavy sigh. "Where do you think I'm going?"

Nathaniel glowered at him, then turned and stalked along the cell block.

Before Sarah had a chance to speak, the vampire grabbed Dan by the throat. "Why is this dog here?"

Both Sarah and Charlotte screamed, "Don't!"

"Let him go, Nathaniel," Ed told him. "He's one of the good guys. Or so it seems."

Nathaniel's large hand remained clamped around Dan's neck. "And why should I believe that?" His dark eyes remained steadfast on the cop.

Charlotte spoke. "Because he's my ex-husband and I know him. He wouldn't do anything to jeopardize my safety or anyone else's."

Nathaniel stared into her eyes, searching her soul for the truth before he unclenched his fingers. "Very well."

Dan coughed and clutched at his throat. "Thanks," he said, his voice raspy.

Nathaniel turned on his heel and was about to stalk back to his post when he noticed Josh was not where he had left him. He turned around. "Did anyone see Josh pass us?"

Sarah gazed down the cell block. "No." She turned to Ed. "Did you see him?"

Ed gave her an incredulous look. "I think we were a little preoccupied, don't you?"

Reece walked through the door. The look on Sarah and Ed's faces worried him. "What's wrong?"

"Josh has gone," Nathaniel told him. "We are not sure how he got away."

"I knew we should've kept him locked up." Reece paced, then stopped. "Ok. Get organized and I'll go find him."

"I'm sorry, Reece, I thought he'd keep his word." Sarah felt responsible.

"That's Jamieson. He'll do whatever it takes to protect himself. Don't let it get to you. You did what you thought was right." He gazed into the dark corridor. "He can't have gone far." He debated whether to go after the detective or leave him to his own devices ... and the wolves.

CHAPTER FIFTY

Josh raced through the infirmary, the flashlight beam bouncing along the floor ahead of him, to the locked evacuation exit. He assumed it was the same door Reece had let Charlotte and her ex into the prison through. A smug smile crossed his lips as he reached into his pants pocket and pulled out a duplicate set of skeleton keys. Did Borenko and the others think he wouldn't have a backup plan?

He snatched his jacket off the trolley, where he'd left it, pulled it on over his flak jacket and rushed to the door. Fumbling through the numerous keys, he realized it would take some time to get the door unlocked. Time he didn't have. The first key slid into the deadlock and wouldn't budge. He struggled with it for a few seconds and gave up in disgust. "Shit!" He fingered through several keys, holding them in the circle of light—flashlight wedged between his knees—to see if the serial numbers matched the locks. They didn't. Why did he think it could be that easy?

Josh continued to push keys into locks.

One lock opened with a loud metallic snap that echoed around the room, and the detective peered over his shoulder. He knew they'd be coming for him soon. He rammed another key into each lock and padlock. Another lock snapped free. He worked systematically until all the locks were open and breathed a sigh of relief. He was about to pull the door free when it burst from its hinges, hurtling him across the room. He crashed into the wall and fell in a heap on the floor.

Three hulking werewolves with glowing red eyes stomped into the infirmary, their roars booming around the room.

Josh pretended he was out cold, hoping they would bypass him and head straight to the cell block. They didn't.

The first werewolf lifted its huge snout and sniffed the stale air, then locked its gaze onto the ward and gave another booming roar. The three creatures stalked across the room. The leader raised its massive foot and thrust it into the door, sending shards of glass and wood flying everywhere.

Savage snarls and ear-splitting sounds of crunching metal and breaking glass echoed out of the room. The wolf shackled to the gurney didn't stand a chance.

Adrenalin and fear pumped through Josh's rigid body. He wasn't lying in wait of his own death. He had to make a run for it. He eyed the pulverized exit and checked the other doorway. The cacophony reached a crescendo and Josh knew it was time to move. He counted down in his head: three, two, one, sprang to his feet, and dashed across the room. As he was about to dissolve into the night something grabbed him from behind and dragged him back inside.

The roaring and smashing continued.

Reece pulled Josh into a dark corner. "We have to get out of here or we'll be next."

"How are we going to do that? They'll hear us, or smell us."

One snarling wolf stalked out of the room, its huge form silhouetted in the gloom by a beam of moonlight filtering through a high set window. As it moved toward the outside doorway, it stopped, turned its head and sniffed the air.

Both men hoped it couldn't detect them in the dark.

The creature changed direction and headed their way.

Reece prodded the floor around him for anything he could use as a weapon. His fingers touched something cold and cylindrical and he gripped the small glass test tube in his hand. He had an idea. He pushed himself off the floor and tossed the glass vile as far as he could to the other end of the room. It smashed somewhere in the dark.

The hulking creature swung around, snarled, and followed the sound.

Reece and Josh jumped to their feet, flew out of the open door and raced along the corridor. Peering over their shoulders, they expected to see the wolf in hot pursuit. It wasn't.

When they reached the open doorway to the first cell block, Reece slammed the door and secured it with the steel rod. He knew it wouldn't hold for long, but it would keep the wolves busy long enough for the team to gear up.

Nathaniel's huge form filled the second doorway. He stepped aside and Reece and Josh rushed into the cell block. The vampire secured the door and followed the pair back to the team.

"Listen up," Reece blurted. "Three wolves are in the infirmary doing a number on the one we had in chains. They'll be here once they're done in there, and with reinforcements. Let's be ready for them."

The team Ed had called in strutted over to Reece. One cop said, "We'll handle the frontline, you guys cover us."

Reece studied the hulking cop and something slithered in his gut. "All right. Thanks."

Ed noticed the look on Reece's face. He barreled over to the PI. "What's up, Daniels?"

Reece's jaw tightened. "What do you know about those cops?"

Ed frowned. "What do ya mean?"

The muscles in Reece's jaw flexed.

Ed shrugged. "They've been on the force a few years. They seem on the up and up, and they owed me a favor. Why?"

The cop Reece had been talking to walked over to them. "Because he's figured out what we are."

Ed's face wrinkled. "What are ya talkin' about?"

The cop laughed. "Borenko, come on, you can't be that stupid."

"Hey, who are you callin' stupid, punk?" He made a swipe at the young cop's nose.

The cop grabbed his fist. "Easy old man, wouldn't want to break somethin'."

"Why you…" Ed launched himself at the cop, but Reece held him back.

"Ed. Stop. These guys are wolves." He hadn't figured it out, although his gut did tell him something was off about them, he was given the information by the wolf in the infirmary.

CHAPTER FIFTY ONE

Ned sat at a table in the late night café, sipping a mochaccino. He enjoyed a hot, sweet aperitif after a meal. And what a meal! His hunger had been sated and he felt good. No one would recognize him in the attire he had on. It didn't fit his usual professional profile. He was a shadow in the night and the anonymity pleased him.

He thought about Sonia Edwards. She was a problem that needed to be extricated. One he could do nothing about. He'd been warned.

The DA's surreptitious gaze swept the clientele. No one he recognized. Good. He finished his coffee, threw a couple of bills on the table, made sure his face was hidden beneath his dark hood, and left the café.

While he strutted along the sidewalk, hands in his pockets, he thought about Brendan Caldwell. What would the detective be doing right now? Would he, once again, be delving into matters that were not his concern? Ned needed to know.

When Ned rounded the corner, the detective was getting out of his old-model sedan parked on the street in front of his house. He had a bag with Chinese takeout. A very late dinner, the DA thought. Ned stood in the dark and watched him for a while before moving along the sidewalk and slipping behind a tree not far from the trunk of the detective's car.

Caldwell ambled up the path to his front door. He stood there checking his pockets for his key and Ned considered how easy it would be to sneak up behind him and...

No.

He had a better way of removing the detective. A manic smile spread across the DA's face as he visualized what could be the demise of Brendan Caldwell. He was not about to let someone as insignificant ruin his plans. He waited until the detective was *safely* inside before leaving.

Brendan locked the front door and headed to the study with his meal. He'd been waiting on the electronic file on Ned Bowers from his informant. If it was there, he'd probably pull an all-nighter.

He pushed the bag of assorted Chinese cuisine onto the desk, sat down and opened up his laptop. When he heard the *ding dong* sound, he knew the email had arrived. The Detective began sifting through the documents.

In the wee small hours of the morning, further research on the Social Security website disclosed that before 1983 Ned Bowers had no Social Security number. Where had he been before that time? And why hadn't the department picked up on it?

ℰ᙭

A news bulletin roused Ned from sleep as his television automatically switched on and the urgent voice of the news reporter echoed into his bedroom. It was his wakeup call. He much preferred the news to a beeping alarm clock. One eye peeled open and he gazed around his room, then down at himself. He had slept in his clothes again. It had become a bad habit, one he would have to break.

The DA's drowsy demeanor jolted awake when he heard the news reporter announce that Detective Brendan Caldwell had been killed by an unknown assailant in his home the previous evening.

It was reported that when the detective arrived home someone had been inside his house. It appeared to be a robbery gone wrong. The department would continue to investigate.

A smile replaced the initial shocked expression on the DA's face as he realized there was no longer a threat of anyone discovering his identity. It also occurred to him that someone else had done his dirty work for him. He wondered who.

CHAPTER FIFTY TWO

Everyone in the cell block scrambled for position, weapons, wolves and vampires as ready as they could be for what was about to come at them. The roars grew louder as the beasts stormed the secured door. The four wolf cops at the forefront swore nothing would get past them without a fight.

Reece moved Charlotte behind him. His heart hammered so loud he could hear it in his ears. This was it! Make or break. People would die. As far as he was concerned it wouldn't be anyone close to him, especially Charlotte.

Ed sidled up to him, his eyes surveying the dark cell block. "Have you got a backup plan, Daniels?" His voice wavered and he coughed.

"Yeah, we eliminate those motherfuckers and make sure no one gets killed in the process."

Ed's eyebrows rose. "That's it? That's all you got?"

The PI wiped the sweat from his forehead. "You got a better idea? Because if you do I'd like to hear it."

Ed remained silent, digesting the information. This was the final battle. Not everyone would make it, and no, he didn't have a clue what their backup plan should be. They were trapped. The only way out was to fight. And win. He snorted a breath. "We'll fight, and we'll win!" He felt for Reece's hand and shook it.

"Ok, everyone this is it. Lock and load people!" Reece yelled, his voice echoing around the concrete walls.

The door burst from its hinges and six snarling monsters stormed inside. The four cops on the frontline turned—skin stretching, bones cracking, hair sprouting all over their bodies, their roars as fierce as those who had broken through. The wolf cops hurled themselves at the intruders, claws and teeth attacking, ripping, shredding. Blood and fur flying.

Dan's body transformed, his clothes ripping from his huge frame, and he joined the fray.

Nathaniel and his team flew across the room to join the fight.

At the other end of the cell block, the already breached door, holding on by a thread, burst open and six more monsters stormed into the prison. The group was surrounded.

Reece and Ed raced across the block, swung the twin M2 BMG around and fired continuous rounds at the second pack of werewolves. The high-powered shells torpedoed through the air and the creatures raised their heavy paws and swatted the fast-moving missiles like flies.

Sarah took position and fired off the silver arrows in her high-powered crossbow. One creature went down with an agonizing roar, his body convulsing as the pungent smell of singed fur and smoke permeated the air.

The other five kept coming.

Reece continued to fire the M2 in the hope of knocking them out of the battle.

Two agitated wolves stalked toward Sarah. Ed and Adrian spotted them at the same time and made a dash for her. Adrian reached her first, using his powers to whip across the cell block, and shove her out of the way. She slid across the floor backwards. Charlotte raced to Sarah, helped her to her feet and both women threw themselves into the space behind Reece and the huge gun.

Before anyone could react, Adrian and Ed were jumped by the creatures and went down hard. The wolves were on top of them clawing and ripping.

Andre turned and hurtled himself through the air onto the back of one wolf. He sank his fangs into the creature and it staggered backwards. Raising its huge arm, the wolf attempted to swat Andre off its back. The venom injected into it would take effect in a matter of seconds. The beast bucked and roared and toppled backwards snorting its last breath, and Andre jumped free before it hit the ground.

At the other end of the cell block, the wolf cops had eliminated four of the six creatures with the help of Dan and Nathaniel and his team. The remaining two wolves knew they were outnumbered, so they turned tail and fled. With Nathaniel's team and two of the wolf cops on their tail, they wouldn't get away.

The large black vampire stalked across the cell block, grabbed the two werewolves attacking Adrian and Ed by their tails and hurled them across the room. Both crashed into the wall and hit ground, their huge bodies splitting the concrete floor. Andre and Nathaniel flew across the block and latched onto the struggling creatures, sinking their fangs into them. A double dose of venom would finish them off.

Nathaniel pushed himself off the dead creatures, repulsed at having to be in such close proximity. He wiped the blood from his lips and raced over to Adrian and Ed.

Andre pushed between Nathaniel and a cop and fell to his knees beside Reece. He couldn't sense any life force or immortal energy.

Charlotte and Sarah rushed across the cell block. Sarah swiped at a single tear sliding down her cheek. She had to be strong. Always.

Reece pressed his fingers to Ed's throat for a pulse. His fingers slipped in the blood and he pushed harder, praying for even the weakest beat beneath his fingertips. He looked at Andre and shook his head.

Andre's eyes widened. They couldn't fight this hard to lose the ones they loved.

Sarah sucked in a startled breath and turned away, hand to her mouth to stifle a sob.

Charlotte wrapped a comforting arm around her shoulders. What more could she do?

Andre leaned in, using his immortal senses. All of a sudden, he raised his arms; hands clenched and wielded a sharp blow to Ed Borenko's chest.

Reece grabbed his arm. "What the hell are you doing? He's gone."

Andre shrugged out of Reece's grasp and repeated the procedure several times. He was not giving up.

"Let him try, Reece. What have you got to lose?" Dan stepped next to the PI. He'd gone to find a pair of pants from among the spare clothes stacked in the last cell.

A blast of air whooshed from Ed's lips and he inhaled a ragged breath.

Sarah turned with a gasp, dropped to her knees beside him and grabbed his hand. "Ed, can you hear me?" She glanced up at Charlotte. "He's alive!"

"Yes." Charlotte gave her an uncertain smile.

Andre moved to Adrian, he knew it was too late. He closed his eyes and a single blood-stained tear slid from the corner of his left eye. Adrian had taught him everything he knew about survival in a human world. He had rescued him when he hadn't wanted to be saved. He'd become his immortal father. What would he do without him?

Reece placed his hand on Andre's back. "I – I'm so sorry, Andre. I wish there was something I could do."

Andre turned to him, his features contorted with grief, bloody tears sliding down his pale face. "There is. Help me kill the Alpha."

"That's a given."

Sarah stood up. "We need to move Ed somewhere safe."

"We'll put him in one of the cells. At least he'll be more comfortable," Reece told her.

Andre and Reece lifted the older man off the floor, carried him into a cell and laid him on the cot.

Sarah prayed over Adrian. It was the least she could do. He had been an integral part of their team and would be sadly missed.

Once Ed was settled, Reece and Andre returned to the others.

Charlotte huddled against Reece, tears running down her face, and he wrapped an arm around her.

Sarah gave the final blessing and made the sign of the cross over Adrian, and as she did his body disintegrated. She blinked back the urge to cry.

Josh Jamieson appeared from his hiding place. All he wanted to do was go back to his apartment, shower, change, and forget any of this ever happened. But that was impossible.

There would be consequences for what had taken place here tonight.

CHAPTER FIFTY THREE

The orange hue of the morning sun had just appeared behind the buildings as Reece pulled the van into the curb outside his office. It wouldn't be long before the street was in full sunlight. Sarah and Charlotte were in back with Ed. There had been no way to take him to a hospital. Too many questions.

Nathaniel and his team had returned to the night club, with the assurance that if Reece required their assistance they would be there, and the cops had left the facility saying they'd be in touch. They had finished off the entire pack and Reece knew the Alpha would seek retribution for his fallen wolves.

Andre had taken off from the facility, telling Reece he needed some time alone. Reece didn't want him to leave, even though he understood why his friend had to go. He hoped Andre wouldn't be gone too long.

It was around five o'clock and as Reece gazed out of the windshield he noticed there were no pedestrians on the street. Now was the perfect opportunity to get Ed upstairs without being seen. If anyone witnessed the mess he was in it wouldn't be long before a squad car screeched to a halt out front and cops filed into the building to knock down his door and ask a lot of difficult questions he wasn't prepared to answer.

The one thing that worried Reece right now was Ed turning. It was something he didn't want to contemplate. His main priority was to get medical assistance for his ex-boss ... and fast!

He told Sarah and Charlotte to remain in the van while he raced upstairs to unlock the door. When he got to the top of the landing, Dennis Miller was outside the office. This was either a coincidence, or…

"Hi Dennis, what brings you here?"

"I received a voicemail message from Andre saying to meet you here and to bring medical supplies." He stepped aside to reveal a large gray plastic suitcase standing against the wall, the kind you checked in before boarding a flight.

Reece frowned. "And you just did what he asked?"

"Yeah." Dennis nodded. "I trust him."

The PI sighed, walked over and unlocked the office door. "Okay, well you'd better get set up. We'll bring up the patient."

Dennis raised an eyebrow and stared into Reece's eyes. "How bad is it?"

"Bad. I hope you've got something in that magic bag of yours to put him back together."

"Who are we talking about?" He gripped the handle on the suitcase.

"My old boss, Ed Borenko."

Dennis was inside before the PI left the floor.

Reece was back on the street in seconds. Time was of the essence. Daylight was breaking. Soon there would be people on the street heading to their day jobs.

He flung open the back doors of the van. Sarah and Charlotte gasped in surprise. "What took so long?" Sarah asked.

Reece wiped the sweat from his brow on the sleeve of his shirt and gave her an uncertain look. "We've got company."

Sarah's face paled. "The police?"

He shook his head. "Dennis Miller."

Charlotte looked at them both. "Who's Dennis Miller?"

"He's a friend of Andre. A doctor," Sarah told her.

Charlotte stared at Reece. "Does he know?"

"Not that I'm aware of. Andre kept his identity a secret for a long time. I don't think he told Dennis, but I can't be sure of anything right now." He reached in and shuffled Ed forward.

The women stepped out onto the street.

"So why is he here?" Charlotte asked.

"Andre contacted him." Reece climbed into the van. "You two get his legs and ease him forward and I'll get his shoulders."

After struggling with Ed's dead weight, the three managed to get him into the doorway.

The building had an unused freight elevator and Reece wondered if it worked. He was prepared to give it try because he knew the three of them wouldn't be able to carry Ed up the two flights of stairs.

They struggled to get Ed behind the staircase to the elevator door. When they got there, they eased him onto the floor while Reece checked the lift. There wasn't a sign to say it was non-operational, so he slid the gated door open and stepped inside.

Dennis had cleared one of the desks and laid a sterile sheet over it. It would have to do as a makeshift treatment table. He had also set up a desk lamp for better examination of the injuries and a pole for fluids. He dressed in blue scrubs, washed his hands with Ecolab, and snapped on a pair of purple latex gloves ready to start work as soon as they brought Ed in.

He wondered what had happened to cause the kind of injuries Ed had sustained. Andre had been vague about the details. There had always been something about Andre he'd wondered about, something hovering in the background. Maybe now he'd find out.

The elevator key was in the lock and looked as ancient as the building. Reece imagined when he tried to turn it, either it would be stuck solid or it would snap off in the lock. He held his breath as he turned the rusty metal key. To his surprise the dim overhead light flickered and flashed on and he could hear the dull hum of the electrical cables.

Sarah and Charlotte did a little jump for joy, relieved they wouldn't have to struggle to get Ed up the stairs.

After moving Ed inside the cubicle, Reece pressed the button for his floor. With a clatter and a jolt the elevator lifted off the ground and made its sluggish ascent.

Dennis heard the buzz of the cables and rushed around the stairwell. When the elevator stopped, he shoved the metal gate open and helped Reece carry Ed into the office.

"What the hell happened to him?" Dennis asked. He'd never seen injuries like it before.

"Look, I don't have time to explain right now. Just do whatever it takes to keep him alive." Reece gripped Dennis' arm. *"Please."*

Dennis pulled on the surgical mask from around his neck, hooked up a blood bag, pushed the catheter into a vein in Ed's arm and secured it. Once the blood was travelling down the tube, he picked up a pair of sterile scissors and cut away Ed's clothing to evaluate the damage. *Lord have mercy!* He ran his eyes over the decimation.

From where he stood, the man was lucky to be alive at all. And he wasn't sure how long he could keep him that way.

CHAPTER FIFTY FOUR

Andre didn't need time alone. He needed to find the Alpha. His red Ducati Monster skidded to a stop in the alley behind Decadent Desire and he stepped off his bike, removed his helmet and sat it on the seat. He gazed up at the foreboding building, remembering what his twin brother had tried to do to him and the people he cared about. Thank God Jacques was gone, never to return. At least, he hoped not.

He was a shadow during the time between night and morning in his black leather riding gear: A cliché to the vampire race. A flicker of a sorrowful smile tugged at his lips. It amused him in a way, because he was nothing like his so-called race.

Andre pulled the door open and stalked along the dark hallway to the back entrance into the night club. When he reached it, the door opened and Nathaniel greeted him.

"I did not think it would be long before I saw you again." The vampire stepped aside and Andre entered the club.

"I need your help." He stared into the black vampire's eyes with earnest determination.

Nathaniel arched a curious eyebrow. "What kind of help?" he asked, already aware of the answer.

"I want you help me get rid of the Alpha." He paced.

"And how do you propose we do that when we do not know who the Alpha is?" Nathaniel crossed the night club to the bar. Andre followed.

The fury inside Andre shifted to the surface and he spat the words out.

"I don't know. What I do know is we have to *find* and *destroy* him before he can do anymore damage!"

Nathaniel was behind the bar pouring two Vodka shots. He slid one across the counter and downed his in one swallow. He could feel the heat plummeting into the pit of his stomach. The only warmth he felt these days.

Andre eyed the clear fluid in the glass before picking it up and downing it. He coughed and slammed the glass on the counter. "Are you going to help me?"

Nathaniel studied him. He could sense the immense pain inside Andre and understood why he wanted to exact revenge. At what cost? Perhaps his own immortality.

Andre's rage fueled his impatience. "Well are you? Because if you don't I'll find him myself." He turned to leave.

"Wait." Nathaniel was over the bar and beside him. "I did not say I would not help you. It will be very dangerous. You must understand that if you are bitten or scratched, as was your mentor, you *will* die."

Andre's determined eyes met his. "I don't care. I want this monster gone!" He stormed toward the door. "Bring your team and meet me at Adrian's tonight. Reece won't be there and that's the way I want it." He gazed over his shoulder at Nathaniel. "And don't bother following me out it's almost daylight."

He turned on his heel and evaporated into the dark hallway.

₮ℂ

It was after eight and Nathaniel and his team hadn't arrived. Andre paced the entrance hall, lost in thought, wondering where they were. A sharp rap on the door startled him and he whipped the door open. It was Reece.

"What are you doing here?"

Reece frowned. "Thanks for the hello, buddy."

Andre glanced at the floor and sighed. Looking up again he said, "Sorry. I was expecting someone else."

Reece entered the hallway. "Nathaniel?"

"How do you know that?" He closed the door.

The PI folded his arms across his chest. "Because he asked me to come and talk some sense into you."

"I don't need you to talk sense into me. I can handle this."

"Nathaniel thinks it's far too dangerous. He's worried about your welfare, Andre. He doesn't want to see you get yourself killed. And neither do I."

Andre climbed the stairs. Reece followed.

"The Alpha has to be stopped. And I have to stop him."

"Look, I understand how distraught you are about losing Adrian, we all are, but you can't go off half-cocked and expect a good outcome because you're not going to get one. We need a strategic plan. So far we've been blindsided at every turn. Next time we want to be one step ahead of the Alpha."

Andre glared at him. "I'm doing this without you, Reece. It would be easier for you to be infected than me, and I don't want that on my conscience. I don't want to lose any more of the people I care about."

Reece walked across the room and rested a hand on his friend's shoulder. "Let's talk to Nathaniel together and put a plan in motion that will work."

"It would better if you took care of Charlotte and Tommy. She needs you more than ever now that Tommy is part of a pack. Help her deal with that and let me do what I know."

The PI gripped his friend's arm. "Don't tell me what I should be doing. Charlotte's a strong girl, she'll cope once she gets her head around it. What needs to be done to protect her and her son is to get rid of the Alpha, and I *will* be a part of that. Like it or not."

Andre wanted to protect his friend. He couldn't deal with losing him too. He knew once Reece had made up his mind nothing would stop him. "All right. But don't say I didn't warn you."

CHAPTER FIFTY FIVE

Sarah stood beside Ed holding his lifeless hand, tears spilling down her face. She never allowed herself to show signs of weakness, but how could she help it? Ed looked like death and her heart ached.

Dennis had been doing everything he could to keep him alive, and there was no guarantee. It was touch and go with the element of infection spreading rapidly through his system. Both kinds: Lycan and bacterial. He was hooked up to two drips—one containing blood, the other high-dose antibiotics. Would they help? Only time would tell.

He checked Ed's vitals every half hour and when he did, he'd start to ask Sarah a question, but stop himself.

She watched him for a while, contemplating what she should do, and decided to tell him the truth. Regardless of how Reece felt, Dennis needed to know what he was involved in.

"Dennis?"

He moved his gaze from the blood pressure machine to her. "Yes?"

Sarah swallowed the lump lodged in her throat and stared into his eyes, trying to determine if he would stay once he knew the truth. Ed wouldn't survive without him.

"What is it, Sarah?" He walked around the desk to her.

She released Ed's hand and gazed up at Dennis. "You must have questions."

He sighed and removed the surgical mask. "I do. I'm just not sure if…"

"If you'd stay?"

He nodded.

"What do you think happened?"

Dennis gazed at the unconscious man lying on the makeshift hospital bed. "I think … something unnatural. I'm right, aren't I?"

It was Sarah's turn to nod. She explained what happened, omitting some of the details.

Dennis was shocked. He'd imagined something was going on in Andre's life, but not this. He paced for a few minutes, contemplating what to do.

She stopped him and squeezed his arm, her eyes welling with tears. "Will you stay? Please? He won't make it without you."

Charlotte had taken Ed's house keys so she could pick up some fresh clothes for him. As she pulled up outside Reece's office building, Dennis came down the stairs and out the front door.

When Charlotte got out of her car he bypassed her and rushed along the sidewalk. She watched his car pull away from the curb. Where was he going?

Charlotte snatched the bag of clothes from the back seat, closed the door and rushed into the building.

Sarah was outside the elevator when it reached the landing and opened the gate.

"Where's Dennis going?" Charlotte asked, crossing the hall with her and entering the office.

Ed was hooked up to all kinds of devices: Blood, clear fluid, a blood pressure cuff and an ECG machine.

Charlotte dropped the bag on a nearby chair and turned to Sarah. "What happened? Is he coming back?"

Sarah gave a weak smile. "He was called into the hospital and said he'd be back as soon as he can get away. We're to monitor Ed. Check his blood pressure. That's all we can do for now."

Charlotte gave a relieved sigh. "Oh, thank God. For a minute there I thought he'd left."

"I thought he would too after I told him. What else could I do? He had questions and suspicions about Andre."

"You know, I never was suspicious. To me, he seemed like an all-round, nice guy. Who would've known he was a vampire."

"He's still a nice guy, despite the fangs thing." A smile tugged at her lips.

Charlotte smiled too. "You're right. And he's been there for all of us."

"Yes, he has."

Ed moaned. Both women swung around.

Sarah rushed over and took his hand. "Ed, can you hear me? Open your eyes. Can you squeeze my hand? Ed?"

No response.

Charlotte crossed the office and stood by Sarah. "Give it time. Dennis is doing the best he can."

"You're right. Can't expect miracles." She gave Charlotte a surreptitious look. Was her faith slipping?

"You like Ed, don't you?"

Sarah's gaze met hers and she frowned. "Is it that obvious?"

"Only to me." Charlotte shrugged. "And I think it's wonderful." She gave Sarah a hug.

Sarah eased out of her embrace. "Can we please keep it between us? I don't want the guys making it uncomfortable."

"Absolutely. Your secret's safe with me. I won't tell a living soul."

The priest's right eyebrow arched. "Does that mean you can tell a non-living soul?"

Charlotte balked. "Oh, no, I didn't mean…"

"I know. I'm just playing with you." She gave a humorless chuckle. It was hard to be cheerful while Ed was fighting for life and Adrian was gone.

Charlotte crossed her heart. "I won't tell anyone living or not."

Ed moaned again.

The women watched him, wondering if he might wake up soon. Sarah hoped with all the faith she had left that he would.

CHAPTER FIFTY SIX

When Reece and Andre entered Decadent Desire it was too quiet. Neither Nathaniel nor anyone from his team was anywhere downstairs. Reece's hackles immediately went up. He whipped his 9 mm Glock out of its holster and pulled a small pistol from an ankle holster and handed it to Andre. Andre took the weapon, stepped up behind him and scanned the club with his eyes and senses.

"Something's wrong, Reece. I sense Lycan." His eyes darted to the spiral staircase.

Reece nodded and moved across the night club with caution, gun raised.

The pair climbed the circular stairs, their senses on high alert.

Reece wondered how many there were and how he and Andre were going to handle them on their own, especially if the others had been put out of commission. "How many?" he whispered.

Andre picked up Lycan vibration. "Three. In the office with Nathaniel."

Reece frowned over his shoulder. "Where are the others?"

"Good question. Maybe the cellar." There was no time to check.

They reached the landing and scanned downstairs once more before moving along the hallway.

Reece was glad his gun was loaded with silver bullets. These days, he never left home without them.

The office door was ajar when they reached it and before they had time to plan their next move it swung open and Dan appeared in the doorway. "It's about time. You'd better come in."

Reece stepped inside and scanned the room. He didn't sheath his weapon.

Nathaniel was seated beside the desk with a second Lycan male beside him. He didn't look happy.

Reece recognized the woman behind the desk. "I assume you're the Alpha female we've heard so little about."

Her glossy red lips spread into a gratified smile. "You know what they say, 'You should never *assume* anything.'" She stood up, walked around the desk and sat on the front edge. "Yes, I am." She held out her hand.

Reece ignored it. "What do you want?"

She lowered her hand. The smile disappeared. "I want what you want. To be rid of the Alpha. I think we can come to some arrangement, don't you?" She folded her arms and kept her steel gaze on the PI and his partner. "With him out of the picture we both get what we want and the city will be safe again."

Reece's eyes bored into hers. "Will it? You'll still be here."

"I don't recruit. The Lycan in my pack are ancients, not children."

"Dan isn't."

She glanced at the cop sideways. "That's true." She didn't elaborate.

It occurred to Andre she would know who the Alpha was. "Who's the Alpha?"

Her eyes snapped to him. "I can't tell you that. Not yet. We have an … understanding."

"That's bullshit! If you know who it is you can tell us." Andre grabbed her by the throat and squeezed.

Dan and the other wolf hurtled themselves across the office and tackled him to the floor.

Reece stepped up to her. "And this is how you expect us to trust you?"

She rubbed her throat. *"He attacked me!"*

"You're playing games with us and I don't like it." Reece glared at Dan, who still had Andre pinned down. "I warned Charlotte about you. Seems there was good reason."

Dan stood up. "She's trying to help you. Don't you get that?"

Reece pulled the other jerk Lycan off his friend and helped him to his feet. "You'll have to do better than this if you expect to us join forces."

Sonia Edwards stepped between the men, her hands raised. "Enough." She turned her serious gaze on the PI. "All right. We'll try it your way."

Dennis was longer than expected and by the time he arrived back at Reece's office it was 9.23 pm. He'd acquired a number of essential medical supplies he hoped wouldn't be missed, and had loaded them into the trunk of his sedan during a break. He had also moved his car close to the exit so once his shift was finished he'd be on his way.

Pulling into the curb outside the older-style, shop front building, he turned off the engine and sat. *Why did Andre pull me into this nightmare? Am I prepared to see it through?* He gazed into the rear view mirror, stared deep into his eyes, and searched them for a reason to start the engine and drive away. He was caught between a rock and a hard place, whatever that meant. He couldn't let Andre down, but more importantly he couldn't let a man die because of his own insecurities.

Dennis pulled the keys from the ignition and opened the door. He had a job to do. A life hung in the balance. He left the supplies in the trunk and entered the building. He would need some help getting the equipment upstairs later.

He glanced at his watch. 9.29 pm. He'd been away too long and hoped everything had been all right while he was gone. When he reached the office the door swung open and Sarah appeared in the doorway. "What took you so long?"

The doctor swallowed. "I had to fill in for another doctor. I couldn't just pick up and leave, I had to finish the shift." He stepped around the priest, crossed the room and checked Ed's pulse, blood pressure, and fluids on the portable stand. "So far, so good."

Sarah followed him over. "We heard him moan a couple of times."

Dennis took a pen light from his pocket and checked Ed's pupils. They reacted. That was a good sign. He rechecked his pulse. Weak but steady. Also a good sign.

Charlotte entered the office with a bag of Chinese takeout from a little place down the street. "Oh, good, you're back. We were getting worried." She carried the bag of food over to the small kitchen in the corner of the office. "There's enough for all of us."

"Thanks. I've already eaten," Dennis said. "You two go ahead while I keep working."

Sarah walked over to Reece's desk where Charlotte had laid out the plates and sat down. It felt good to sit. She was tired.

Dennis remembered the things in his trunk. "Charlotte, would you mind helping me bring up some more medical supplies from my car?"

"Of course. Just give me a few minutes to finish my food and I'll be right with you."

"No hurry. Take your time. You both deserve a break."

Ed was naked under the sheet, and Dennis noticed the travel bag sitting on the chair. "What's in the bag?"

"Oh, that's some fresh clothes for Ed. Pajamas, underwear and some other clothes for later on." Charlotte wanted to stay optimistic about Ed's recovery.

"Great." Sifting through the clothes, he pulled out PJs and a pair of boxer shorts. He cleaned Ed up and dressed him.

Once Charlotte finished her meal she joined the doctor at Ed's bedside. "He looks a lot better. Thanks for doing that." She touched his arm. "So, let's go bring up those things."

As they came out of the building, Reece pulled into the curb. He and Andre got out of the Mustang and walked up to them. "Where's Sarah?"

Charlotte gave him a curious frown. "Upstairs. Why?"

"Because we have some things to discuss in private."

Dennis walked over to his car and opened the trunk.

Charlotte glanced over Reece's shoulder. "Andre, would you give Dennis a hand with those?"

"Sure."

Dennis realized it was a distraction as Reece wasn't aware he knew.

The two men took the medical supplies upstairs.

Charlotte reached for Reece's arm. "Sarah told him."

He frowned into her eyes. "Why would she do that? The fewer people that know the better, for everyone's sake."

"Because he had questions. He'd always been curious about Andre apparently, so there was no point keeping him in the dark. He's here to help us, Reece. He needed to know." She leaned into him and rested her head on his chest. He put his arms around her. "Besides, we need him on our team."

Reece sighed. "I guess you're right." He took her hand. "Let's go up. I want to tell everyone what we found out tonight."

CHAPTER FIFTY SEVEN

Josh Jamieson left his apartment around 10.00 pm and headed to the parking garage. He climbed into his Mercedes and checked the glove compartment for his pistol. A safety precaution. As he pushed the key into the ignition, someone climbed into the passenger seat beside him.

Josh whipped his head around. "What the hell are you doing here? I told you I'd meet you outside the zoo so no one would see us."

The guy glanced around the empty garage. "Doesn't seem to be anyone here, Jamieson, so what's the problem?"

Josh glowered at him. "The *problem* is people I work with live in this building. I can't afford to be seen with you just in case things take a turn for the worse."

The guy chuckled. "You think things are *going* to take a turn for the worse? Things couldn't get much worse, could they?"

The detective sighed. "It could get a lot worse. You know that. Especially if Ned Bowers has anything to do with it. Keeping track of him has solved nothing."

The guy locked his serious gaze on Josh. "He's been warned off. Whether or not he takes that advice is anyone's guess. You know what an asshole he is."

Josh started the engine and backed out of the parking space. "Yes, I do. I know he's up to something, I just can't figure out what. He's not one to confide in people so we'll need to be extra cautious."

The guy fastened his seatbelt. "Yeah, he's like a dog with a bone."

The white roller door to the parking garage curled upward and Josh drove his car out of the building, heading for Griffith Park.

Night had set in and the drive up to the park was in shadow. When Josh pulled into the empty parking lot outside the LA Zoo he surveyed the area in case there were teens making out. It was a hotspot for that kind of thing.

He turned off the engine and headlights.

The guy unclipped his seatbelt and got out of the car.

It was a balmy night, the air thick. The moon was almost full too, offering just enough light to see by.

Josh opened the glove compartment to retrieve his pistol and tucked it into his belt at his back. He didn't trust anyone and he wasn't taking any chances. He got out of the car.

The guy leaned against the back door and folded his arms. "So why'd you bring me up here? Got a job for me?"

Josh walked around the vehicle and stopped a few feet away. "Yes. Something has to be done about Sonia Edwards. Can you make that happen?"

The guy threw off his hood. Even though the weather was warm he never went anywhere without his jacket. It kept him hidden from the rest of the world. "You know who I work for, right?"

Josh swallowed hard. "Of course I do. What has that got to do with this?"

"Who do you think warned Bowers off?"

Josh paced. "She could ruin everything. Doesn't he understand that?"

"I'm sure he does. I think he's letting her run her course, if you get my drift. We may not need to do a thing if that detective and his crew have anything to do with it." He pushed himself off the car. "They want to rid the city of the Lycan population, and now that Daniels knows who the female Alpha is … well, I'm just saying if things go bad between them he might off her himself."

A devious smile spread across Josh's face at the thought of being rid of that bitch. "I don't understand why he'd want to keep her alive anyway."

"One step at a time. If the detective doesn't do it, she'll be dealt with in due course."

Josh kept a cool façade, even though he was scared inside. "Tell your boss I'll wait to see what happens between the PI and the Alpha female." *Should be interesting.*

CHAPTER FIFTY EIGHT

The following morning, Ned entered the precinct and headed for the elevators, business as usual, at least for now. He pushed the call button and as the door slid open Josh Jamieson appeared out of nowhere, stepped into the elevator beside him and pushed the close button before anyone else got in. He wanted a private discussion with the DA.

"We need to talk," he said tightly, glancing sideways at the shorter man.

Ned stood holding his briefcase in front of his knees with both hands, and gazed at his reflection in the closed doors. "What about, Jamieson?"

"I believe you've become privy to certain facts that could be detrimental to our cause. There are things you have no knowledge of, things that could potentially expose those involved."

A smug smile spread across the DA's face. "Could *you* be one of those people?

Color rose in Josh's cheeks. "You're not listening, Ned. This situation could explode into something far more dangerous."

Ned swung his head around and glowered at the detective. "I'm aware of that. Nonetheless, I won't be threatened by anyone. Do I make myself clear?"

"Who threatened you?"

"I think we both know who, don't we?"

The detective cleared his throat. "He means business, Ned."

"You think I don't know that? I'm on my way out. As soon as I can clear things I'm leaving."

"Leaving? Are you insane? He'll track you down and you'll be dead. He won't leave loose ends, especially if it can be linked back to him and the force."

"I'm done with it. The world can run amok for all I care. I have plans in place. He *won't* find me." Ned chuckled. Something he never did. "And if you have any sense at all, you'll do the same."

For the first time in his life Josh was afraid. He knew every one of them was expendable. He also knew more would follow.

ℰᎧᏟᎡ

Even after a few hours' sleep the information Reece had imparted on them the previous evening still hadn't sunk in. Someone who worked with them was the Alpha. The Alpha?

Charlotte tried to wrap her mind around the frightening thought. It made no sense. How could *he* be the Alpha? She sprang up on the cot stretcher. HE had taken her son!

Reece, Andre and Dennis were at the small kitchen table having a break. When they heard her sit up, they all looked across the room. "Everything all right, Charlotte? Reece asked.

She looked at him, her mind a jumble of sleepiness and unsettled thoughts. It took her a minute to answer. "No. Everything isn't all right. That bastard took my son. How could he do that?" Charlotte swung her legs off the stretcher and stood up.

Reece walked over and pulled her into his arms. "It's all over now. Tommy's safe and we're going to get that sonofabitch. I owe him one for hitting you."

Ed moaned and they all turned to look at him. Dennis jumped off his chair and rushed over to the unconscious man. He checked his pupils, his blood pressure and listened to his heart. He also checked the wounds. They were healing faster than expected.

"Any improvement?" Charlotte asked.

Dennis pulled the stethoscope from his ears. "His heart rate is steadier and his blood pressure is at a more normal level."

Reece frowned. "What does that mean?"

"Hopefully, it means he's on the mend," Dennis smiled.

"How long before he wakes up?" Reece walked around the desk.

"Hard to say." Dennis looked at Reece. "He's improving by the hour, so it could be any time. If the Lycan virus has integrated, and it appears it has, it could be sooner than we think."

"Scary thought," Charlotte said. She turned to Reece. "There isn't a chance he won't change, is there?"

"No. Until the Alpha is dead anyone connected to him will turn on the next full moon, which is only two nights away. At least that's the theory."

Charlotte shivered. "How will Sarah cope with that?"

"How will Sarah cope with what?" Sarah asked as she came through the door.

Charlotte swung around in surprise. "Oh, Sarah, hi. We were just..."

Reece stepped into the conversation. "Dennis thinks the Lycan virus has integrated. You know what that means."

Sarah's expression turned serious. "Yes, I do." She crossed the office and stood beside Dennis, gazing down at the man she had grown so fond of. She turned to the doctor. "Are you sure?"

Dennis rested a comforting hand on her arm. "Yes, I'm sure. He's healing too quickly and his vital signs are improving at the same rate. I'm sorry."

"I understand." Sarah reached for Ed's hand and squeezed it gently. "Hang in there, Ed, we're going to get you and everyone else out of this nightmare." She turned her stern gaze on Reece. "Aren't we?" It was a statement, not a question.

Reece returned the intense stare. "Yes, we are. And this time there'll be no mistakes."

Andre joined them. "In the meantime, don't you think it would be a good idea to move him to a more secure location? Now that the Lycan virus has taken hold there's no telling what could happen when he does wake up. He might change without the influence of the moon."

Reece frowned. "Yeah, you're right." His mind was ticking over. "We could lock him in the cellar at the club. Nathaniel won't be happy about it, but we don't have a choice."

CHAPTER FIFTY NINE

Douglas MacKinnon, Chief of Detectives, sat behind his large desk and scowled at the man standing before him. The whole situation had gotten way out of hand and he was ready to execute a clean sweep. The detective on the other side of the desk was a trained professional, only somehow during the course of all this madness he had overlooked his appointment. It was time to return things to order and this man was one of a chosen few who could facilitate that outcome.

"Do you realize what's at stake here? We are part of an order that serves to protect humans from the otherworld. If anyone was to discover who we are it would destroy everything that has kept this world safe for the past thousand years. You were meant to keep things under control." He stood up and walked around the desk, staring into the eyes of the man in front of him. "What do you have to say for yourself?"

Josh looked his superior in the eye and bowed his head. "I apologize, my Lord, I got caught up in this world. I should have been better prepared. Please allow me to put things right." Josh had seen what this man could do to those who didn't follow the laws of the order—The Order of Night, a secret organization that had been in existence for over a thousand years. MacKinnon was almost as old as the order. He had been a teenaged boy when he became a novice—a warrior in training.

"No one is to lay a finger on Sonia Edwards. Is that understood?"

"It is, my Lord. But…"

"But what?" MacKinnon's intense gaze remained on the detective.

Josh cleared his throat. "We will never find the Alpha male if she keeps interfering. And it is essential we find him so that the teenagers can be released from the lupine curse."

His superior sighed. "Yes, I understand that. I believe Reece Daniels will assist us with that task. He is hell-bent on locating the Alpha and destroying him because his friend has been attacked and will surely turn on the next full moon, if not before."

"Do we want to wait that long?"

"The teens are contained, so there is no concern about them running amok. I think we can afford a little time for the PI to implement whatever plan he has formulated."

"I'll go to his office and see what he's come up with. Perhaps I can offer…"

"No. You were meant to know nothing about any of this. If you start offering advice they may become suspicious. Leave it to him. Stay close, and if necessary work behind the scenes. *Do not* give him reason to suspect you."

"He already detests me. I think any reason would be enough for him."

MacKinnon walked back to his chair and sat down. "Then make damn sure he doesn't find one."

The detective bowed his head. He knew the audience with his superior was over.

As Josh closed the door and walked along the corridor to the elevators he felt every nerve ending in his body quiver. MacKinnon was a formidable individual and not only the Doyenne of the order, but also a half breed vampire. Dangerous? Definitely!

Would Ned take heed of MacKinnon's warning? He would, if he knew what was good for him. Josh wondered what was going on in Ned's mind. He should know by now that MacKinnon was no one to mess with. The DA needed to shelve his ego and do as he was told.

Josh pressed the ground floor call button and stepped back. He wondered how much longer he could keep his identity secret. Reece Daniels was no fool, he had come to realize, and the detective wasn't sure how long it would be before the PI started putting the pieces together.

When the elevator doors slid open he came face to face with his nemesis.

Ned stepped into the corridor. "You've been to see MacKinnon?"

Josh nodded.

Ned's Adam's apple bobbed up and down above his collar and tie. "Do you have any idea what this is about?"

Josh shook his head and stepped into the elevator. "Good luck. You'll need it."

The elevator doors slid shut and Ned glanced at the Chief's office door at the end of the hallway. Taking a deep breath, he headed along the hall feeling like a dead man walking. At least they hadn't uncovered his secret. Yet. And he would be long gone before they discovered the truth.

When he reached the door he stopped. His palms were sweaty and his mouth dry. He hated coming here. It was humiliating. He knew if he'd ignored the request someone would have come to collect him, and not in a good way. He would have been taken somewhere out-of-the-way. Here was better.

He opened the door and stepped into the outer office. A young blonde behind the reception desk smiled and greeted him, telling him to take a seat. How long would he have to wait? Was this some kind of tactic in an attempt to unnerve him? If so, it worked.

CHAPTER SIXTY

Andre entered the night club through the front door. Staff were preparing for tonight's gig. He passed the dance floor and headed to the spiral staircase. When he reached the top, Nathaniel was on the landing. The club was a safe haven for nightwalkers, as there were no windows. Nathaniel rarely slept anymore.

"To what do I owe the pleasure?" he asked.

"We need to work out some details about finding the Alpha, and I suggested we bring Ed here and put him in the cellar." He gave Nathaniel a sheepish look.

"What?! You expect me to house a dog on my premises?"

"He's a *friend*, not a dog. He would help you if you needed it. We need somewhere safe to keep him contained."

Nathaniel was not pleased. "All right. Only because he is a friend."

"Thanks." Andre smiled. "Now, can we discuss our plans?"

Nathaniel turned on his heal and stalked along the hall toward the office. "Of course. Is there anything else you want from me while you are here?"

Andre followed him. "Just to let you know that Dennis Miller will be accompanying Ed. He's under Doctor Miller's care."

Nathaniel turned around. "Am I to take it he knows? Everything?"

The pair continued into the office and Nathaniel closed the door.

"You would be correct. He already had his suspicions about me. I don't understand how. I was always careful not to give anything away about myself. He wasn't sure what his suspicions were, but he knew there was something different about me. Sarah told him the rest."

The black vampire growled. "The priest should know her place and not be involved in all of this. It is … sacrilegious."

Andre sat in one of two chairs in front of the desk, while Nathaniel returned to his seat. "Why do you say that?"

Nathaniel frowned. "There are things about her. Things she has not made known to you."

Andre sat forward. "What things?"

Nathaniel's intense gaze locked onto Andre. "It is not for me to disclose. Ask her."

"I'm asking you."

"I am sorry, I cannot tell you. It needs to come from her." He clasped his hands in front of him on the desk. "She has a reason for her hatred of vampires. That is all I am saying."

Andre sat on the edge of his chair. "Is she a threat?"

"I do not think so. She genuinely wants to help you."

Andre sat eyeing Nathaniel intensely. He wanted to know more. He wanted to know what secret Sarah was keeping from them. Was it something that would put the group in jeopardy? He knew it would be pointless pushing Nathaniel further. His integrity wouldn't allow him to divulge something that was not his to share.

He thought it strange that Nathaniel had been with his brother Jacques. They were two very different immortals. His brother wouldn't have hesitated in handing over information if it benefited him, and he also wouldn't have hesitated in killing without a reason.

Andre's thoughts returned to the present. "So what are we going to do about the Alpha? Reece wants to talk to you, once Ed is settled in the cellar. We need to get things moving."

"Very well. I will organize for the team to be here. I have an idea that may work. I want to *run it by all of you*. Is that the phrase?"

Andre stood up. "Yes. You're learning modern English. Cool. I'll head back and let them know we can move Ed. Thanks Nathaniel."

"It is all good." Nathaniel sat at his desk and gazed out of the tinted glass wall at staff downstairs preparing for the evening. His mind troubled him. Should he have told Andre about Sarah? Should he have told him about Dracula?

ಐಂಿ

Andre could hear the alarm going off the minute he walked through the front entrance of the building. He flew up the stairs and threw open the office door.

Dennis was administering CPR to Ed, while Reece performed mouth to mouth. Sarah and Charlotte were standing near the door and gave him an anxious look as he rushed across the room.

When Andre reached the desk, Dennis looked as though all hope was lost. "He went into cardiac arrest. We've been working on him for fifteen minutes. He's flatlined."

Andre pushed Dennis aside, clenched his fist, and issued a heavy blow to Ed's chest. The monitor continued to flatline. He balled his hands together and tried again. This time he heard a crack and knew he'd broken one of Ed's ribs. The monitor's line beeped a couple of times and went flat. He tried again. Nothing.

He looked at Reece and Sarah, his expression dazed. "He – he's gone. I'm sorry."

Sarah rushed over to Ed, threw herself across him and wept. "You can't be gone. You can't be." With tears tumbling down her face she stared at Dennis. "Do something! Anything!" she screamed.

ಐಂಿ

The group arrived at Decadent Desire late afternoon and Reece parked the van in the alley near the rear exit. With everything that had happened that afternoon, Reece had considered not coming, but knew it was imperative to make plans to eliminate the Alpha once and for all. Too many lives were at stake.

Reece and Dennis unloaded Ed's stretcher from the back of the van, carried it through the back entrance and into the night club. When they'd finally conceded that Ed was dead, somehow his heart had started beating again. The Lycan virus had to be the reason he was alive, there was no other explanation.

Staff would return in a few hours to finish setting up for the night's events. Until then, it was the perfect time to get Ed down to the cellar and set up the medical equipment without being seen.

Sarah followed the pair down the stairs, holding the fluid bag attached to Ed's arm. She wanted to be near him.

Charlotte was close behind, carrying sterile linen and a cold bag containing more fluids.

Andre remembered being confined in the cellar and sleeping on the tiny cot when his brother, Jacques, had held him prisoner a few years ago. The feeling settled on him like a heavy weight.

Dennis and Reece eased Ed onto the cot stretcher and Sarah hooked the fluid bag on a nail protruding from the wall. It would suffice until they could get the portable stand from the van.

Once Dennis had Ed hooked up to the heart monitor, and had completed a thorough check of his vitals, Reece asked the rest of the group to follow him upstairs.

Nathaniel and two members of his team were in the office. The black vampire had seen them carry their injured friend through the club and awaited their arrival.

Reece came through the open door, followed by Andre, Sarah and Charlotte.

Nathaniel stood behind his desk and gestured for them to take the seats in front of it. Reece declined. He was antsy and wanted to stand.

"We have been devising a plan that will draw the Alpha out and leave him vulnerable. Once he is where we want him, he can be dealt with," Nathaniel told them.

Reece folded his arms across his chest. "So what's the plan?"

Nathaniel came around the desk and stood opposite the PI. "I believe he has a weakness for ... how shall I put it politely? Ladies of the evening. One of my team, who will be planted in the whorehouse, will *persuade* him to accompany her to a private location for a better time. We have a property in the country that would suit this purpose, and once she subdues him we can go in and put the dog down."

Reece's expression was skeptical. "And you think he'll go for it? Surely he would know she's a vampire. Doesn't both your kind have built in radars for that kind of thing?"

A knowing smile spread across Nathaniel's face. "A half breed gives off human scent. He would not even consider that she was anything more than a pleasant distraction."

Reece gazed at Andre, expecting him to confirm or deny what Nathaniel had told him, the way Adrian would have. Andre didn't respond. He didn't know the answer.

"Andre, do you know if that's true?"

He turned his head and glanced over his shoulder. "Just because I'm a vampire doesn't mean I know everything about our kind. Nathaniel knows what he's talking about, you can trust him."

Reece sighed. "Who's going in undercover?"

Nathaniel directed Reece's gaze to one of his team. She walked over to the pair. "This is Arianne. She is 550 years old with the strength and abilities of her age, among other assets. She will seduce the Alpha, transport him to the location and keep him there until we arrive. By the time he is suspicious it will be too late."

Sarah stood up. "Arianne? Are you ok with this? What if something goes wrong and he attacks you? You'll die."

Arianne's gaze moved to Nathaniel. He gave her a single nod.

"As Nathaniel has said, I have incredible strength and other abilities. I will be fine. This is something that has to be done otherwise we will have the city overrun with dogs. I'm not being forced to do this, Sarah. I volunteered."

Sarah was uneasy about sending a lone woman to do men's work. It didn't matter how strong she was or what abilities she had, things could go wrong if the Alpha suspected her. He wouldn't hesitate in killing her as a warning.

Nathaniel turned his intense gaze on Sarah. "We will not be far behind them. She will have a tracking device, and I'll have other team members on standby. The dog won't have a chance to do anything to her. I give you my word."

Sarah met his dark gaze with one of her own. "Talk is cheap, Nathaniel, and I've seen this kind of situation turn on a dime and people have died. There has to be another way."

Andre turned to Sarah. "Let's remember why we're doing this, okay? Arianne seems qualified to handle the situation, so let her do what she knows."

Sarah sat down, gazed up at Nathaniel and sighed. "Ok, it's your call. Just remember I did try to warn you."

After the meeting, Sarah rushed downstairs to the cellar. She wanted to see how Ed was doing. Reece and Andre were going to pick up some much needed ammunition and Charlotte had already gone to the precinct to see if there had been any developments on the case. She had to make an appearance some time otherwise people would ask questions.

As Sarah walked along the short corridor to the cellar she had a strange feeling. Something was wrong. She backed up the corridor, climbed the stairs and burst through the door into the night club.

Reece and Andre were on their way out when they heard her. Both men rushed over to her. "What is it, Sarah? What's wrong?" Reece asked.

She was out of breath. "Something's ... wrong down there. I can feel it."

Andre glanced at the door behind her. "What do you mean?"

Sarah shook her head. "I'm not sure."

"Did you see anything?" Reece placed both hands on her shoulders to steady her nerves.

"No. I didn't go all the way to the door. I got the feeling before I reached it." She frowned up at him. "So I suppose you're going to say I'm imagining it. Right?"

Reece frowned back. "I think we should take a look before we start sounding alarm bells. Don't you?"

She nodded. "I guess you're right."

Reece turned to Andre. "Do you have a weapon?"

Andre pulled the pistol Reece had given him from the back of his belt. "These days, always."

"Good." He pulled his Glock. "Sarah, you wait here."

Sarah glowered at him. "No way! I'm coming down there with you. Don't argue with me. Let me get my crossbow." She marched across the club and out the exit. Within minutes she was back, locked and loaded and ready to face whatever was down there.

"Let's go down quietly." Reece led the way.

Sarah moved behind him and Andre followed her down the stairs, gun ready.

When they were almost to the cellar door Reece stopped them and took the last few steps alone. He jumped into the doorway, Glock raised, then disappeared into the cellar. After a few tense seconds he was back. "They're gone!"

Sarah rushed to the doorway and peered into the dark room. "Where could they go? We would have seen them from Nathaniel's office."

"Not if they went that way." Andre pointed along the corridor at the new door.

Reece and Sarah followed his direction. "When did that go in?" Reece asked, knowing he wasn't going to get an answer.

Sarah's face turned ashen. "Why would Dennis take Ed?"

Reece turned to her and placed a hand on her arm. "What if it wasn't Dennis who took Ed? What if it was the other way around?"

"Ed was unconscious. He couldn't..."

Andre came back from taking a look outside the new door. "He was healing fast, Sarah. He could've woken up and in his confused state of mind thought Dennis was trying to hurt him."

She shook her head. "I don't believe that."

Reece sighed. "Well believe it or not, they're gone." He pulled his cell phone from the back pocket of his jeans and keyed in a number. "Hi, it's me. Do you know anyone on the force that you can trust one hundred percent?" He walked down the corridor toward the newly erected door. "Because Ed and Dennis are missing. Charlotte, Charlotte, hold on a minute." He turned and headed back to the others. "I don't know. We need someone to patrol and see what they can find. Is there someone who can do that, no questions asked?" He stalked along the corridor, heading for the stairs. Andre and Sarah followed. "Ok. Just make sure he's not in Ned's or anyone else's pocket first. All right, I'll keep you posted and you do the same." He rang off.

Nathaniel was at the bar doing a stock take when they came through the door. "I heard. Would Ed go back to the facility perhaps?"

Sarah stepped around Reece and Andre. "What makes you think this is Ed's doing?"

Nathaniel glared at her with an eyebrow raised. "Because dogs can never be trusted."

She flung her crossbow onto a nearby table and stalked across the room. "Ed is *not* a dog. He's a human being. I don't believe he did this." She turned her serious gaze on Andre. "What do you really know about Dennis? Perhaps he knew more than he was telling. He did say he was suspicious of you."

Apart from working together and only knowing what Dennis had told him, Andre couldn't say for sure that he didn't have something to do with it. Although, knowing him for as long as he had, Andre didn't think so.

Reece stalked over to the bar. "Hit me with a shot of Bourbon." He needed a drink. The whole situation had all gone pear-shaped and he wasn't sure where to go from here.

Nathaniel slid a glass across the bar and Reece swallowed it in one mouthful.

"The way I see it, we can either let Charlotte follow up on Ed and Dennis while we go after the Alpha, or we can go looking for them and give the Alpha opportunity to get away." He smacked his hand on the counter top. "Nathaniel. Again."

Sarah glared at him. "This is no time to be drinking. You need to be clear-headed."

Reece downed the alcohol. "It takes more than a couple shots to get me drunk. I'm fine."

Andre crossed the night club. "What if someone else came in through the new door down there and took them both?" That would mean the Alpha knew where they were.

CHAPTER SIXTY ONE

Ned was in his office. He needed to have everything in order so when the time came to get out there would be no way for MacKinnon to locate him. He did have one more item to take care of first. Once that was done he would disappear.

It was time to move on. He'd grown tired of LA and its degenerates. There were too many variables now. Before long, someone would figure out what he'd been doing all this time; gathering intel against the Chief of Detectives.

He pulled Charlotte's file from his briefcase and placed it under some paperwork in his out tray. His administration assistant would return it without giving it a second thought. Ned smiled. By the time anyone figured out he was gone it would be too late.

Checking his watch, he realized it was later than he'd anticipated. He needed to head to his usual haunt for some much needed TLC. One last night of heated, unconstrained sex with someone he'd never have to see again was on his to do list. The Madame knew his distinct tastes, and she never offered him the same artiste twice.

His body tingled at the prospect and he hurried to pack his briefcase, then strutted across his office and out the door. He needed a pleasurable distraction, even if it was only for an hour. As he marched along the corridor, heading to the elevator, he heard the familiar ding as the doors opened and Josh Jamieson stepped out into the lobby. He stood, motionless, watching Ned coming toward him.

Ned's pace slowed. Why was Jamieson here at this hour? What did he want?

As the DA got closer, he noticed something in the detective's eyes. A gold shimmer slithered across Josh's pupils and he smirked in a way that Ned knew meant danger. There was something incongruous about his behavior. It was as if he wasn't in control of his own faculties.

Ned stopped. His instincts were screaming to run in the opposite direction. The hair on the back of his neck stood static and his breathing quickened. Something was wrong.

He swallowed hard, contemplating what he should do. His legs started to quiver and he locked his knees to prevent him from shaking. His eyes remained on Josh. Why wasn't he moving or speaking?

Josh's demented smile widened, the look in his eyes indecipherable. What was wrong with him?

Ned dropped his brief case and bolted along the corridor toward the emergency exit. He glanced over his shoulder expecting to see Josh in hot pursuit. He was gone.

The DA stopped and stared along the corridor. Where was Josh?

Before Ned could react, the emergency exit door burst from its hinges and Josh flew at him with a large sword in his hand.

Ned woke up screaming and sprang off the bed. He scanned the room with anxious eyes. No one was there, only the shadows of night. His ragged breathing and trembling body were unlike him. He dropped onto his disheveled bed, taking in a deep, steady breath. It had been a dream … just a bad dream.

Why had he dreamed about Josh Jamieson? And why would the detective want to kill him?

He gathered his composure, stood up, walked to the window and gazed up at the moon. A waxing gibbous. LA reacted during a full moon, and it was less than twenty four hours away.

Ned pulled a deep breath into his lungs and blew it out. His dream had rattled him. He glanced at the bedside clock. Almost midnight. He knew exactly where he could go to soothe his jangled nerves. He'd be well taken care of. No need to call, he had a personal invitation allowing him access at any time of the day or night.

He pulled clothes from his closet. Not his usual business attire, a pair of black sweat pants and matching hoodie. He had to remain unidentifiable in case anything went wrong. On occasion, he was known to get a bit carried away. There had been an incident once where he'd unintentionally broken a girl's neck. Unfortunate, he knew, although nothing could be done about it. So she simply vanished.

Ned threw on his outfit, stepped into his joggers and headed out the bedroom door. It wouldn't take him long to get there. And after the dream he'd just had he needed to relax.

He moved through the dark rooms of his house to the garage, opened the door and stepped inside. He had a second vehicle used for this purpose. No one could connect it to him, no matter how hard they tried.

℘ℂ℞

She was a beauty. He'd never seen anyone as exquisite before. His insides quivered with anticipation of how the evening would pan out; her naked on top of him, her sexy body soaked in sweat and her begging for more.

He got out of the car, hit the remote locking device and strolled casually along the street. He passed her, wanting a closer look. Yes, she was the one. His body was already reacting to her and he could feel his erection pushing against his pants, needing release. She would be expensive. He knew that even before he turned around and walked back along the neon-lit sidewalk, but she'd be worth every penny. Long legs and a body to die for. The short black mini and purple, sequined spaghetti strap top she wore didn't leave much to the imagination, too much skin for his taste. He enjoyed peeling away the layers to reach the treasure beneath, but tonight he didn't care. He wanted *her*.

She recognized him right away. She had seen him before. He had been to Decadent Desire on more than one occasion looking for a good time.

Arianne sensed his reaction to her as he passed by and felt a sense of satisfaction. She turned, hand on hip, and flashed him her sexiest smile. The plan worked. He was a fish on a hook about to be reeled in. Not so smart for an Alpha.

When he got closer, she pushed herself off the wall and sauntered over to him using her best seductive moves. He reached out and pulled her to him, breathing in the exotic perfume she wore. There was a hint of something mingled with it, something he didn't recognize, but he let it go. He needed her and only her.

"Can we go inside?" he asked, easing her away from him and staring into her beautiful dark eyes.

She glanced back at the entrance to the Madame's establishment knowing she didn't belong there. She smiled wickedly. "I know a place we can go where we won't be disturbed." She wound a lock of his dark wavy hair around her finger. "Wanna take a drive out of the city?"

Should he be concerned? He let the thought go. She was a hooker, nothing more, and she was trained in how to get a man's attention.

"Why not?" Being alone with her would afford him certain liberties. Taking her by the hand, he led her back to his car.

She played up her role. "Wow! Some set of wheels."

"Yes." He pressed the remote and opened the passenger door for her as though she were a lady. "After you." He gestured for her to get in.

"Thanks."

He moved round the front of the car and climbed in beside her. "Give me the address and I'll key it into the nav."

She gave him the address, sat back and fastened her seatbelt. As they headed out of the city, she gazed out the passenger window and smiled. He thought he was about to have a night of hot sex. He had no idea what was coming.

CHAPTER SIXTY TWO

Charlotte was called into MacKinnon's office. She didn't realize he would still be in the building. It was late. When she approached the door she stopped and took a deep breath. The Chief of Detectives wanted to see her. Why? Had she over-stepped her bounds somewhere during the investigation? Hell, yes. With everything that had happened in the city of late what else could she do? Had Josh caused this meeting? She suspected he had.

She buttoned her jacket, shrugged off the anxiety, opened the door and stepped into reception. The young woman behind the desk asked Charlotte to take a seat while she let MacKinnon know she'd arrived.

The receptionist returned and ushered her into MacKinnon's office, closing the door behind her. Charlotte glanced over her shoulder at the back of the door and swallowed hard.

"Please, have a seat, Detective Delaney," MacKinnon offered, gesturing to the chairs in front of his large desk.

Charlotte crossed the room and sat in the right-hand chair. "Thank you."

MacKinnon watched her for a moment, allowing her nerves time to reanimate. He could sense her apprehension.

She glanced past MacKinnon and noticed numerous awards and photographs with famous people displayed on the shelves behind him. Impressive.

He leaned back in his comfortable office chair and steepled his fingers.

"How are you, Charlotte? I know you've been through quite an ordeal of late."

Charlotte cleared her throat as quietly as she could. "I – I'm fine, sir." It was obvious he had something on his mind, and she wondered why he wanted to delay it with small talk. "Is there a reason you asked me here?"

A smile spread across his face. "You'd like me to get to the point, I take it." He leaned forward and rested his elbows on the desk. "Very well…"

Reece burst into the office, flustered receptionist in tow. "I'm sorry, sir, he … he just barged straight in."

MacKinnon stood up. "What is the meaning of this, Daniels?"

Reece stalked across the room and stood behind Charlotte's chair. "I think it's time we had a little chat about your extracurricular activities, don't you?"

MacKinnon's gaze fell on the receptionist. "That will be all, Felicia. You can head on home now. Please close the door on your way out."

Charlotte looked up at Reece with a questioning frown. He rested a hand on her shoulder. "I received some information. You're the reason why our investigation has stalled."

"What are you talking about?" Charlotte asked.

His serious gaze remained on MacKinnon. "I believe this man knows what's going on."

"Yes, and preventing it." MacKinnon moved around the desk.

Reece raised a warning hand. "Stay where you are. Kids have been snatched off the streets in broad daylight without any witnesses and turned into monsters. And you knew."

"Tell me, have there been any recent abductions?"

Charlotte answered his question. "No, there hasn't."

MacKinnon gestured for Reece to take a seat. After several seconds of resistance, he sat down.

"Thank you." MacKinnon returned to his chair. "What I'm about to tell you *must* remain confidential. Understood?"

Both detectives nodded.

MacKinnon scrutinized the pair, wondering if he should reveal the truth about himself. It appeared Reece had been provided with certain incriminating information. Not the truth. He needed the assistance of these two detectives if the eradication process was to be successful, especially the dispatch of the Alpha.

Where to begin, and how much should he tell them?

"What's the deal? Where do you fit it?" Reece was agitated. He expected MacKinnon to deliberately mislead them to protect himself.

"Have you ever heard of The Order of Night?"

Both detectives said no at the same time.

"It's an ancient order initiated in 1512 by Pope Julius II, known as 'The Warrior Pope'. He believed it was crucial that such an order exist to deal with the otherworldly creatures inhabiting our world, significantly Lycanthropes."

Reece and Charlotte glanced sideways at each other.

"Men were trained in the ways of hunting, battling and destroying these creatures. They were ordinary men, not knights, who risked their lives for the good of their fellowman. Later, however, some became more powerful. In a supernatural sense. It was necessary, for fighting these creatures got more humans killed rather than eliminate the Lycan population. So, by order of the church, some of them became half breeds. A special force."

Charlotte's chest tightened. "What ... kind of half breed?"

MacKinnon glanced at her. "Half human, half vampire. And a few Lycan."

"Are you one of them?" Reece folded his arms across his chest.

"That's for me to know. I'm giving you the facts. Nothing more."

Charlotte moved forward in her chair. "Why would you tell us if there wasn't more to it?"

MacKinnon smiled. "Ah, clever girl. You're right, of course, there is more to it. I'm just not certain I can trust you with that kind of information."

Reece jumped out of his chair. "This is bullshit! If you've known all this time, you need to tell us how to end it. Don't give us half the story and expect us to do your dirty work."

Charlotte reached out and touched his arm. "Reece, please."

He shrugged her off. "No. If he knows how to stop the Alpha he needs to tell us *now*."

MacKinnon sighed. "I have others out there. I don't need you to do my *dirty work*."

"Then why tell us at all?" Reece paced. "Unless..."

"Unless what?" Charlotte frowned at him.

"We know there are Lycan in public service sectors, what if there are others from the order too? Conflict of interest, wouldn't you say? How can they be eradicated when they're serving society?"

"There are certain exceptions. We have our orders and they are to deal only with the renegade pack."

Charlotte remembered Arianne was a half breed and 550 years old. "Why did you situate one of your warriors in Nathaniel's team?"

Reece looked at her. "What do mean?"

"Arianne."

The PI turned his intense gaze onto the Chief of Detectives. "Is she one of yours?"

∞ℭℜ

Ed Borenko came to and scanned his surroundings through blurred vision. Everything looked like it was under water. He balled his fists and rubbed at his eyes trying to clear his out-of-focus vision. *Where the hell am I?* Ed attempted to move. His body ached all over and felt like it had been pummeled by something huge. He dropped back against the wall, realizing he was on the floor.

As his vision cleared, he recognized the prison infirmary. *How did I get here? And where's Reece and the others?* Something moved in the shadows not far from him and his body went rigid. He squinted into the darkness. "Who's there?" His voice echoed off the concrete walls. "I know someone's there. Show yourself!"

A familiar voice came out of the dark. "It's me, Ed. Doctor Miller. Do you remember what happened?"

Ed's brow wrinkled and he strained his brain to remember. "Dennis? Why don't you come over here and help me up?"

"I can't. You handcuffed me to the metal buffer on the wall."

"Why'd I do that?" Ed rubbed his sweaty forehead. "Why're you here?"

"You were critically injured during the fight in the cell block. Andre asked me to help you. Ed, you were attacked by a … a werewolf and you died. Andre brought you back. We took you to the night club to lock you in the cellar. There'll be a full moon tomorrow night. When you woke up you weren't yourself. You knocked me out and brought me here."

The chief's head spun. Everything ran past his brain like film winding back through a projector, only nothing would stick. He talked to himself.

"So I was bitten. Shit! How could this happen? I'll turn into one of those Goddamn creatures." NO! He scrambled to his feet, his weighty body almost toppling over. "Where are you, Dennis? Talk to me so I can find you." He walked in the direction of the doctor's voice, foraging through his pockets for the handcuff key. He must have it somewhere. Found it.

Ed felt around until his hand found Dennis's shoulder. "Lift up your hands so I can find the lock." He unlocked the cuffs and helped the doctor to his feet. "Sorry about that. I don't remember doing any of it. What's going on with me?"

"I think it's the Lycan virus. You've had a few lapses of memory since you brought us here."

"I have?" He shook his head. "I can't..."

"Don't worry about it, Ed. Let's just get out of here." He took the detective by the arm and led him to the open door.

৪৩৫৫

Charlotte and Reece sat in the diner staring at their mugs of cold coffee. Neither one could bring themselves to believe that the force was infested with Lycanthropes and half breed vampires. How could this happen? Charlotte gazed out of the window at the cream hue of the almost full moon above the rooftops of stores and cafés along Sunset Boulevard. It gave the street an eerie feel despite the traffic and people. How could she have been so ignorant for so long?

Reece reached across the table and took her hand. "Some night, huh?"

Charlotte swiped at the tears about to spill down her face and tried to smile. "You could say that."

Wanting to comfort her, Reece moved around the table and squeezed into the bench seat beside her. He slid an arm around her shoulders, pulled her to him and kissed her forehead. "We're going to get through this, you know."

She could hear his heartbeat, it was soothing. "I wish I could believe that. What about Tommy and Dan? They're going to be what they are forever. Maybe Ed too. We don't know how the Alpha was turned. What if he wasn't bitten? What if he was cursed?"

Reece lifted her chin up so he could look into her eyes. "Hey, don't do that. We'll find a way to help them." She gave him a skeptical frown. "I give you my word. We might not be able to cure them, but we can at least set up a safe house for them."

Charlotte reached up and touched his face. "That's why I love you so much. Because you care."

"Tommy's a great kid. I'd do just about anything for him."

"You'd make a great dad, you know. Sometimes I wonder if I'm a good mom. I spend so much time away from him."

Reece pulled her to him and stroked her hair. "You're a great mom and don't you forget it. This will all be over soon and you and Tommy can get on with your lives."

Charlotte eased herself out of his embrace and frowned into his eyes. "Will it ever be over, Reece? If it's not werewolves or vampires, what next? You said there's more out there than we can possibly imagine, so when will it ever be over?"

"Sweetheart, you can't think like that. It will consume you if you do. I've learned to live each day as it comes and battle the demons, even my own, when they appear. That's all we can do. We can't live in fear."

Charlotte gave a wry smile. "You're right. It's just..."

He rubbed her arm. "I know. It's difficult to get your head around, knowing that there's things out there cohabiting with us. Sometimes it ... look, we can only do what we can to keep people safe. That's why I left the force. Once I knew the truth I had to do something."

"What were you going to say? Why did you stop?"

Reece looked at her and smiled. "It's nothing. Don't worry about it. Just know that I'll never let anything happen to you or Tommy ever again. Okay?" He raised her face up to his and kissed her gently on the lips. What he didn't tell her was that sometimes it scared the hell out of him too. His cell phone vibrated and he pulled it from his shirt pocket. "What is it, Nathaniel? Ok, we're on our way." He pressed the button and turned to Charlotte. "The Alpha's with Arianne and they're on their way to the cabin. We have to go."

CHAPTER SIXTY THREE

The headlights of the dark sedan shone across the black, wrought iron gates, their spear-like staves lit up by the double, overlapping circles of light. On the other side, a long driveway led to the property the young woman had talked about on the drive up. Mindless chit chat. He'd listened, what else could he do?

She handed him a key to open the padlock. He wanted to tell her to get out and do it herself, but decided against it. He didn't want to get her riled up, not yet. Keep her cool and calm until he wanted her to be anything more. And he did want her to be more. He wanted her to be a dirty slut in the bedroom. Although she may be an exceptional beauty, have an exquisite body and be trained in the art of pleasuring a man, she was still just a whore. And he'd paid a significant amount for her services.

He opened the door and slid out of the upholstered leather seat, leaving the door open. After unlocking the gates and pushing them back, he returned to the vehicle. He had pocketed the key and she didn't remind him to give it back. It seemed a lengthy drive to the cabin and he began to wonder how far into the forest it was. He was about to ask her when the property came into view.

Excellent. At least now we can get this party started. He was eager to get her into bed. He pulled his sedan up to the front entrance and stopped.

Arianne glanced over at him. "So, what do you think? Elegant enough for you?"

It was indeed quite a remarkable home out in the middle of nowhere.

Cabin? More than just any old cabin. Two story, paneled windows, red timber with a large, welcoming front porch. At least he wouldn't be having sex in some dilapidated hay barn. "It will do."

He got out of the car and came around to open the door for her. She offered him her hand and he helped her out of her seat. She led him to the oversized wood and glass front door and took a plastic swipe key out of her purse. The door popped open with an electronic click and Arianne gestured for him to go in ahead of her.

Something primal stirred in his groin as he stepped over the threshold and into the living room. It wouldn't be long now and he'd have her in bed. He couldn't wait. She entered the room and closed the door, dropping her purse onto a chest of drawers beside it. "Would you like something to drink?" she asked, walking toward the kitchen.

He grabbed her wrist and swung her around. "No. Thanks. I want to get started."

She smiled and wriggled her wrist out of his hot, sweaty grasp. "What's the hurry? We've got all night. That's what you paid for."

He glanced up the stairs. "I don't need to make small talk or get in the mood. I'm in the mood, so can we get on with it?"

"I'd like a drink first." She headed to the kitchen.

His wolf stirred inside him and he growled deep in his throat. She was pissing him off. He wanted her and he would have her *now*. He stalked across the living room to the kitchen doorway. She wasn't there. *What is this, hide and seek? Could be fun, especially when I catch her.*

"Hello?" he called. She hadn't told him her name and he hadn't asked. "Where'd you go?" He walked into the kitchen and gazed around the room. There were two more doors leading to other areas of the cabin. He crossed the kitchen and opened the first door. It led to a back patio.

He stepped backwards out of the doorway and closed the door. He tried the second one. It was a study that led back to the living room through another internal door. He walked through it. *Where could she have gone?* His internal animal rage overtook him and he flew up the stairs, banging open every door on the second floor. "Where are you, bitch? I didn't pay $3000.00 so you could scam me."

No one was on the second floor, which meant she had to have used the back patio door to get outside. He raced down the stairs three at a time, ran through the study and out to the patio. He stood, using his canine hearing.

There. He heard a twig snap in the distance. He followed the sound.

He could hear the whore's heartbeat. It wasn't accelerated. In fact, it was slow. Maybe 45 beats per minute by his calculation. She wasn't afraid, so why had she run? He had her scent now and knew he was on the right trail. He continued through the dark forest. She wasn't far ahead of him. He would catch up to her any second and she would learn not to fuck with him.

There was a clearing up ahead and the waxing moon gave off enough light to see her shadowed silhouette disappear into the bordering trees. He slowed his pace; he didn't want to alert her. She thought she had gotten away from him. Wouldn't she be surprised when he circled around behind her and met her in the middle? He'd take her right here in the forest. Why not? He'd paid for her.

He smiled. It was too easy. She didn't have a clue he was on her tail, nor would she realize he was right behind her when he lunged out of the trees and grabbed her. His wolf felt exhilarated. He hadn't hunted in quite some time. Not this kind of hunt. Perhaps he should take it to its bloody climax. He did need a release of one kind or another, and she was just a whore, who would miss her? The remains could be disposed of out here where they would never be found. The prospect of a kill caused his body to vibrate—his wolf was expanding, threatening to emerge. No, not yet, he had other plans for her first.

Arianne could sense him. He was close. She knew his plan because she could read his thoughts. Where were the others? They were meant to be here by now? She was trained in mortal combat and knew she could hold him off for a while. She wasn't sure for how long. His Lycan strength would overpower her eventually. If she had no other choice she would bite him, which wouldn't kill him because he was an Alpha. But it would put him out of action until the others arrived.

Reece and Charlotte were in the van following Nathaniel and his team. They were almost at the turn off. It would take another few minutes to get to the property. Charlotte hoped Arianne was ok. She knew the young woman was half vampire and had some of their strength and capabilities. Was it enough against a powerful Alpha?

Nathaniel's black van made a right down a dirt road just ahead of them and as Reece made the turn a truck hurtled around the shoulder heading straight for them. Before he could avert the impending collision the truck ploughed into the rear left side of the van, spinning it out of control. The vehicle never stopped.

Both he and Charlotte braised themselves for the impact with the clump of trees on their right. The van didn't hit it. As the wheels skidded across the gravel, it flipped over and landed on its roof.

Nathaniel was at Reece's van before it had time to stop spinning. He ripped the passenger door from its hinges, tore Charlotte's seatbelt out of its retainer and pulled her free of the wreck. He could smell gas.

Once he had Charlotte clear of the van he circled it and did the same on the driver's side. Reece had blood pouring down his face and Nathaniel wasn't sure he was still breathing. He carried the PI across the roadway and laid him on the grass beside Charlotte. She was dazed and had a two inch gash above her left eyebrow and a bruise forming on her left cheek.

The large black vampire leaned down and placed his ear against the PI's chest and listened. A heartbeat. He was grateful. He didn't feel like losing anyone tonight. They still had to find Ed and Dennis. Sarah had volunteered to do a sweep of the city and check Ed's house.

He looked at Charlotte. "Are you able to walk? I need to carry him to the van."

Charlotte gazed up at him still dazed. "I – I think so. Is he all right?"

"He is unconscious. I will have one of my team look at you both in the van. Come." He lifted Reece off the grass as though he were a large, toy teddy bear and carried him along the dark road. Charlotte followed. The wreck would be dealt with later.

Arianne heard the crash in the distance. She hoped it wasn't any of her team or Reece and his crew. She needed their help. Remaining low to the ground, she kept moving so that the Alpha wouldn't catch up to her. It wasn't easy. He was silent and quick on his feet. She hoped the trap had been set. That was the plan. Arianne knew where it was and if all else failed she would spring it herself somehow. She couldn't let him get too close or she would be forced to fight him. She kept retracing her steps and crossing over them to leave her scent in every direction, hoping it would confuse him and keep him at a distance.

She crouched in the long overgrowth and slowed her heartbeat even further. Being part vampire had its advantages. She could appear dead if she wanted to, a tactic she had used on some of her previous missions. It had saved her life many times.

Before she could react, the Alpha had her by the throat. His eyes glowed red and menacing in the dark. "There you are. I've been looking for you everywhere. Why did you run off? I thought we were going to have fun together." He flung her into a tree. Her body crashed against it and landed in the overgrowth. She was on her feet, taking a defensive stance.

"Is that any way to behave, especially since I paid a small fortune for your services? You owe me." He punched her in the gut. She kicked out hard as she flew backwards and connected with his manhood.

The Alpha fell to his knees, holding his groin.

Arianne took off running through the forest and headed to the other side of the clearing where the trap was set. She hoped. She peered over her shoulder as she flew through the trees. Where was he? As she turned around she crashed into him.

He grabbed her long ponytail and raised her at eye level. "Well, that hurt. Now it's your turn to feel pain." He shoved her backwards and a jagged tree branch skewered her through the ribs. She screamed as searing pain burst through her abdomen.

Using her powers she drove herself forward, disengaging her body from the tree. The pain was unbearable but she had no choice. Get free or die. She kicked out and swiped the Alpha alongside the head with her shoe. He stumbled back and landed on his butt, giving her the opportunity to kick his ass some more.

He was down and she wasn't about to let him stand. She kept kicking: the ribs, the back, the legs, anywhere she could to keep him on the ground. He grabbed her ankle and tripped her up. She hit the ground and before she could whip back onto her feet he was on top of her.

The black van coasted into the trees at the edge of the clearing and Nathaniel shut off the engine. He sat, allowing his nocturnal hearing to scan the perimeter and surrounding forest. His ears pricked as he heard the struggle. "Theo, ensure the trap is set. Arianne needs help."

The young vampire was out of the van, the other two team members following him.

Nathaniel turned to Charlotte. "I want you to remain here. You are both injured and would only hinder our attempt to capture the Alpha."

Charlotte couldn't argue with that. Reece was still unconscious and she wanted to be near him. "When you've secured him let me know. I want to see his face when he realizes he isn't going anywhere."

The black vampire gave her a knowing smile. He could sense how much she wanted to confront the man who had taken her son. Every fiber of her aching body raged with hostility and her thoughts focused only on physically hurting him for what he had done. "I will take you to him once he is restrained." With that said he leapt out of the van and dissolved into the dark forest. Nathaniel followed the sound of the struggle, his team fanning out to work their way back toward the pair. As he approached he called out, "Let her go!"

The Alpha flung the young woman aside and turned around. "So, you want to challenge me, do you?"

Nathaniel stepped into the moonlit path between the trees. "I do not need to."

A cage plummeted from the trees encasing the Alpha. He roared and rushed at the bars, but the metal was coated with pure silver and smoke rose from his hands as he grabbed them. He recoiled, growling even louder. "You won't get away with this."

The black vampire stepped closer. "I believe we have." He raised his arm in the air, and the base of the cage, which was hidden under the dirt, snapped into place. The Alpha was trapped.

CHAPTER SIXTY FOUR

Sarah had been to Ed's house and completed a double sweep of the city without locating the missing pair. She spoke to store owners, pedestrians and even night patrol, showing their photos. No one had seen them. As she drove back to the detective's house she wondered who had taken them. Ed and Dennis were small fish in the huge pond of deception taking place in LA. What would be the motive?

She racked her brain trying to figure out where they could be. It didn't seem plausible that someone had abducted them. If they did, it would have to be someone who knew Ed had been attacked and would turn at some point.

Sarah hated to admit it, but Ed could've woken up, his mind affected by the infection, and didn't know what he was doing. If that was the answer, where would he go?

Swinging the car around, she headed for the highway. While waiting at the next set of traffic lights she spotted Dennis's car on the opposite side of the street. When the light turned green, she sped along the road and did a U-turn at the next intersection. She had to catch up to them.

The lights were still green. She was going to make it. Just as she reached them they changed. Sarah smacked the steering wheel. "Dammit!" She looked up and mouthed 'sorry.' The lights flashed green again.

As she drove along the street, overtaking and zipping between cars she kept an eye out for Dennis's silver Nissan. Where was it? They couldn't have gotten away that fast.

She craned her neck to see past other vehicles on the road, hoping a set of headlights would illuminate the doctor's car and she'd know she was on the right track. They had to be just up ahead. At the next set of traffic lights she noticed a silver sedan about six cars ahead. Was it them?

When the cars moved off, she indicated and moved into the outer lane trying to get a closer look. Yes, it was them. All she had to do now was maneuver behind them.

She edged forward and got a break in the traffic, only one car in front now. After two more sets of lights she was behind them. She flashed her lights and the car pulled down the next side street. She followed.

A guy she didn't know got out of the car. "Something wrong?" He looked surprised to see a priest standing on the street.

Sarah wasn't sure what to say. She thought it was Dennis's car. She'd been certain of it. "I'm – I'm terribly sorry. I thought you were friends of mine. They drive the same car."

The guy started to get back into his vehicle but stopped and turned around. "Maybe next time check the license plate first." He got in and drove away.

Sarah climbed into her four-wheel drive and did a U-turn. She'd head over to Ed's house again just to be sure.

When she arrived at the detective's home Dennis's car was in the drive. They were here.

She flew out of the car, leaving the door wide open, rushed onto the front porch and pounded on the door.

It opened.

Dennis was surprised to see her.

"Where is he?" she asked, anxious.

"He's in the kitchen making coffee."

"Making coffee! What the hell are you doing? Why did you take off from the night club? You do realize he's going to turn, don't you?"

Dennis raised his hands. "Hold on a minute. First of all, Ed took me. He had a Lycan moment. And second, yes I know he's going to turn, but right now he's fine. Let him be himself. It's going to be hard enough for the man when it does happen. At least he's got one more day."

Sarah glowered at him, worry evident on her face, then her expression softened and she let out a heavy sigh. "You're absolutely right. I'm so relieved you're both ok."

She stepped inside, headed straight to the kitchen and wrapped her arms around Ed. "I'm glad you're ok."

Ed didn't know how to react. Should he put his arms around a priest? He was going to Hell anyway so why not? He wrapped his arms around her and they stood together in silence. It was nice.

When Sarah eased out of his embrace she looked up at him. "I was so worried about you. We all were. We thought..."

"You thought what?"

Her expression changed to concern. "We thought you were taken by someone who knew you'd been attacked. I thought they'd try to use you against us."

"Nah. I had a lapse of memory." He looked sheepish. "The infection's doin' funny things to my brain." He poked his temple.

"Where'd you go? I've already been here once today."

"The last place I remembered."

Sarah smiled. "I knew it. I was on my way out there until I saw Dennis's car and followed it."

"My car?" Dennis said.

She shook her head. "Long story."

"You were coming out there on your own?"

"Yes?"

"What if I'd turned already? It was a dangerous move."

Ed cared about her. It was nice to know. "I can take care of myself. What were you looking for out there?"

"Don't know. Where's Reece and the others?"

"They set a trap for the Alpha." She glanced at her watch. "And they should have him by now, if all went according to plan."

He smiled. "You mean I won't turn into a monster tomorrow night?"

Her eyes looked pained and she rested a hand on his arm. "In theory. Trouble is we don't know for sure, Ed. We can only hope the information Adrian gave us was accurate. There are so many variables to consider."

Ed's smile disappeared as he thought about the prospect of becoming a werewolf. Not something he ever thought he'd have to think about. Then it dawned on him. "Who's the Alpha?"

That was the Million Dollar question.

ℰ⅃ℭ℞

Reece jolted awake and gazed around the van disoriented at first until his focus rested on Charlotte. "Hey."

"Hey, yourself. How are you feeling?"

"Like I've been hit by a truck." He gave a wry smile and rubbed his aching head, wincing when he touched the gauze pad on his forehead. "How about you? You look…"

"Don't say it or I'll curl up in a ball and stay there. I'm holding on by a thread right now." Tears welled in her eyes and her voice became a whisper. "When Nathaniel carried you from the wreck … I thought you were dead."

Reece moved beside her and wrapped an arm around her shoulders. "Hey, I'm here. I'll always be here. You have my word." He kissed her forehead and glanced out of the open back doors. "Where is everyone?"

"Doing what we came here to do. Nathaniel wanted us to be safe until they had the Alpha caged. He's coming back to take me to him once he's restrained. I want to look that bastard in the eye and tell him how happy I'll be when he's *dead*."

Reece held her close. "That's not you, Charlotte. Don't let him change who you are. Hasn't he done enough already?"

Charlotte burst into tears and wept against his chest. He stroked her hair and let her cry.

Nathaniel appeared at the back doors and Charlotte and Reece jumped.

"Shit, Nathaniel, can you not do that?" Reece frowned at him.

"Do what?" The black vampire mirrored the PI's expression.

"Sneak up on people."

"I did not realize I was sneaking up on you. It is my nature to move silently through the night. I am sorry if I frightened you." He gave a thin, amused smile.

Reece slid across the floor and climbed out of the van, stretching and rubbing his aching ribs and shoulder. "You didn't frighten me, just…"

"Caught you off guard." Nathaniel finished his sentence.

"Exactly."

Charlotte stepped out of the van. "Did you get him? I want to see him."

Nathaniel gave an affirmative nod.

Charlotte wanted to face the fiend who had taken her son.

"Would it not be better to leave the unpleasantness to us?"

Charlotte shook her head. "No. I want to be there. He deserves to die for what he's done. I hold no sympathy for him whatsoever. He's a monster, and I don't know why I didn't see it sooner." She was angry with herself for not picking up on the oddities of the man she was acquainted with. She should have noticed something was off, other than his deplorable behavior.

Reece touched her arm. "Remember what I said, Charlotte? Don't let him do this to you. Not after everything he's put you through."

Charlotte glowered at him. "I know you mean well, but I need to do this. I need closure otherwise it will haunt me for the rest of my life. Can you understand that?"

"I want to." He stared into her eyes, trying to make sense of what she was thinking and feeling. This wasn't her. And that's the reason he'd tried for so long to protect her from it. As much as he didn't want to admit it, it changed who he once was. He had become a different person and he didn't want the same thing to happen to Charlotte.

Nathaniel strode ahead of the pair, his nocturnal vision guiding them to the clearing. His senses honed in on the vibration of immense fear as he continued through the cluster of trees. He heard a twig snap nearby and stopped. "Wait here," he told them and dissolved into the darkness.

Charlotte clung to Reece. "What do you think's going on?"

Reece strained his ears to listen, but could hear nothing other than the night sounds of the eerie forest. "Whatever it is, Nathaniel is worried. He wouldn't have left us otherwise." He moved Charlotte and himself closer to a massive tree and pushed her against the trunk, keeping his body against hers to camouflage them in the dark. He hoped Nathaniel wouldn't be long.

A shrill scream shattered the silence.

Charlotte's body went rigid in his arms. "What was that?"

"I don't know." Something had gone wrong.

They could hear someone moving through the trees: branches snapping, heavy footfalls in the undergrowth. Was it Nathaniel?

Reece wanted a better vantage point. It was too dark and they were sitting ducks on the path. He moved Charlotte around the tree trunk and stepped behind her. She caught her breath and Reece covered her mouth to stifle the sound.

Something large thundered past them through the trees. Reece grabbed Charlotte's hand and took off running in the opposite direction. What had happened to Nathaniel and his team? Was that the Alpha who had just hurtled past them?

Reece led Charlotte through the dense forest, heading for the clearing. As they got closer, the moon filtering through the thinning tree line helped his eyes to adjust.

Should he call out? Were more wolves laying wait in the overgrowth? There was no movement, no sign of life. Reece's heartbeat shuddered against his ribs and he braced himself for what he was about to see.

Charlotte followed in silence. Her head felt light and her breathing came in short bursts. If the Alpha was free none of them were safe. Eyes wide, she scanned the darkness expecting to see a wolf pack emerge from out of the trees. She moved closer to Reece. "Where's Nathaniel and the others?" she whispered.

"Good question," Reece whispered back, his body and senses on full alert. Neither of them had a weapon. They were defenseless.

He was about to push the low-lying branches aside and step into the moonlight when a hand grabbed him.

Reece released Charlotte's hand, shoved her behind him and assumed an attack pose, hands raised.

Sarah stepped out of the dark with the tranquilizer rifle in her hand.

"What are you doing here?" Reece asked.

"I came to help."

"Do you know what's going on?"

"Some of the Alpha's first pack tried to attack us. They didn't stand a chance. We were ready for them."

Charlotte stepped around Reece. "We heard a scream."

"Arianne. She was grabbed by a wolf, but I shot him before he could attack her."

"And the Alpha?" Charlotte asked.

"A stay of execution. Tranquilized for now." She held up the rifle.

"Did you find Ed?" Reece pushed through the remaining trees and out into the clearing. Sarah and Charlotte followed.

"Yes. He's here." She pointed across the grassy patch of land. Ed was on the other side helping Andre and Nathaniel drag the dead wolves into the cluster of trees. They would have to dispose of them later.

Reece turned to Sarah. "How did one get away?"

She frowned at him. "None got away. We have all six carcasses."

Charlotte and Reece stared at each other.

"There must have been seven, because one passed us back there." Charlotte pointed in the direction they had just come from.

The priest shook her head. "Must have been something else because we have all the wolves. A mountain lion or deer maybe? "

Reece was disturbed. "No. Not a deer or a mountain lion. Something much bigger."

"You're sure?"

"Of course we are," Charlotte told her. "It was definitely a wolf. It was too big to be anything else. We thought the Alpha had escaped."

Sarah's gaze moved to the center of the clearing and the cage sitting in the middle of the moonlight. "As you can see, Ned's still here."

"I need to talk to Andre and Nathaniel." Reece stalked across the grass.

Sarah moved beside Charlotte. "You're absolutely sure you saw something? Nathaniel said you were involved in an accident earlier. Could it be some kind of delayed reaction?"

"Sarah, I know what we saw. It was a large dark-colored animal with the power to propel itself through those trees at an incredible speed."

The priest turned and stared through the dark forest. They had the Alpha and his pack, so who was that?

CHAPTER SIXTY FIVE

Dan McCredie pounded on the front door, his body twitching from the change back to human form. It was imperative he speak with his Alpha right away. The door opened and he pushed past the muscular pack member standing in the doorway and charged up the stairs, heading to her office. He knew she would want to be informed about what had happened in the forest. The guy at the door followed him up the stairs, along the hall, and knocked on the door. When it opened Dan stalked inside, followed by his escort.

Sonia Edwards sat behind a large desk working on the computer. Dan rushed across the room and waited for her to acknowledge him. As much as he felt the need to interrupt, he knew better. She finished typing and turned her intense gaze on him. "What's so important that you had to come charging in here like hell's demons were hot on your ass?"

"Reece's team has captured Ned Bowers."

The female Alpha was out of her chair and around the desk. "What?"

"I followed them out to Angeles National Forest. They set a trap for the Alpha. The vampire, Nathaniel, has a property out there. They lured Ned to the cabin using one of their team as bait, a half-breed vampire, posing as a hooker. I stayed hidden in wolf form and when the other wolves attacked…"

"What other wolves?"

"The Alpha's first pack. The one my ex-partner, Paul, belonged to. They took all of them out."

"They're dead?" Sonia folded her arms. "Reece and his team have no idea, do they?"

"No. And Charlotte's out there with them. They plan on executing Ned."

"What?!" She gazed around the room. There were four of her pack present, and two more downstairs. "All right. We're going to have to get out there and clean up this mess. It'll be daybreak soon. Everyone get into camouflage gear. Leo, bring the van around. Dan, take Patrick and Jackson, collect the necessary weapons and meet us out front ASAP. And on your way to the armory tell Neal and Eric they're needed."

ℰↃ℘

The van traveled out of the city, heading for the forest. When it turned onto the road leading to the cabin they noticed Reece's damaged van lying on its roof by the side of the road.

"I wonder what happened there," Sonia said, glancing over her shoulder at the wreck.

"Don't know," Dan replied. "Reece and Charlotte weren't in the field, although I could sense them. Maybe they were involved in that wreck."

Sonia turned her gaze back to the road. "Obviously they weren't injured too badly. By the look of that van it could've been a lot worse."

Dan frowned. "Yeah."

When they reached Nathaniel's black van, Leo parked alongside it. Everyone exited and joined Sonia for a recap of their plan. They would go in as humans, knock everyone out with tranquilizers, including the vampires (which would be difficult, but doable), take Ned and leave. He was not to be harmed.

The group advanced through the trees without a sound and when they came upon the clearing they moved into position. They wore black clothes and balaclavas to blend into the night. Sonia gave the signal and they stormed in. The humans went down first. The vamps took longer, although it was over in minutes and they never knew what hit them.

Sonia strutted over to the cage to assess the situation. Ned was out cold. Good. It made their job easier. She turned to Dan. "Tape his mouth, zip tie his hands and feet, and load him into the van. And make damn sure he's secure." She turned around and studied the scene. Nathaniel and a couple of his team were already moving. "Come on, let's get out of here. They're waking up."

℥

Nathaniel was on his feet in one swift movement. Everyone was down. Two members of his team were coming to. The others were still out cold. He turned to the cage. Gone!

He gazed up at the sky. It would not be long before daybreak. They needed to get out of the forest and back to the nightclub. Nathaniel wandered around the unconscious bodies. He and his team would have to load them into the van. The two members were on their feet. They knew what had to be done and set about carrying the humans to the vehicle.

Nathaniel sniffed the air. Wolves. The female Alpha. But why? Would she not want him dead?

Arianne was on her feet and so were the other two members of his team. They had to go. Now.

As the black van sped along the road back to LA, Reece and Ed came out of it around the same time. They both sat up and looked blankly at each other before realizing where they were.

Reece crawled across to Charlotte and lifted her head off the floor. "Charlotte? Charlotte?" Nothing. He turned to the front of the van. "What the hell happened back there?"

Nathaniel glanced over his shoulder. "We were ambushed. And I believe it was Sonia Edwards' team."

Reece crawled through his unconscious team to Nathaniel. "How do you know that?"

"I smelt wolf on the air."

"We had the dead wolves in the trees."

Nathaniel shook his head. "Living wolves. They have a distinct odor. And so does the female Alpha's choice of perfume."

Reece rubbed the stubble on his chin. "Why? She wants the Alpha dead just as much as we do."

The black vampire's left eyebrow rose. "Yes, you would think so. It appears there is more going on there than we realize."

Reece squeezed through the gap between the front seats and sat beside Nathaniel.

"Then we need to go pay her a visit."

Nathaniel scrutinized the PI. "Do you think that is wise?"

"We've been played. She was supposed to let us do our job." He stared at the vampire. "She knows something we don't and we need to find out what that is."

When the black van turned into the alley behind Decadent Desire, two figures stood in the bright circles of the headlights—Sonia Edwards and Dan McCredie.

Reece was the first one out of the van. He stalked up to the pair, his intense gaze locking onto Charlotte's ex. "So this is what we can expect from you, is it? Betrayal?"

"Wait a minute…"

Sonia grabbed Dan's arm. "Don't."

Nathaniel stepped out of the passenger seat and joined Reece. "Your team was in the forest. You disabled us and seized our prisoner. Do you not believe it to be treacherous?"

Sonia stepped up to Nathaniel, something malevolent skimming across her eyes. She had no time for bloodsuckers any more than they had for Lycan. "We did you a favor."

"And how is that?" Reece asked, stepping between her and the vampire.

She turned her serious gaze to him. "You were about to make an irreversible mistake."

Sarah, Ed, Charlotte, Andre and the others stepped out of the van and joined Nathaniel and Reece. They had to show the Alpha a united front.

Reece gave her a skeptical look. "What kind of mistake? From where we stood, we had the one person who is the key to this whole situation, and you took him."

Dan stepped up beside his Alpha. "Ned Bowers isn't the Alpha. He was just in the wrong place at the wrong time. And, as it turns out, he belongs to MacKinnon."

CHAPTER SIXTY SIX

MacKinnon roused from sleep, the sound of his cell phone vibrating across the bedside table was enough to disturb his preternatural senses. He grabbed the annoying contraption, pushed the button and pressed the phone to his ear.

"What?" he barked. He didn't care who was on the other end of the line, he didn't want to be disturbed.

"Ned's been abducted."

He sprang up into a sitting position and swung his legs over the side of the bed. "When?"

"Sometime between last night and this morning. He left his house around midnight and didn't go back. What do you want done?"

Douglas MacKinnon was one of a long list of people who despised Ned Bowers. Even though he was a member of their order, he was a hypocrite and a horrid little man. Should he care that someone wanted to get rid of him? If it were anyone else he wouldn't. Knowing how Ned's mind worked, he had to protect the order, first and foremost. MacKinnon sighed. "Find out what you can and get back to me ASAP. I'll work something out." He ended the call and tossed his phone onto the bedside table. "That little man is more trouble than he's worth."

He was about to stand when his cell phone went off again. "What is this, a call center?" He snatched the phone off the table. "What is it now?"

"Good morning, sir, it's Josh."

"Oh?" He sighed. "What is it?"

"I wanted to let you know I'll be heading over to Daniels's office in a couple of hours to see what I can find. Anything in particular you want me to look for?"

Josh was another human MacKinnon didn't care for. He was self-centered, self-righteous and arrogant, a dangerous combination. He had no idea why Jamieson was ever inducted into the order. It had happened while MacKinnon had been on sabbatical, and once initiated you can never leave, at least not by walking away.

"Something that links them to Ned's disappearance."

"Ned's disappearance? When…?"

"Do you think they could be behind it?" He paced.

The detective hadn't known Ned was missing, until now. "I don't … They have been clutching at straws as to the identity of … well, you know." He remembered he had company. "They must've thought Ned was the one they were looking for."

MacKinnon realized Josh had someone with him by his cryptic response. "We need to get this situation under control. Now. I can't have someone running amok and abducting people that will be missed. It will raise serious questions and suspicion. Find out what you can and get back to me pronto!"

"As you wish." Josh ended the call and pushed his cell phone onto the night table. He'd deal with the PI later. Right now he had other things that required his attention. He turned over and smiled at the young woman lying naked beside him. There was still an hour and a half until sunup and he knew exactly how she could utilize the time.

CHAPTER SIXTY SEVEN

Out of the early morning sun, inside Decadent Desire, the discussion continued. Sonia had no intention of telling Reece where they'd hidden Ned Bowers. And she wasn't divulging information regarding who the Alpha was either, because she didn't know. It would remain a standoff. The PI would continue to ask and she would continue not to answer.

Sonia knew the black vampire could read minds. He was unable to read a Lycan mind, fortunately; otherwise they would already be on their way to where she had sequestered the DA. She had to convince Reece Daniels and his team that Ned was not the Alpha, because it was the truth.

"Why won't you believe me when I tell you I don't know who the Alpha is?" She folded her arms and paced.

"Because you've lied to us all the way through this ordeal." Reece stood with his arms folded watching her strut back and forth, the heels of her high-heeled shoes clicking on the concrete floor.

She stopped abruptly. "I may have given you the wrong impression. Trust me, it was necessary. Besides, we saved your asses back there."

Reece glowered at her, his expression incredulous. "We had everything under control. The pack wolves were dead and Ned was sedated, so how did you save our lives?"

Sonia mirrored his stance. "Because the real Alpha has more than one pack. There may have been others out there waiting for his order to finish you."

Reece frowned into her eyes. "How do you know that?"

"I have my resources." She smirked and stepped away from him. "The Alpha is clever. Do you really think he wouldn't have another plan?"

"Let's just say I believe you. How many wolves do you think he has running around LA?"

The smug smile was erased from her face. "That I don't know."

Charlotte got up from the round table on the perimeter of the dance floor and walked over to her. "If we've eliminated one pack and the kids are the second pack, wouldn't he only have one more?"

Sonia liked her. She was smart. "Possibly. He wouldn't continue to create packs because he wouldn't be able to control them. They would have to be in separate locations. Different packs, even if sired by the same Alpha, don't get along."

Ed Borenko had had enough. "This pissin' around isn't makin' a lot of headway, so why don't you cut the crap and tell us somethin' useful?"

Sonia turned her scrutinizing gaze on the detective. "I understand your concern, Lieutenant Borenko, you've got a lot riding on the demise of the Alpha, but what I'm *not* telling you has the potential of keeping you safe. At least for now."

"Yeah? How much longer do you think I'll be safe for? It's the full moon tomorrow night. Right?" Ed got up and charged over to the counter. "Hit me." He looked at Nathaniel with a grim expression and the vampire slid a double shot of whiskey across the bar.

"Sonia?" Sarah got up and walked over to the woman. "If we can locate the Alpha and eliminate him, those teenagers along with Ed will be released from the Lycan curse. Isn't that right?" She needed confirmation that killing the Alpha would allow the people he'd initiated and those bitten by them to return to normal.

"Yes, in theory."

"So you don't know either." Sarah returned to her seat.

Sonia wanted to console her. "I've never seen it happen before, because I've never known an Alpha to be killed. It could work, but until the Alpha is gone there's no way of…"

Josh strutted into the club through the rear exit. Reece was the first to vocalize his distaste. "What are you doing here? No one invited you."

The detective crossed the night club, and in a matter-of -fact tone said, "I've been looking for you. When you weren't at your office I thought you might be here. Do you have any idea what time it is?"

Reece glanced at his wrist. He didn't have his watch. It must have come off during the accident.

"It's almost nine." Charlotte moved up beside Reece. "Why were you looking for us?"

Josh gave her a disgruntled glare. "Because, Charlotte, I wanted to let you know that Ned is missing." No one looked surprised.

His irritated gaze scanned every face in the room. "It appears you already know." He folded his arms. "Mind telling me how?"

Ed crossed the room. "News travels fast in our circles, Jamieson. You should know that by now," he bluffed, moving next to Charlotte.

Sonia and Dan remained silent.

Josh turned his gaze to Sonia Edwards and the cop. "You wouldn't happen to know where the DA is, would you? You seem to have feelers everywhere." He raised his hands and wriggled his fingers. "Heard anything?"

She stared at him without responding.

"What's wrong? Cat got your tongue?" A wry smile crossed his lips. He turned to Reece. "MacKinnon wants intel on Ned ASAP. If you find out anything let me know." He marched back across the night club and stopped in the doorway. "Oh, and one more thing, I have a lead on the Alpha." He disappeared through the exit.

By the time Reece got out to the alley Josh was gone. Was he playing mind games with them or did he have the answer they needed?

CHAPTER SIXTY EIGHT

Late that afternoon, Reece received a text message from Josh asking him to meet him at the old state prison. He had something important to tell him. Come alone. Reece was in two minds about going, except he needed to know who the Alpha was and Josh had the answer. Or so he said.

Reece parked his midnight blue Mustang under a tree about five hundred feet down the deserted road and walked to the compound. He had his Glock tucked into his belt under his shirt, just in case. It was difficult to trust anyone these days, and Josh was one of the least people he'd stake his life on right now. This whole meeting in secret in the middle of nowhere left a bad feeling in his gut.

He stepped through the unlocked gates and headed to the heavy outer door leading into the administration building. The door stood open. He peered inside, his heightened senses telling him to stay alert. He didn't pull his weapon, not yet. He used his hearing and wits to navigate to the warden's office without being jumped or attacked by Josh or anyone else roaming the prison.

Reece checked the time on his cell phone. It was a quarter after five. Josh said he'd be waiting. The PI picked up his pace. The warden's office was left at the end of the corridor not far from the infirmary. He turned the corner and walked along the short hallway to the door. It was open. He thought Josh would be waiting in the inner office. He wasn't.

He wanted to get the meeting over with as soon as possible and get out of the facility before nightfall. It always seemed to get darker sooner out in the wilderness than in the city and he didn't want to be caught in a dark place without a flashlight. Safety first. Always.

Reece opened the solid wood and reinforced glass door with apprehension and stepped inside. Something felt off. He moved with caution toward the closed door to the warden's office, contemplating whether to draw his pistol. His heartbeat kicked up a notch and shuddered against his ribs and he blew out a sharp uneasy breath.

He walked over to the second door and was about to open it when the outer office door slammed shut behind him. Reece pulled his Glock and whirled, ready to defend himself. He scanned the office with his eyes and his weapon. No one. He let out the breath he'd been holding. "Get a grip. Probably just the wind." He stalked over to the door and turned the handle. Locked. "What the hell?"

Reece pounded on the door. "Jamieson! This isn't funny. Open the goddamn door." He gripped the handle and tugged. The door wouldn't budge.

The connecting door leading to the infirmary had been open the last time they'd been there. Reece rushed over to it. Locked. Was the warden's office locked too? His breathing quickened. Who was playing cat and mouse with him, and where was Jamieson? His gut clenched, the hairs on the back of his neck stiffened. He moved around the old reception desk toward the door.

Where was he being led to? And why?

Reece stepped up to the honey-colored, wooden door and pressed his ear against it. Not a sound. Was someone waiting for him in there? Had he been set up by Jamieson? Was he about to die? A light bulb flashed on inside his head. Could Josh be the Alpha?

He took a wide step across the closed doorway and positioned himself near the jamb, so he'd be shielded by the wall when he flung the door open. His heart did the Rumba against his ribs as he took a deep breath and reached for the handle with his left hand, Glock in his right. Staying behind the wall, he pulled the handle down and shoved the door back. He waited a heartbeat, then threw himself into the doorway and assumed a *ready to fire* stance. He scanned the office. No one.

This could be Josh's way of unnerving him. A twisted game. It worked. He was spooked.

Reece noticed another closed door on the right-hand side of the room.

Could it lead back to the hallway between the office and infirmary? A way out? He crossed the room and stared at the door. With his weapon raised, he reached for the handle and pulled it open. A closet-sized bathroom. He closed the door.

If someone wanted him dead, he'd be dead. So what was the point of all this?

He entered the reception area again and scanned the room. The hallway door was still locked, but the infirmary door stood ajar. Reece felt like a mouse in a maze, being led to the prize at the end. What?

ഇ)രു

Ed was fidgety. He didn't feel quite himself. Only a few more hours and the full moon would be staring down at him, willing him to turn into a werewolf. He swallowed the wad of nerves lodged in his throat and gave a heavy sigh. He didn't want to become a monster. He hated goddamn monsters, with the exception of a few he knew personally.

Sarah had decided to stay at Decadent Desire. She wanted to be close in case he needed anything.

Nathaniel was not happy about accommodating Ed at his club. The fact remained, either they contained him in the cellar before the moon came up, or he ran amok and killed people. Easy choice.

The detective sat at the bar absentmindedly drumming his fingers on the counter top. He'd had a skin full of whiskey and felt rather mellow, despite his anxiety. Maybe the alcohol would lessen the effect of the change. Perhaps he wouldn't feel the agony of twisting bones and stretching muscles and skin. Who was he kidding? It would be *hell* and he was too old for that shit.

Sarah crossed the club and sat on a stool beside him. "How're you doing?"

Ed's frown softened. "How do ya think?"

She rested her hand on his. "Maybe Reece will get the answers we need and put the Alpha out of commission before the moon rises."

Tears welled in the detective's eyes and he coughed back a sob. "Yeah. We can hope."

Sarah wrapped her arms around him and squeezed, trying to impart some of her strength to him. She was glad he was alive, although she hated seeing him this way. Hated the fact that he would turn into a beast if something wasn't done to prevent it. And she knew he felt the same. He was a man's man and showing weakness was not easy for him. He had some dignity.

He swiped the moisture from his cheeks and sniffed. "I wish I could say 'why me?' but I can't. That would be selfish. It could've been any of us."

Sarah looked into his eyes and smiled. "You're a good man, Ed Borenko, and don't you forget it." She noticed something red shimmer across his eyes. The wolf was ready to escape. She stepped down off the stool and took his hand. "Why don't we get you settled in and comfortable downstairs, hm?"

Ed frowned into her eyes. "That soon, huh?"

She nodded.

The detective swiveled around on the stool and stood up. "Let's do it. I don't want to put anyone in harm's way."

Nathaniel followed them down the concrete stairs and into the cellar. Shackles had been fitted to the massive steel beam in the ceiling and also bolted into the concrete floor. He crossed the cellar to the chains. "Are you ready?"

Ed gave Sarah a forlorn smile. He sighed and nodded. "Yeah, let's do this." He walked across to the black vampire and held out his wrists. He was petrified. This changing thing scared the shit out of him.

𝕊ᴑℂℛ

The sun had started to set and Reece's jangled nerves were electric. Pure animal instinct had kicked in. When he left the warden's office and entered the infirmary the door to the ward had been locked. Whoever devised this plan knew exactly how to unravel a cop. To his mind it had to be Jamieson. Which only confirmed his suspicions about him being the Alpha.

He paced. There wasn't any point in going back to the warden's office; he couldn't get out that way. All he could do was wait until the infirmary door was unlocked. Which he hoped would be soon. He checked his phone. 6.55 pm. How much longer would this scenario play out?

When he found the detective blood would be spilled. That bastard deserved a nose reconstruction and Reece was in the right frame of mind to accommodate him.

Five loud bangs echoed through the door from along the hallway. Reece rushed over and stared into the gray haze. It sounded like it had come from the cell block where the kids were. He was in the process of having them moved to a safe house, but until then they had to remain locked up out here.

Reece stepped out of the doorway and edged along the wall until he reached the corridor. Peering around the corner, he scanned the shadowed length as far as he could see. He eased his way along to the first cell block. It seemed too quiet. He knew one of Nathaniel's team had been out to check on the kids and give them some food, so maybe they had eaten and called it a night.

He sidled up to the doorway and used his phone as a flashlight.

Reece's heart thudded in his chest.

He rushed into the block and aimed his phone at each of the cells. No, no, no!

Melinda, Claire and the three young men were dead. A single gunshot to the head. That's what he'd heard. Their execution.

Could the killer still be here somewhere? Reece whipped around and backed out of the block, keeping his eyes and senses alert. He had just enough light to find his way back to the infirmary, and once inside he stayed in the shadows, edging his way around the wall to the treatment room.

A broken fluorescent tube cast a bright swatch of intermittent light through the single, fractured doorway. Reece's anxious gaze darted around the dark ward. He wondered if someone could be lurking in a corner waiting for him to enter that room. If he did he'd be trapped. Just like the kids.

One way in, no way out. Game over!

CHAPTER SIXTY NINE

Charlotte left the precinct staring at her cell phone and willing it to ring. She was worried about Reece and wondered why he hadn't called. He said he would as soon as the meeting with Josh was over. They were to meet up and drive back to Decadent Desire together. She wanted to be there for Sarah and Ed. She knew how difficult it was watching the man you love go through something so devastating. And she knew Sarah loved Ed.

She made the decision to head to the night club without him. Maybe something had come up and he'd be there by the time she arrived. She crossed the parking lot to her car and when she reached it MacKinnon came up behind her.

"I want to speak to you for a moment."

Charlotte spun around, gasping. "You scared the life out of me."

He could feel her fear of him. "I apologize." He gave a thin smile. "Breeding."

"What can I do for you, sir?" She opened the car door and tossed her purse onto the passenger seat. She wanted to be ready to leave as soon as the conversation ended.

"Have you heard from Jamieson?"

"What makes you think he'd contact me?" She brushed a stray wisp of hair off her face and noticed her fingers were trembling. She wondered if he could read her mind, and recited Mary Had A Little Lamb over and over in her head, just to be sure. She wasn't about to tell him where Josh was, even if she knew.

He frowned into her eyes. "You are partners, aren't you?"

"That's as far as it goes. He never tells me what he's up to and I don't ask. Is there anything else, sir?"

MacKinnon pursed his lips and studied her for a moment longer. "No. That's all."

Charlotte got into her car and started the engine.

MacKinnon tapped on the window and she lowered it halfway. "Sir?"

"If you do hear from him ask him to call me."

"I will." She backed out of the parking space and drove off.

As she merged into the evening traffic, she realized she was still trembling. Her commander and chief unnerved her. He was a vampire half breed, after all. How could that happen? How many more supernatural beings were on the force that no one was aware of?

She checked her rear view mirror and breathed a sigh of relief when none of the cars behind her looked familiar.

Charlotte arrived at the club around 7.30 pm. She parked on the street and walked across the road to the front entrance. It was locked. She sighed and made her way down the alley. When she reached the back door Sarah stepped out of the building for some air.

"Hey. Everything ok?"

Sarah tried to smile. "As ok as it can be. Ed's secured in the cellar waiting for the inevitable. In less than four and half hours he'll become a werewolf." She rested her head in her hands. "Can you believe that? I still can't get my head around it."

Charlotte heard her sniffle. She wrapped a comforting arm around her. "I wish Ned had been the Alpha. I wish we knew who the damn Alpha was. I wish none of this was real."

Sarah looked up at her, tears streaking her face. To hell with being strong, she cared too much for Ed to continue hiding her feelings. "I do too. I don't want Ed to go through this agony." She burst into tears.

Charlotte hugged her. Without knowing the identity of the Alpha, Ed would turn into a werewolf tonight. She hated the thought too.

₭ʠ

Reece heard a moan coming from the room. Was he hearing things? He strained his ears to listen as he scanned the darkness around him one more time before considering his options. Lucky for him he had on dark-colored clothes. Great camouflage.

He kept his back to the wall and eased himself closer to the doorway. His breathing was shallow and he felt light-headed. He sucked in a large mouthful of air and let it out.

Another moan.

Reece stepped up to the venetianed window and peered through the smashed glass and mangled slats. Josh!

With no further regard for his own safety, Reece rushed over to the detective. He crouched beside him. God, what a mess. Blood everywhere. Josh wasn't going to make it, Reece could tell by the extent of his injuries. What the hell happened to him? He'd been attacked by ... a wolf. *Shit! Josh isn't the Alpha.*

Reece was on his feet, gun in hand, his nervous eyes scanning everywhere around him. Whoever did this was still in the building. The one who had played games with him.

Josh moaned Reece's name.

The PI dropped to one knee and leaned in to hear him.

"I – I know..." He pushed the jagged words out on a groan.

Reece leaned closer. "Know what, Josh?"

Josh coughed and bright red blood poured from the corner of his mouth. His chest rattled and Reece knew the detective didn't have much time.

"The Alpha..." He coughed again and more blood sprayed from his lips. He gasped and moaned.

Reece squeezed his arm under Josh's head. "Who is it, Josh?"

The detective wheezed moist air into his lungs. More blood ran from the corner of his mouth. "It's ..."

"Who?" Reece was desperate for the answer.

The detective coughed once, gasped and stopped breathing, his eyes staring blankly at Reece.

"Shit!" Reece lowered Josh's head onto the floor and stood up.

He heard a noise in the dark and dropped down behind the broken window next to the doorway. Someone knew exactly where he was. He was stupid to allow himself to be cornered.

Reece glanced up at the broken light. It needed to be off. He gazed around the room. The switch was on the opposite wall. He would have to cross the doorway and stand up to turn it off. Bad move.

He felt the vibration of his cell phone. Thank God it was on silent. He pulled the device from his jeans and checked the screen. It was Charlotte. He pushed the phone back into his pocket. Explain later.

How could he get out of this game?

ℰᏣ

Charlotte had taken Sarah back into the night club and the women were sitting at the bar drinking coffee. Nathaniel had made them a couple of cappuccinos and they were taking some time to do something normal for the first time in a long while. Normal really wasn't in their vocabulary anymore. Nothing about their lives would ever be normal again. Charlotte tried to contact Reece as she became more and more concerned about him not showing up at the club. She removed the phone from her ear and frowned at it. "That's strange."

"What is?" Sarah asked, taking a sip of her hot frothy coffee.

"Reece isn't picking up." She slid her phone onto the counter.

"Maybe he's still busy and doesn't want to be disturbed."

Charlotte sighed. "The meeting with Josh is taking much longer than expected, if that's the reason."

Sarah leaned across and rested her hand on Charlotte's arm. "I'm sure he'll call when he can. Don't worry."

ℰᏣ

Reece scanned the floor for something to throw at the light. His second option was to shoot it out, which, he decided, was a bad idea. He needed to hold on to his bullets.

Staying crouched behind the window, Reece's eyes darted around the floor again and this time he noticed a stainless steel flask poking out from underneath a mess of strewn medical records. He reached across and snatched it from the damp sheets of paper. It was heavy enough to throw. He hoped it would connect with the center of the long fluorescent tube and smash it in two.

Reece remained low to the ground and moved back to where he'd been hiding. He tossed the flask as hard as he could. It hit the light, dropped onto the gurney and bounced onto the floor with a metallic clang. Instant darkness. Now it was time to get the hell out of there.

He edged up to the door, still on his haunches and peered into the dark ward. Straining his ears, he held his breath and listened to the sounds inside and outside the prison. He couldn't remain cornered in the room any longer. He had to make a run for it.

With his weapon in his hand, Reece moved out into the dark and kept his back to the wall. He knew the layout, so all he had to do was make it to the door. Once he made it to the warden's office he'd call Andre for help. Should've thought about that sooner. He was annoyed with himself for not bringing backup. He'd always maintained it was the most important thing, and yet here he was alone in a deserted prison while someone toyed with him. Stupid move!

Reece wasn't more than a few feet from the open door. When he reached it he jumped to his feet and bolted along the corridor. Once inside the warden's office, he slammed the door and braced a chair under the handle. He pulled his cell phone from his pocket and hit speed dial.

"It's me. I'm trapped out at the facility in the warden's office. Someone's playing cat and mouse with me and there's no way out. Josh is dead. Can you get out here ASAP?"

"Nathaniel and his team can get to you faster than we can. I'll call him the minute I hang up. Don't worry we'll be there as soon as we can."

"Thanks." Reece pushed his cell phone into the front pocket of his jeans and breathed a relieved sigh. The cavalry was on its way. Hoorah! He walked over to the window, folded his arms across his chest, and gazed at the night sky, wondering how he was going to break it to Charlotte about the kids.

CHAPTER SEVENTY

Nathaniel and his team moved silently through the facility heading toward the warden's office. They had arrived fifteen minutes after the call to Andre, faster than any vehicle could make the distance. The black vampire stalked along the corridor ahead of his team and when they reached the short hallway, he told them to wait while he went in to retrieve the PI. He entered the reception area and crossed the room to the open office door.

His huge frame filled the doorway. "Reece?" He was not there.

Nathaniel returned to the four waiting outside. "Something is wrong." He stood in silence, allowing his immortal senses to search the facility.

Andre, Charlotte and Sarah raced along the corridor to the warden's office. When they turned the corner, Nathaniel and his team were in the short hallway. "Where's Reece?" Charlotte asked, anxious.

"He was not here when we arrived."

She pushed past him and rushed into the room fanning the dark space with her flashlight. "Reece, are you here?" She moved across to the closed door on the right and jerked it open. No one.

Andre and Sarah followed her in.

She turned and looked at them. "Where is he?" Her voice was thin with worry.

"We'll find him, Charlotte," Andre reassured her.

Nathaniel stepped up behind them. "He is still alive, I sense his mortal energy."

Charlotte crossed the office to him. "Do you know where he is?"

"In the infirmary."

"Why are we standing here? Let's go." Charlotte squeezed between Andre and Sarah and moved out to the corridor.

Nathaniel's team had weapons that would take down human or Lycan. Andre, Sarah and Charlotte also carried weapons. Sarah had her crossbow and Andre and Charlotte had pistols loaded with silver bullets.

They were ready to move in when a voice echoed out of the darkness of the long corridor. "Wait. You're going to need our help." It was Sonia Edwards and her pack.

Everyone turned around.

"How did you know we were here?" Andre asked.

Sonia stepped up to him. "We've been following you for your own protection. Looks like you could use our help."

"Why would we need your help? This is a rescue operation with one assailant."

Sonia's lips spread into a knowing smirk. "Is that what you think? Let me tell you what I think. Reece was led here by Josh because he discovered who the Alpha was. Josh was a pawn to get Reece here, which serves the Alpha's purpose."

"Which is?" Charlotte asked.

Sonia glanced at her sideways. "Luring us all here for the final battle."

Charlotte thought out loud. "He wants to eliminate anyone who knows."

"Yes, and we're all here, except for Lieutenant Borenko."

A gravel voice came out of the dark. "I am here."

Sarah rushed over to him. "How did you get out of the cellar, Ed? How did you know where to find us?"

"Someone let me out. And my hearing is super-sensitive. I heard Andre talkin' to you." He took a step toward her. She stepped back. "I'm ok."

She rushed into his arms. "I…"

"Yeah, me too." He gave her a crooked grin. He knew she cared for him and hoped she knew he cared for her too.

Sonia marched up to him. "You shouldn't be here."

Andre followed her. "Ed, she's right. You don't know how to control the wolf yet. You could turn on us."

Ed eased Sarah away from him. "I get that, but I want to help find Reece. He's not only an ex-employee he's a friend. He's saved my ass more than once, it's the least I can do for him."

Sonia folded her arms. "The sentiment is touching, but you're a danger to us all."

He frowned at her. "If I feel anything different I'll leave. I wouldn't put my friends at risk."

Sonia sighed, threw her hands up and turned to Andre. "It's your call."

Nathaniel stepped between a team member and Charlotte. "He could not only get one of us killed he could also get himself killed. He should not be here."

Andre stared into Ed's eyes. "We may need his help. Who knows how many wolves the Alpha has now? He can stay. I think he knows whose side he's on. Right, Ed?"

"You bet."

Sonia glowered at Andre. "Don't say I didn't warn you."

"I won't."

Nathaniel moved back to the front of his team. "We need to move."

Everyone followed the black vampire and his team as they forged ahead along the dark corridor. When they reached the infirmary, Nathaniel told them to wait while he and his team checked the ward.

All clear.

Charlotte was the first one through the door. "Where is he, Nathaniel?"

"In the treatment room." He led her over to the room. They stopped at the door and she swept the beam of her flashlight around the interior.

Reece was unconscious and strapped to the blood-soaked gurney their captive wolf had been slaughtered on.

"Oh!" she gasped, and rushed across the debris strewn room. She set the flashlight down on the gurney and tried to loosen the restraints. "Reece? Reece, can you hear me?" Tears welled in her eyes as she struggled with the straps.

Nathaniel strutted across the room and ripped the straps from the metal.

Charlotte looked up at him, tears sliding down her cheeks. "Thank you."

Andre appeared at the door. "We need to get out of here. Now."

Nathaniel threw the PI over his shoulder. Charlotte grabbed the flashlight and they followed Andre across the dark ward to where the others were waiting.

As they headed to the doorway the overhead lights flashed on. The cat and mouse game was over.

CHAPTER SEVENTY ONE

Ned awoke to a splitting headache pulsing in his temples, his wrists and ankles bound with zip ties. Where was he and what had happened? It took a few seconds for his foggy brain to recall the circumstances. The hooker bitch! And that damned private investigator and his team had abducted him and had him caged like an animal out in the forest.

Why?

A light bulb flashed on in his brain. Because they thought he was the Alpha. They must have planned to kill him. Thank God they hadn't. Using his elbows for leverage, he struggled to force his bound body into a sitting position. He gazed around his tight surroundings.

Who brought me here?

Could it have been one of MacKinnon's cronies? Had he found out the DA was about to expose him for what he really was? Or was it the Alpha? But why would it be the Alpha? Ned didn't know his identity. MacKinnon had ordered Caldwell's execution, so why not his? Ned swallowed the nervous wad in his throat, the rhythm of his heartbeat kerthumping against his ribcage. His anxious gaze moved around the concrete walls.

The room reminded him of work space in a subway tunnel, the kind you see in the movies, although he hadn't heard a train pass. No windows and the solid green door was a snug fit in the frame. The only air circulating in the tiny space was through a narrow air conditioning duct in the center of the ceiling. If someone turned the AC off he'd be dead in less than two days. Suffocated. Was that the plan?

Beads of cold sweat dotted his forehead. Carbon dioxide was poisonous to the body; he had read that somewhere. Even small doses could cause muscle spasms, high blood pressure and reduced brain function. Higher levels caused heart fibrillation, body convulsions and death. Was he to die a slow agonizing death, unable to breathe?

Ned called out, hoping someone had been posted outside. "Is anyone out there?" His voice echoed around his small concrete tomb. No one responded. A more gruesome scenario came to mind. What if they left him here? What if no one came back for him? No water, no food. He'd be dead in a few days from starvation and dehydration. A horrible, painful death.

"Stop it!" he barked. "Don't put stupid ideas in your head that won't happen."

He twisted his wrists over and over trying to loosen the ties, but they were so tight they chafed his skin. He had to get free somehow. He needed to move, needed to think of a way out of this. He studied the tiny space with more precision. No other means of escape. Even the air conditioning duct was too small to get through.

Ned's worst case scenario became a reality when the grilled halogen globe above the door buzzed and went out and the quiet hum of air conditioning ceased. He was trapped in the dark with no air.

CHAPTER SEVENTY TWO

"Go. *Now!*" Nathaniel ordered, carrying Reece out into the corridor. "This way." He stalked along the dark passage heading to the compound. He needed to get Reece to safe ground. Everyone raced out of the infirmary, except his team who lagged behind in case they were attacked from the rear.

Ed, Sarah and Charlotte were on Nathaniel's heels. Their chances of survival were better outside. Sonia and her team were right behind them. Andre had slowed his pace to wait for Arianne. He wanted to be sure she was all right. He didn't have a chance to ask her after the forest incident and he knew she'd been injured. Half breeds didn't heal as fast as immortals.

When they reached the door, Dan stepped into their view.

He waved them out and moved aside.

Once outside, Nathaniel laid Reece under a set of security stairs and joined the group.

Sonia strutted up to Dan. "Where the hell have you been? You were meant to be here when we arrived."

Dan glowered at her. He'd had enough of her bullying tactics. "I had something else to do before I came out here. You'll understand in a few minutes."

"What are you talking about?"

"You'll see." He folded his arms across his chest and smirked at her.

Charlotte stepped up next to Sonia. "Dan, is everything ok?"

Shit! Charlotte and Reece weren't meant to be here. They'd been injured in the accident he had set up and should have been at the hospital.

"No, Charlotte, everything isn't ok." He paced.

She frowned at her ex-husband. "I don't understand."

Dan swung around. "That's just it, you never did."

Charlotte's eyes widened. "So tell me now. What's going on?" She had an awful feeling something terrible was about to happen.

He took hold of her hand and looked deep into her eyes.

She snatched her hand from his and stepped back. "You're the Alpha?"

"I always knew you were a great investigative detective, Char." His smirk broadened.

Rage surged through her and she threw herself at him and pounded her fists into his chest. "You told me you were bitten in the alley. How could you do that to our son? To me?" She remembered the stakeout at the cabin. "You knocked me out, you bastard."

"I was an Alpha long before I lied to you about the dog bite. Paul knew what I was and he wanted in. That night he got scared, changed his mind, only it was too late. I'd groomed him to be part of my pack. He was mine."

"And you had him killed so he wouldn't tell?"

"Of course I did. He would've spilled his guts. I couldn't have that."

"So what now?"

He glanced at his watch and looked over his shoulder. "My packs are on their way. In fact, some of them are here already."

Everyone's eyes darted around the compound. Everywhere they looked, eyes glowed in the dark. Dan had enlisted more into the ranks of Lycan than just a handful of wolves. He had an army.

"You and your boyfriend weren't meant to be here. You should've been at the hospital." He brushed her cheek with his fingertips and she turned her face away. "I planned to spare you both. For Tommy's sake. But Reece came out here to meet Josh Jamieson and I couldn't let him go, once he knew the truth." He'd thought the detective had told the PI who he was.

Charlotte's expression darkened. "Don't do me any favors." She thought about when they first met, and the day she found out she was pregnant. He'd known their child would be born a Lycan. "You knew our baby would be a ... wolf, didn't you?"

"Only the male children become Lycan. We still don't understand why, but yes, once we knew it was a boy. It doesn't matter if it's only the male offspring, as long as we keep populating the world."

"You're crazy," Charlotte whispered, tears glistening in her eyes.

His thoughts turned to the DA trapped in that tiny concrete cell with no air. "It's funny how you all thought Ned was the Alpha. I suppose it was easier to think a pompous, self-absorbed pariah could be. He had the right characteristics." He smirked, knowing that in just a day or two Ned would be dead. Pretentious prick. No one would miss him.

Dan's expression turned somber and he stared at Charlotte. "If you want to save yourself and your lover leave now while you still can."

Charlotte stood tall, squared her shoulders and said, "I'm not going anywhere. If you plan on killing everyone you'll have to kill me too."

Ed backed away from the group unnoticed, while Charlotte kept her ex busy. He hunkered down, made his way over to Reece and dropped his heavy frame onto one knee. He slammed a hand on Reece's shoulder and shook him hard. "Daniels? Daniels, wake up. Wake up!" Nothing. He shook him harder. "Come on, Reece. Wake up, we need you."

Reece didn't have any serious injuries on his body that would keep him unconscious for this long, so the only deduction Ed could make was that he'd been drugged. And depending on what he was given, it could keep him out for hours.

He was about to get up off his aching knee when a hand grabbed him in the dark. "Shit! You scared the livin' crap outta me." He helped Reece into a sitting position and didn't even bother to ask if he was all right. "You want the good news or the bad?"

Reece did a couple of neck circles and blinked a few times to clear the haze from his brain and his vision. "Is there any good news?"

"Charlotte's ex is the Alpha."

Reece straightened. "What the Fuck?"

"Yeah, who would've figured? He's got an army out there. More than we can handle. Charlotte's keepin' him talkin', but that could change at any second."

Reece felt around his jeans for his cell phone.

Ed gave him a quizzical frown. "What are ya gonna do?"

"Call MacKinnon. He's got an army and weapons to deal with this kind of situation."

"How long ya think it'll take for his team to get here?"

"Don't know. But we need major help."

Charlotte knew she had to keep Dan talking, otherwise the werewolves would attack. She was furious with her ex-husband, regardless of the fact he was the Alpha. He had attacked her and abducted their son. How could he put their lives in that kind of danger? She wished she knew if Reece was all right. She needed him beside her right now, needed to draw on his strength to get through this nightmare.

"What are you going to do, kill us all?" She folded her arms.

"That was the plan until I knew you were here."

"Does that mean you're going to call off your pack?"

"No. It just means I have to work out a different strategy." His expression grew darker. "You shouldn't be here."

"You said that already. I am here so make your choice." She hoped any feelings he still had for her would influence his decision. She could see the turmoil in his eyes.

Reece ended the call and pushed his phone into the front pocket of his jeans. "They'll be here as soon as they can."

"Well that's somethin'." Ed's brow wrinkled and his eyes glazed over.

Reece noticed. "Are you ok, Chief?"

The older man didn't answer right away. When coherence returned to his eyes he looked at Reece and said, "I'm good."

"You sure?"

Ed swallowed hard. Something had begun and he didn't want to unnerve Reece. "Yeah."

Reece gripped his arm. "You'd tell me, wouldn't you?"

"Do you think I'd put any of you in danger?" he replied, his voice gruff.

"Just asking." Reece removed his hand. "I'm concerned about you. You know that, right?"

Ed's scowl softened. "Yeah, I know."

"We have to look out for each other. We're all we've got in this crazy world right now."

He knew. Still, something stirred inside him. Something he wasn't sure he could control.

CHAPTER SEVENTY THREE

Ed helped Reece to his feet and they remained in the shadows under the stairs. Ed realized his vision had altered. He could see in the dark. He gave Reece a sideward glance and wondered if he should say something, but decided to wait and see what other changes occurred before volunteering the information.

Reece didn't know how long it would take MacKinnon to organize his team or whatever they were … knights? They needed to be prepared for the onslaught of aggravated werewolves. He remembered the twin M2 BMG had been left in the second cell block. The windows to the building faced out to the compound. If they could get the gun high enough he could fire on the pack and knock some of them out of the fight.

He turned to Ed. "If we can set up the M2, we can take out a large proportion of those things before they have a chance to attack."

Ed considered the scenario. "If we start shootin', the wolves outside the fence will attack instead."

Reece gave a heavy sigh. "We have to do something. Who knows how long MacKinnon's team will take to get here. And another thought crossed my mind. What if he doesn't send them? It would serve his purpose, wouldn't it?"

"Shit. You're right. He's just as much a bad guy as Charlotte's ex, and he has a lot more to lose."

"Yeah." Reece headed for the door.

"Where ya goin'?" Ed followed him.

"I think we'll take our chances with the M2."

Ed shook his head. "Wait a minute. Those things are hungry for blood."

Reece turned around. "How do you know that?"

The chief cleared his throat. "Because I … uh … noticed a couple changes."

"What kind of changes?"

"I can see in the dark, for one, and I can hear better too."

"Anything else?" Reece couldn't help the tightness in his tone.

"I can sense those things. That's how I know they're hungry."

Reece folded his arms across his chest. "You're connected to them and you didn't say anything?"

"I was waitin' for somethin' big to happen. You know?"

"Like you turn and attack me?"

"I would *never* attack you."

"You wouldn't be able to stop yourself." He kept moving.

Ed caught up to him. "Sorry, Daniels."

"Stay close and let me know if you have any more *changes*."

"You got it," he said, and followed Reece into the prison.

The pair stalked along the unlit corridor shoulder to shoulder and as they did Reece remembered the kids. He grabbed Ed's arm and stopped. "Wait. There's something you should know."

"What is it?" Ed gave him a quizzical frown.

"The kids. They're…"

"Yeah, I know. I could sense that too." He gazed along the corridor. "Glad I'm not the one who has to tell Charlotte."

Ed had taken the death of the teens too well. Were his emotions being altered by the beast lurking inside him? Reece didn't want to think about that because it could mean the difference between him living or dying if his ex-boss lost control.

When they reached the cell block, they stepped through the pulverized doorway and kept moving. Ed didn't look in the cells as they passed and Reece realized he was avoiding the situation rather than acknowledging it.

Once they were in the second cell block, Reece and Ed formulated a plan to eliminate as many of the werewolves as they could with the M2.

The window sill was too high; they needed something to set the gun on.

Ed suggested the lockers against the far wall. If they put them under the middle window and sat the table on top it would be the perfect height.

"Ok, let's try that," Reece said, marching along the cell block. "We have to be quiet otherwise they'll hear us."

Ed nodded, hoisted a locker onto his shoulder and set it down under the window, then returned for the second locker. Reece stood and watched him in amazement. Once the lockers were in place, they picked up the table together and stood it upside down on top. Reece pushed a couple of chairs over and climbed up onto the makeshift platform. The M2 was a monster of a gun, but Ed handed it to him like it was a toy. Another side effect of the wolf virus, no doubt.

When the gun was in place, Reece scanned the compound and counted at least thirty wolves waiting for Dan's signal. "Shit, there's an army out there. Who knows how many more are outside the fence."

Ed climbed onto a chair and craned his neck to see out of a window. He could sense the wolves were restless and wondered how much longer they would wait before attacking without the order. "They're agitated. They want to move on the group, especially the humans."

"The only humans out there are Charlotte and Sarah." He peered through the eye piece. Charlotte still had Dan's attention. Good. "We need to do this now."

"I got a bad feelin' about this." Ed stepped down off the chair.

"Well I don't see MacKinnon's team arriving, do you?"

Ed was twitchy. He paced.

Reece remained perched on the lockers watching him. "Ed?"

He continued to pace the way a dog does when it's agitated.

"Ed!" he whispered loudly. This was not good. Reece checked his watch. 11.36 pm. He squinted through the viewer again. Dan was in the right position for Reece to take him out. If he didn't, Ed would turn right in front of him. And that could be deadly.

Charlotte felt the cold steel of the pistol in her pocket. She wanted it accessible, in case she had to use it—in case she had to use it on him. She didn't want to process that thought. He planned to kill them all and she couldn't let that happen.

She stared into her ex-husband's eyes realizing she never knew him at all, even though he was the father of her son. He'd deceived her in the most despicable way. And he'd fathered a child he knew would become a werewolf one day.

"Well, Dan, what are you going to do?"

His eyes narrowed. "Go through with my plan, what else?" He raised his arm high in the air. The wolves would attack the second he lowered it. His top lip twitched, his conflicted emotions wreaking havoc on his conscience.

There was no time to deliberate. Charlotte snatched the pistol from her pocket, aimed and fired a shot into the middle of Dan's forehead.

He recoiled and remained standing. The disbelief on his face as he stared into her eyes caused her stomach to clench, and as his body hit the ground she threw up at his feet.

Sarah rushed to her side, eased the pistol from her hand, and gave her a quick tight hug. There was no time, they had to move.

Reece couldn't believe what he'd just seen. Charlotte had killed her ex. He pressed his eye to the viewer and fired round after round at the looming wolves. He continued firing to cover the group as they made a dash for the prison door.

Wolves were bounding toward them at a hundred miles an hour. Reece watched Charlotte and the others, hoping they would make it inside before the monsters reached them. He fired off more rounds to keep the beasts at bay. Andre grabbed Arianne's hand and whisked her along at super speed. The members of Nathaniel's team waited and attacked. Reece could hear their snarls and roars above the noise of the M2. Fur and flesh flew everywhere and finally the vampires sank their fangs into the subdued beasts, administering their venom.

The monsters outside the fence retreated.

Reece stopped firing and turned to check on Ed.

He was gone.

Oh God, could he have turned into a werewolf and raced out there into the fight? Could I have shot him by mistake?

Reece scanned the cell block before climbing off the lockers. He stood in the center of the concrete space with hands on hips, wondering where Ed was. He prayed he hadn't killed him.

Charlotte ran through the doorway and flung her arms around his neck. "I'm so glad you're ok. Thank you for covering us. You're my hero, as always." She hadn't noticed the dead kids in the unlit cell block. She had been too preoccupied with getting to Reece.

He didn't answer her, his mind elsewhere.

She frowned. "Something wrong?"

His thoughts returned to her. "You didn't see Ed anywhere, did you?"

Charlotte slid her arms from around his neck. "No. Why?"

Reece looked at Nathaniel. "You?"

"No. Was he not with you?"

The PI gave a long sigh. "He was until I started firing. When I turned around he wasn't here."

Sarah rushed over to them. "Then where is he?" The horrible scenario she didn't want to think about prodded her mind. "You think you shot him, don't you?"

Reece wiped a hand over his sweaty face. "I don't know. I hope not."

Andre let go of Arianne's hand— he'd forgotten he was still holding it—and walked over to them. "Did he have time to change? Maybe when Charlotte shot Dan…"

Sarah turned in Andre's direction. "He could have changed at any time before midnight." She looked at Reece, her voice quivering. "Where is he?"

Nathaniel's gaze moved to the back door and he pointed. "I think he can better answer your question."

Sarah rushed into Ed's arms. "Don't you ever scare me like that again."

"Yes ma'am." He kissed her forehead.

"Where were you?" Reece asked.

Ed moved Sarah aside. "Who do ya think was takin' pot shots at the wolves gettin' too close? Sure as hell wasn't you, Daniels."

Sarah gave Reece a wry smile and shrugged. "At least he didn't turn."

"Yeah. That's a good thing." He strutted over to Ed and wrapped his arms around him. "I'm glad you're ok. I thought…"

"Don't, Daniels." Ed patted his back. "It's all good." He cleared his throat and stepped back. "Don't go gettin' all soppy on me now." He sniffed.

"Ok." Even though Ed could be a pain in the ass sometimes there was still that seed of affection between them.

Everyone prepared to leave, and as they moved along the corridor Reece pulled Charlotte into the small hallway between the infirmary and the warden's office. He kissed her hard on the mouth and held her close, stroking her hair.

Charlotte knew he wanted to say something. "What is it, Reece?"

He stepped back and sighed. "Something happened tonight. Something … terrible.

"What?" Her stomach tightened and she steeled herself for what he was about to tell her.

"I heard gun shots while I was trapped in this section of the prison, and when I went to check it out I…" He couldn't bring himself to say the words. It would make it all too real. Too horrible.

"You what?" She rested her hand on his arm.

Reece swallowed hard. "The kids are dead, Charlotte. Dan killed them."

ℴ⇛

Nathaniel thought it wise for everyone to return to Decadent Desire. It would be safer for the humans to be under his watch, at least for the time being. No one knew if the remaining wolves would plan some kind of retaliation, and he did not want to risk his friends' lives by acting without caution.

When the van and four wheel drive pulled into the alley behind the club everyone was relieved. What they all needed right now was time to recoup their strength for the next battle with MacKinnon.

Nathaniel had called ahead to have three of the upstairs rooms made up for his guests. They would be safe and comfortable for as long as they required it.

Everyone climbed out of the vehicles and followed Nathaniel. When they reached the interior of the club they were welcomed by MacKinnon and several of his crew. "Come in. Make yourselves at home," he mocked with an overindulgent smile. "Ah, Miss Arianne, I see you've defected to the other side."

Arianne gave Andre a furtive sideward glance. He squeezed her hand. It didn't matter.

Reece stepped out of the group. "Why are you here, MacKinnon?" His gut told him they were in serious trouble.

MacKinnon pursed his lips. "Well, we've eliminated all of the Alpha's pack. Funny business that. Who would've suspected Dan McCredie was the unscrupulous Alpha?"

"And?" Reece asked. They'd stepped into a trap, one they should have seen coming.

MacKinnon sighed. "Bottom line is you know too much and that could be detrimental to my position in this city. It's as simple as that. Don't take it personally I would do the same to anyone who knew my secret."

Charlotte stepped next to Reece, took his hand and squeezed it, her mind in turmoil. *This can't be happening. We've fought too hard for it to end like this.*

Nathaniel wasn't sure if the Chief of Detectives and his cronies possessed the ability to read minds. Being a half breed might prevent it. He decided to give it a try. If they couldn't read thoughts, Nathaniel would give instructions to his team and Andre.

"Andre, can you hear me?"

Andre continued to look ahead. *"Yes. What if they can too?"*

"That is what I want to find out. If none of them react we will know."

"And?"

"I have a plan."

Andre continued to keep his eyes to the front. *"They don't seem to be able to hear us."*

"We must be certain of that. They may be faking."

MacKinnon gave quiet instructions to his team, turned on his heal and left the night club through an exit near the bar. An obscure retreat.

Everyone braced themselves.

Nathaniel advised his team and Andre of his plan.

The half breed vampires moved forward, their gazes darting from person to person. As they moved closer their canines snapped into place.

Nathaniel, his team and Andre stepped to the front, fangs in place.

Charlotte had never seen Andre in his vampire state before, in fact she'd never seen any of them as vampires before, it scared her. She pulled Reece out of the way. "Can't we get out of here?" she whispered.

Reece leaned in to her. "You, Sarah and Ed should go. I need to stay."

Sarah and Ed backed up to Reece and Charlotte. "What's the deal?" Ed asked.

"You and Sarah should take Charlotte and Arianne and get out of here while Nathaniel and his team keep MacKinnon's guys busy."

Ed frowned at him. "I'm not goin' anywhere, Daniels. I'm stayin'."

"I'd appreciate it if you'd get the ladies out of here."

Reece was right the women needed to be gone. "All right. But I'm comin' back as soon as I've secured the girls."

The PI nodded. "Ok. Move toward the exit and when it's clear make a run for it."

"You ready?" Ed asked, turning to face the three.

The women gave the pair an incredulous glare and said, "No."

"What makes you think we're leaving?" Sarah asked.

Charlotte pulled her pistol and checked the clip. Eight silver cartridges. Would they affect half breeds? She didn't know nor care. She opened fire.

Arianne raced across the room, jumped on one of MacKinnon's men and had him in a choke hold.

Sarah had left her crossbow on a table not more than a few feet away. She hurled herself toward it, loaded silver arrows into the chambers and fired. She hit one of MacKinnon's team and he went down. She continued moving. Another one down.

Reece pulled his Glock and fired. He had to be careful not to hit any of his or Nathaniel's team. He waited until he had a clear shot, fired again and just missed Nathaniel's ear when the vampire flew across the room and pushed Arianne out of the path of a fast-approaching bullet.

One of MacKinnon's team threw himself across the room and, before she had a chance to react, grabbed Sarah by the throat. She dropped her weapon as he lifted her into the air, choking her.

Ed raced across the room and snatched the crossbow off the floor. He aimed at the attacking half breed, but was smacked in the face. The weapon flew out of his hands and he stumbled backwards, hitting the floor.

Sarah's mouth gaped as she gasped for air. Before she knew what had happened, her attacker sank his fangs into her throat and gorged her blood. Sarah could feel herself falling into a black hole. She had been there once before.

Ed and Reece were on their feet running to her at the same time. The PI aimed between the half breed's shoulders and fired off three shots. He hoped one of the silver bullets would hit a vital organ.

The guy dropped Sarah, turned and staggered toward Reece, a fountain of blood pouring from his mouth. He was dead before hit the floor.

The fight was done. Nathaniel and his team dragged the bodies across the club and down to the freezer room in the basement.

Sarah lay unconscious in a pool of blood. Ed dropped to the floor and lifted her head into his lap. "Sarah, can you hear me?" He tapped her face with gentle fingers. "Sarah?" He felt for a pulse. "I can't find it."

Reece crouched beside her and checked her carotid artery, a faint unsteady beat. "There's a weak pulse."

Ed rocked her in his arms, tears sliding down his ruddy cheeks. He gazed up at Reece with tear-filled eyes. "Don't let her die, Daniels. Please."

Andre and Nathaniel carried Sarah across to the bar and laid her on the counter. The doctor in Andre kicked in. He felt for a pulse. Shallow and unsteady. He checked her eyes, using the night club's flashlight. Pupils dilated. Shallow breathing.

"We need to give her blood. There's no time to cross match."

Charlotte was concerned. "Isn't that dangerous?"

"It's risky, but if we don't do it she'll die." His gaze rested on Ed. "Sorry."

"Do it." The chief rolled up his sleeve. "I'll go first."

Sarah let out a huge sigh and stopped breathing.

Andre went into rescue mode, pumping her chest.

Reece rushed behind the bar and commenced mouth to mouth. After twenty minutes, and no sign of life, Andre pronounced her dead at 3.27 am.

Ed howled. Tears poured down his face. He sounded like a wounded animal in pain.

Charlotte sobbed against Reece's chest. "It's not fair. First Adrian, then the kids and now Sarah. Why?"

Reece held her close. "I don't know."

Ed fell across Sarah's body and continued to howl.

Nathaniel joined the grieving group. "I am sorry for your loss."

Ed lifted his head, his face as red as beetroot. "Thanks."

Nathaniel wasn't sure he should broach the subject of moving the body, but tried to do so with delicacy. "May I suggest we move Sarah to a more suitable place?"

Reece looked at him and shook his head.

Ed sniffed back the urge to sob again, pulled a handkerchief from his pants pocket, blew his nose and wiped his eyes. "Where'd you have in mind?"

"I thought perhaps on the cot stretcher in the cellar. The others are in the freezer room. She would be safe. We can use a bed cover from one of the beds upstairs. There's a floral one in Charlotte's room."

Ed nodded. "Yeah. Thanks. That would be nice for her."

Reece sat Charlotte in a chair and walked over to the bar. He and Ed lifted Sarah off the counter and carried her to the cellar.

Nathaniel covered the folded bedspread over her, leaving her face visible. Everyone made their way into the hallway except Ed. He pulled up the only chair in the cellar, sat down beside the cot, took Sarah's hand out from under the cover and kissed it.

Charlotte buried her face in Reece's chest.

Reece felt immense pain for his ex-boss. He didn't want to leave him down here alone. "You want to come upstairs for a drink?"

Ed peered over his shoulder and gave a crooked half smile. "In a couple minutes. Ok?"

"Sure, Chief. Take all the time you need."

CHAPTER SEVENTY FOUR

Reece, Andre, Charlotte and Ed sat at the bar in silence. Nathaniel had left a bottle of Vodka and four shot glasses on the counter an hour ago. The bottle was empty. He glanced at the ornate clock on the wall above the liquor shelves. The sun would rise in an hour. "Perhaps you should try to get some sleep," he said. "It will be daylight soon."

"Thanks, Nathaniel. I don't think any of us can sleep right now," Reece told him.

"I understand how you feel, and I am sincerely sorry, but not taking care of your own needs is not going to bring Sarah back."

Ed glanced along the bar. Everyone was exhausted. "He's right, Daniels. We still have to deal with MacKinnon and we'll need all the strength we can muster for that."

The PI frowned at his empty glass. Ed was right. Besides, the Chief of Detectives wasn't going anywhere. He thought he was safe.

"Thanks for the hospitality, Nathaniel. Appreciate it." Reece slid off his stool.

"It is the least I can do."

Reece helped Charlotte off her stool, took her hand and led her toward the spiral staircase. Ed and Andre followed.

As they were about to climb the steps a voice from behind stopped them in their tracks.

"Where are you going? We've got work to do."

Everyone swung around.

"Sarah?" Ed rushed over and pulled her into a bear hug.

"Ed, you're cutting off my circulation," she joked.

He pulled back and stared into her eyes.

"What is it?" She could see confusion on everyone's faces.

Ed took both her hands in his. "You were attacked…"

"And I thought I was going to die until Reece shot the guy."

Ed cleared his throat. "Sweetheart, you … you did die."

She slid her hands from his and stepped backwards. "Oh."

Reece watched her reaction. "How can you be alive?"

A sheepish look crossed Sarah's face. She had hoped she would never have to reveal her secret.

"Let's sit down." She walked over to a table.

Everyone followed her and took a seat.

"A long time ago, I hunted a vampire." She looked at Reece. "Remember when you first came to me for help and I told you I'd had dealings with these creatures before?"

Reece nodded.

"I'd traveled all over the world in search of the elusive Dracula, although I never encountered him face to face. Society believed he was a myth, a dark, fictional character created by Bram Stoker to frighten young Victorian women into holding onto their virtue. Unfortunately, he's very real and travelling the world in search of another human companion.

"During my travels, I was attacked by an errant vampire, one of his minions no doubt, and for some unknown reason I didn't turn and I didn't die. It prolonged my life, and for that I was grateful. One day I would come face to face with the monster that killed my family and I would repay him." She gazed around the intimate group trying to discern what they were thinking.

"So, you can't die?" Reece asked.

"Oh, I can die. It just takes more than the usual methods to make it permanent."

"How old are you?" Charlotte asked.

Sarah gave her a wry smile. "I'm a hundred and forty nine."

Ed reached for her hand and squeezed it. He didn't care *how* she was alive all he cared was that she *was* alive. He looked at Reece. "We need to figure out how to get MacKinnon out of the picture for good. Let's work on that."

ഇറ

Reece called Sonia Edwards to ask for her help. She declined. Her pack was leaving LA. She was running scared rather than staying and seeing it through. Reece tried to understand her reasoning. She'd told him if they didn't leave they would be picked off one by one until they were all dead. She said MacKinnon would have strategies implemented in case something happened to him. He never left unfinished business.

The PI stepped out of the van and joined the others in the precinct parking lot. They arrived early, before the building was converged on by administration staff and officers heading to their jobs. Would MacKinnon be waiting for them?

"So is the she wolf gonna help?" Ed asked.

Reece shook his head. "She and her crew are leaving LA."

"Why?" Charlotte asked.

"She's afraid of the fall out after MacKinnon's dead. She thinks the Order of Night will come gunning for us."

"Do you believe that?" Sarah asked.

"Even if I do, I'm not backing off. It's more likely that once he's out of the way the members of the order will move on. Why would they stay in LA when the Alpha and his pack have been eliminated? That's the reason they were here in the first place."

Ed gazed up at the building behind them. "Let's get this done."

Everyone headed for the main foyer. Once inside they took the elevator to MacKinnon's floor. On the way up, Reece went over the plan to make sure everyone knew what they had to do. The elevator stopped and the electronic female voice gave the floor number as the doors slid open.

Andre was the first to go in. He carried a syringe containing a sedative in the pocket of his jacket. A safety precaution so the receptionist couldn't warn MacKinnon or press the distress button under the desk. It would take effect in less than a minute. He also had four more syringes containing liquid silver just in case any of MacKinnon's cronies showed up. Because the vampire gene was stronger than the human in a half breed, silver would poison them in a matter of minutes.

He entered the office and gave the receptionist a dazzling smile. She smiled back, preening her hair and running her eyes over his body. Andre moved to the desk, making small talk for a couple of minutes. The receptionist couldn't believe her luck—a gorgeous-looking man flirting with her.

Andre asked if he could step around the desk and she said yes. He sat on the edge close to her and continued their flirty conversation. When the chance presented itself, he covered her mouth and stuck the injection into the side of her throat. She was out before he laid her on the floor.

He hit the button on his phone to send a pre-typed text to Reece and the group came through the door.

"Where is she?" Reece asked.

Andre pointed behind the desk.

They moved to MacKinnon's office and Reece pressed his ear against the door. There was no sound. "Ready?"

Everyone nodded and raised their weapons.

Reece gripped the handle, flung the door open and they charged in.

The office was empty.

They checked the closet and emergency exit. MacKinnon was gone.

Reece stalked along the corridor. Without knowing the Chief of Detectives' whereabouts their lives were still in danger.

At the elevators, he pressed the call button and stood with his arms folded. Charlotte moved up beside him. "We won't be safe while he's out there, will we?"

"I don't know, Charlotte. We can't be sure of anything where he's concerned."

"So what are we going to do?" Her expression was grim. She had a son to raise and didn't want to be looking over her shoulder every day wondering if someone was going to kill them.

"There's nothing we can do unless we can find him."

The elevator doors opened and they got in. Ed pressed the ground floor button and the lift moved off. As it descended, he frowned at the numbers moving above the doors and wondered why the elevator hadn't stopped at any floor. "Hey, Daniels, don't you think it's strange this crate hasn't stopped on the way down?"

Reece gave him a curious frown. "Not really. Maybe no one wants in or they got into another elevator."

Something didn't feel right, and Ed always trusted his gut.

The elevator continued its descent and when it reached the ground floor it moved straight past, heading for the basement.

Ed stared at Reece. "What did I tell ya?"

Reece jabbed the stop button. Nothing happened.

The elevator came to a stop on the LB floor. They were in the bowels of the building.

The doors slid open and the answer revealed itself. MacKinnon stood outside with four of his men, weapons aimed at the occupants.

"Out!" MacKinnon ordered, motioning with his pistol.

The group stepped out into the basement and the elevator doors closed, leaving them trapped.

"How did you know we were in that elevator?" Reece asked, eyeing MacKinnon's men and wondering if they could attack them and survive.

He smirked. "There's security CCT all over the building. Not difficult to tap into." The smile left his face. "You were meant to be dead. You all seem to have nine lives, perhaps we can remedy that."

Charlotte was out of plain sight behind Reece. She had her pistol in her shoulder holster under her jacket and wondered if she could reach it without being noticed. Sarah saw what she was about to do and warned her with her eyes not to try it.

MacKinnon's gaze fell on Sarah. "And you, priest, you're definitely not easy to kill. Why is that?" He raised a dismissive hand. "Could it be because you're a half breed too?"

Sarah didn't answer.

"I'm talking to you!" MacKinnon bellowed. "You will address me with a response."

Ed had had enough. "Hey! Don't talk to her like that. She's a woman of the cloth, so show a little respect."

MacKinnon's dark gaze fell on Ed and he shot him in the knee.

The women jumped backwards, letting out a shriek that echoed down the long pipe-filled corridor.

Ed fell hard gasping in pain, blood pooling in his pants leg and turning the gray material murky brown.

"Now, do I have your undivided attention?" MacKinnon pointed the gun at Andre. "You. Do something for him and hurry up about it."

Andre tore a strip of material off the bottom of his shirt and tied it above the wound to staunch the bleeding.

Charlotte touched Reece's arm and he turned his head. She was as white as a sheet.

MacKinnon spotted the pair. "Detective Delaney, would you be so kind as to stand on the other side of the priest? There's a good girl."

She did as she was told, moving around behind Reece and Sarah and at the same time pulling her pistol from its holster. When she stepped up beside Sarah she raised her weapon and fired at MacKinnon and two of his team. They hit the floor.

All hell broke loose.

Reece pulled his Glock and fired, taking out one of the guys still standing. Andre dragged Ed out of the way. Sarah rushed to his side. Andre flew at the other member of MacKinnon's team and knocked him to the ground. He sank his fangs into the man's neck and drained him in less than a minute.

The Chief of Detectives wasn't dead.

Reece kicked the gun away from MacKinnon and hauled him to his feet. "You have a lot to answer for you sonofabitch."

Andre took the syringes from his pocket. The silver in them would kill MacKinnon. He walked over to Reece. "Here. These should finish the job."

Reece studied them. "That would be too good for this monster."

MacKinnon laughed. "I always knew you were a pussy, Daniels."

The PI glowered at him, pushing him back against the sewage pipes. "Shut the fuck up."

Charlotte walked over to them. "Andre's right. Let's just get it over with so we can get on with our lives."

"I agree," Sarah said.

Ed groaned. His knee was on fire. "Me too. Let's not give this bastard the satisfaction of livin' any longer than he has already."

Reece pushed his arm under MacKinnon's chin and shoved his head further against the pipes. "Looks like your death sentence is unanimous." His eyes moved to Andre. "Go ahead."

MacKinnon wrestled with the PI but Reece had him in a choke hold.

Andre administered all four injections.

The Chief of Detectives sagged to the floor, his body going into spasm.

Everyone watched as he gasped his last breath.

"Thank God," Sarah said, "maybe now we can have some peace. At least for a while."

"What are we going to do with the bodies?" Charlotte asked.

"There's a furnace at the end of this passage," Reece told her.

☙❧

Charlotte was at her desk when Reece came into the workroom. She had come to the conclusion that she couldn't be a detective any longer and handed in her resignation on the spot. She wanted to work with Reece. Wanted to help him eradicate the monsters that lingered in the shadows waiting on unsuspecting humans. Wanted to make the city a safer place for her son.

When Reece reached her desk he pulled up a chair and sat down. "Are you sure about this?"

"I couldn't be more sure." Charlotte finished packing her things into a cardboard box and handed it to him. "How can I do this when I know what's out there?"

Reece stood up, tucking the box under his left arm. "I know exactly how you feel. After I found out I did the same thing." He smiled. "Ready to go?"

She took one last look around the workroom. She was as ready as she'd ever be.

Charlotte was quiet on the drive back to her apartment, and Reece knew something was on her mind. "You ok? Something you want to talk about?"

She sighed. "I feel so bad that we couldn't save those kids. Their families will never know what happened to them. It's not like we could bring their bodies home, is it? God what a disaster."

Reece reached across and squeezed her hand. "Look, we didn't do this. Remember that. We tried our damnedest to save those kids. We gave everything we had. Lost people in the process. You can't blame yourself."

Charlotte glanced at him sideways, thinking about Adrian and Josh. "I know. I'm sorry. It's just … I promised the Grahames I'd bring their daughter home."

"You did your best, Charlotte. No one could argue with that. We all did."

CHAPTER SEVENTY FIVE

One month later:

No one really knew what had happened to Ned Bowers. A letter of resignation was found on his computer, so maybe he had done what Sonia Edwards did and fled LA.

Whether MacKinnon had orchestrated a hit on them before his death, they would never know. All Reece and his team could do was watch each other's backs, and hope life would return to some kind of normal, at least for a while.

Tonight, Reece was in front of the television with Tommy by his side, watching the news while Charlotte prepared dinner.

The CBS presenter reported that the investigation into the disappearance of Chief of Detectives, Douglas MacKinnon was ongoing. It was believed he may have been abducted and murdered by members of a renegade biker gang. His connection with a task force that brought down a drug syndicate recently may have been the motive.

Reece didn't want to know, he picked up the remote and turned on the game channel. "Hey, buddy, want to play a game before dinner?"

Tommy's face beamed. "Sure do. And I'm gonna kick your butt, too."

Reece ruffled his hair. "You think so, huh?"

Tommy giggled. "I know so."

"Ok. Let's see what you've got." Reece passed him a controller.

Charlotte walked to the kitchen door. "Sorry guys, dinner's ready. Tommy go wash up please."

"Aw, Mom, can't we have one game? Pleeeeease."

"Nope, dinner will get cold so get to it pal."

Reece stood up. "Better do as your mom says, buddy."

"Ohhh, ok." Tommy shuffled to the bathroom in his socks, unimpressed that dinner had interrupted their game.

"Got a minute?" He stood in the kitchen doorway.

Charlotte turned around. "I have to dish up. Can it wait till later?"

Reece moved up behind her and slid his arms around her waist. "No, it can't wait till later." He turned her around to face him.

Charlotte smiled unsurely. "Sounds serious."

"You know how I feel about you. And I'm sure I know how you feel about me."

"Yes." Her cheeks grew warm. She wiped her hands on her apron and blew a stray strand of hair from her face.

He reached into the back pocket of his jeans and pulled out a small, black velvet box. "After everything that's happened, I couldn't imagine you and Tommy not being in my life." He flipped open the lid, turned the box to face her and got down on one knee. "Charlotte Delaney, will you do me the honor of becoming my wife?"

She looked into his eyes and saw her heart's desire. Charlotte knew she was in love with him and also couldn't imagine her life without him in it. She smiled. "Yes, Reece Daniels, I will marry you."

The smile on Reece's face grew wider and he stood up, plucked the gold and diamond ring from the box and slid it onto her finger. "You've made me the happiest man in the world."

He was about to kiss her when Tommy ran into the kitchen. "What are you smiling about?"

Charlotte showed him the engagement ring. "Reece asked me to marry him. What do you think about that?"

"I think it's the best news ever!" He rushed over and hugged them both.

After dinner Tommy went to bed without argument. He knew his mom and Reece wanted to talk about grown up stuff.

As they sat snuggled on the sofa watching a reality TV show they weren't paying attention to Charlotte turned to Reece and said, "As far as the wedding goes, I'm happy with something small. Just close friends and family." She didn't want to go through the 'big wedding' thing again. In fact, she didn't want a wedding at all.

Reece had been turning the whole scenario over in his head. He wasn't one for pomp and ceremony. He had another idea in mind. "Charlotte, how do you feel about eloping?"

Charlotte gave him a curious frown. "Where'd you have in mind?"

"Vegas."

Her smile widened. "The Little White Wedding Chapel?"

"Whichever one you want."

"What about witnesses?"

"I'm sure we can find somebody in Vegas to witness our marriage." He smiled and kissed her forehead.

"I love it. I love you. Let's do it." She hopped onto his lap, wrapped her arms around him and kissed him. She knew their life wouldn't be easy, but she didn't care as long as they were together.

ACKNOWLEDGMENTS

Thanks and love to my daughter, Amy, for the wonderful cover design. It fits the story perfectly! Your help and support means everything to me. Thanks to my daughter, Sarah for talking me out of changing the design. I'm so glad we stayed with this cover. Thanks also to my family and friends, and my social media friends on Facebook and Twitter for your support. Each of you have motivated me to get this second book in the Dark Legacy series finished and I'm very grateful.

The series continues with the thrilling

SOUL CHASER

Book three in the Dark Legacy series

M. A. Anderson

Coming in 2016

Read the first chapter…

CHAPTER ONE

Three days after Reece proposed he and Charlotte were at LAX waiting for their flight to Las Vegas. Charlotte was excited as she'd never been to Sin City before. It was going to be a wonderful vacation—honeymoon, and she couldn't wait to arrive at their hotel. Eloping had been a perfect idea.

Their flight would be boarding in twenty minutes, enough time for her to pop to the ladies and freshen up. "Reece, I'm just going to the bathroom before we board. Won't be long." She picked up her flight bag and headed to the ramp leading to a selection of takeaway stores, vending machines and public conveniences.

No one knew about their plans. Reece told Andre, after everything that had happened he and Charlotte needed to get away for a while. If anything urgent came up, Andre could contact him on his cell. Only Tommy and Mrs. Jenkins knew the truth.

While Reece waited, he gave Tommy a quick call. He felt guilty for leaving him behind, but this trip was their honeymoon, and you couldn't have a honeymoon with your kids around, could you? "Hey, buddy, how's things?"

"Hi, Reece, everything's good. Mrs. J is making pancakes again. I looove pancakes."

Reece laughed. "I think you love food in general."

"Yeah, I think I do," Tommy agreed. "Where's mom?"

"She went to the bathroom. When our flight lands I'll get her to give you a call. Ok?"

"Sure. Tell her I love her."

"I will. We'll bring you back a special surprise from Vegas."

"Gee, thanks. Now I'm excited."

Reece checked the time on his cellphone. "Hey, buddy, I better go hustle your mom up. Our flight's almost ready to board."

"Ok. Have fun. Take lots of photos. See you when you get back."

"We will. Love from mom … and me."

He stood up and gazed around the waiting area to see if Charlotte was on her way back. She wasn't. She said she wouldn't be long and it had been fifteen minutes since she'd left. He pressed speed dial. The phone rang for a few seconds then her voicemail kicked in. He left a message. "Hey, hon, where are you? Our flight will be boarding in five."

Reece collected his flight bag, Charlotte's purse and jacket and followed the direction she had taken. When he reached the ladies restroom, he waited outside contemplating whether or not to go in. He was worried all of a sudden. He tried her number again. As he did, he heard the ring of her phone getting closer and thought she was on her way out. Instead, a woman came out of the restroom with Charlotte's things.

"Excuse me, those belong to my fiancé," he said, pointing to the bag and phone in the woman's hand.

"Oh? Here you go." She handed them to him. "They were sitting on the vanity. I was going to hand them to security because I thought someone must have left them by mistake."

Reece frowned at her, then at the bag and phone. "No one was with them or near them or…?"

The woman shook her head. "Sorry, no."

"Ok, thanks."

The woman smiled. "I hope you find her before your flight."

"Yeah, me too." He headed back to where they'd been sitting. Charlotte wasn't there. *Where'd she go? She wouldn't have gotten cold feet, would she?* Reece didn't know what to think. He continued past the waiting area and made his way to the airline counter. "Excuse me."

The young woman smiled. "Yes? Can I help you, sir?"

"Can you broadcast a request for Charlotte Delaney to come to the counter, please? Our flight is boarding and I can't find her."

The woman gave him a concerned look. "Oh? That's no good. Of course." She picked up the telephone receiver and pressed a button on the base. "Would passenger Charlotte Delaney please come to the Alaska Airlines reservations counter? Charlotte Delaney. Thank you."

"Thanks." Reece turned around and scanned the people moving about the airport. No sign of Charlotte.

"I hope you find her. If you have any problems we can change your reservation to a later flight."

"I appreciate that, thanks." Reece moved to the side and waited. After ten minutes he asked the young woman to change their reservation and went back to where he'd been sitting. He dropped the bags onto a chair and sat down. *It doesn't make any sense. Charlotte wouldn't have run off like this.*

Reece sprang forward and snatched Charlotte's flight bag off the seat beside him. He unzipped it and pulled it open. Sitting inside was a note. He picked it up, his heart hammering in his chest, and unfolded it. Had she changed her mind? Had she taken off?

He read the words scrawled in black.

'If you want to see your lady again, alive, you'll do exactly what you're told. DO NOT inform the authorities. Board your flight and act as though nothing has happened. If anyone asks, your companion got sick and couldn't make the trip. You'll be given further instruction in Vegas.'

Could this be the work of MacKinnon? Was it his revenge from the grave?

ॐ

Reece couldn't relax during the flight. All he could think about was Charlotte and what could be happening to her. No one knew where they were going, except for Tommy and Mrs. Jenkins, and he knew neither of them would give the information to anyone. Not even Andre. So who had found out their flight information and how?

The flight was twenty minutes into its forty five minute journey and Reece wished they were already on the ground. He felt confined and useless sitting in the half empty plane unable to do anything. He wanted to get off, head to the hotel and wait for the next communication from whoever had Charlotte. This trip was meant to be a wonderful beginning to their married life and now it had turned into another horrible nightmare. Would they ever be free from it?

He'd contacted Andre before boarding and hoped he was on the next flight out. They had to figure out who these people were, if they were people at all. Could be more monsters for all he knew. Why Charlotte? Hadn't she been through enough? Was this whole scenario something to do with her or something to do with him? Some kind of payback?

A flight attendant asked if he needed anything and he said no. What he did need was to know Charlotte was still alive.

He pulled the window shade down and closed his eyes.

When he opened them again, the captain was announcing that they were five minutes out of McCarran International and gave a running commentary of the weather conditions. Passengers were requested to fasten their seatbelts and to put away all devices before landing.

Reece was relieved and fastened his belt. He wished he could check his cellphone. Why couldn't someone develop a way for passengers to use their goddamn phones inflight?

The landing was smooth and Reece was glad he had a seat close to the exit. As soon as the plane taxied up the tarmac to the terminal and the door opened he'd be out of the plane.

Inside McCarran International, Reece headed to the luggage pickup carousel to collect his and Charlotte's luggage. This should have been the happiest moment of their lives, preparing for their wedding tonight. Instead he was heading to their hotel alone wondering if he'd ever see her again.

His cellphone vibrated and he whipped it out of his shirt pocket to check the text message. 'At LAX. On next flight out. See you soon.' Reece breathed a sigh of relief. At least with Andre here they could cover more ground. And, if anything or anyone supernatural was part of it he'd know. That might give them an advantage.

Reece picked up his rental car, threw the luggage in the trunk and drove out of the parking garage, heading for the older part of Las Vegas, Fremont Street and the Golden Nugget hotel.

Vegas was a 24/7 hustle. No one slept. Even the roads were congested with a sea of traffic with tourists making their way from one venue to the next. It was right on sunset, the time when the city looked her best, and Charlotte would have been in awe of the glitz and glamour of sparkling Sin City. He had seen it all before and it didn't impress him, but he would have loved showing his beautiful bride around.

Reece turned onto Casino Center Boulevard, continued through the menagerie of pedestrians and cars and pulled into the Golden Nugget's valet parking. He popped the trunk, left the keys in the rental and grabbed his flight bag. A bellhop informed him that his luggage would be in his room by the time he finished at the front desk. Reece handed him five dollars and headed through the brass and glass doors into the foyer.

While he waited in the queue, he noticed a woman dressed in a gypsy costume standing by the steps, watching him. At first he thought he'd imagined it, but after a few minutes he knew he was her target.

After collecting his plastic swipe key for the room, he made his way along the carpeted walkway, past the huge pool and assorted restaurants, to the elevator banks. He pushed the button and waited. While he stood in the center of the lobby, he spotted movement from the corner of his eye and turned his head. The gypsy was at the entrance.

"Is there something you want?" Reece asked, his voice tight. Seeing her again made him feel uneasy. He didn't like it.

The gypsy woman sauntered up to him. "Perhaps there is something *you* want. You are missing something, yes? I have seen your future Reece Daniels. There is *death* in it." With that said she turned on her heel and disappeared into the hotel.

Reece rushed to the entrance and scanned the area. She was gone. How did the woman know his name? And whose death did she mean?

The next exciting installment...

Book four in the Dark Legacy series

Coming soon

M. A. Anderson